CW00827872

Wild Calm

Jane Pentecost-Wild

First published in 2023 by Blossom Spring Publishing
Wild Calm Copyright © 2023 Jane Pentecost-Wild
ISBN 978-1-7392955-4-7
E: admin@blossomspringpublishing.com
W: www.blossomspringpublishing.com
All rights reserved under International Copyright Law.
Contents and/or cover may not be reproduced in whole or in
part without the express written consent of the publisher.
Names, characters, places and incidents are either products of
the author's imagination or are used fictitiously.

Acknowledgments and sincere gratitude to those who helped me believe in myself.

My husband Rick for being forever positive, patiently reading each and every word multiple times, and for being my walking dictionary. Sally for proofreading and being an enormous help with editing. Denise, Phil, Lee, Rosie, Claudia, and Nigel for being volunteer readers and for your faith in me to tell a story. My brother Dick for sound advice as an experienced writer. Ben, Joe, George, Jaime, and Harri, for your loyalty and love.

Blossom Spring Publishing for making this happen.

A heartfelt thank you to each and every one.

Chapter One

Do not wake.

Sleep there softly with your pale skin, translucent, free from anxiety, troubled stare gone.

Sleep away your fears, and free yourself.

I cannot see who you are anymore. My arms reach out but…your hand no longer comforts mine.

Maggie lowered her head respectfully, sitting towards the back of St Peter's amongst a handful of faithful supporters, the congregation dutifully following the order of service.

"Almighty and most merciful Father. We have erred and strayed from thy ways like lost sheep. We have followed too much the devices and desires of our own hearts."

If only!

The service was drawn to a close, accompanied by a shaky organ recital of 'Zadok the Priest' minus vocals, leaving one feeling short-changed.

Despite an attempted hasty retreat, she was summoned…

"Maggie, Maggie… I know you're in a hurry, but I would just like to say…"

The vicar held his hand towards her, and smiled.

"We will be starting the community fellowship meetings again next week. I was hoping you would be able to join us?" Her expression, rather than cutting him short as hoped, only succeeded in encouraging him further.

"Bring your mother, dear, if that helps. We haven't seen her for quite some time."

Maggie chose her words carefully.

"Can I phone you, Patrick? Without my diary in front of me, I'm hopeless and I really have to fly now, but okay, yes, put me down as a possible... Thank you Patrick... lovely service and a thought-provoking sermon..."

*Damn, **damn**... just say you can't go.*

"I will call your landline tomorrow morning, my dear. God bless you."

Hastily retreating from the churchyard, she depressed the key to unlock her car, ensuring a fast exit preventing further unwanted encounters.

*

Maggie drove away. Glancing in the mirror, her lips devoid of gloss looked dry and pale.

She looked away. She hated mirrors. She felt every bit her fifty-five years and more. She switched radio channels to some light classical music.

She drove the coastal way home. A mellow sea to her left with a clear road lifted her spirits, and she inhaled and then exhaled slowly, preparing herself for home.

"Hi Susie... oh, am I late?" Maggie glanced at her watch whilst removing her jacket.

Susie was sitting by the dining table, clearly agitated, massaging a screwed up damp tissue in her palm.

"What's wrong? Where's Mum?"

Maggie's eyes turned towards the bedroom. The door was closed.

"She hit me." Susie did not raise her voice. It was a statement.

"Oh, Susie! Are you hurt?" Maggie quickly walked towards the table. She reached out, wanting to embrace Susie's delicate frame, but felt her gesture might be overbearing and make her feel awkward. "I am so sorry."

Susie looked up. "I'm not hurt. Not physically. It was a shock. I'm just shocked because she always liked me coming. It was so sudden. There was no warning, and I handled it badly."

Maggie wasn't sure how to respond. *Did you hit her back?*

"I'm afraid I burst into tears… I shouldn't have done, I know…"

"That's not handling it badly though, is it? That's completely normal. I'll phone the Social Services. It's a… safeguarding or something like that, I think."

"No, no Maggie, I don't want you to do that. I think I'll have a break for a while. I'm okay, just a bit shaken up." She smiled, firm lips pressed together. "She's in the bedroom." Susie nodded towards the closed door. "I'll head off now, but I'll call you."

Maggie sat in silence. Of course it hadn't always been like this. There had been 'pre carer' a life before this. Free, regular and orderly.

Her husband Craig had been particularly fortunate, finding himself in the right place at the right time, securing a senior post with a large building company. His working hours were long, but the daily commute allowed breathing space between deadlines and home life. He and Maggie had been married a couple of years prior to the birth of their son Hugh.

Maggie had wanted a conventional nuclear family. She had hoped for a brother or sister for Hugh, but without medical reason, or lack of trying, Hugh was to be an only child. Blond, tall, wiry, he grew awkwardly as boys often do. He was quiet, retiring, and learnt to play the guitar. He did not inherit his father's arrogance or ambition, but settled into teenage life unsure how it was all going to turn out. He had a particularly warm endearing smile, and was happy enough, and did not demonstrate any inappropriate behaviour when his parents split up.

Monday morning. Maggie avoided answering the phone to Vicar Patrick. The message he left was long-winded and she pressed save, giving her some time to reply. She then dialled a familiar number.

The receptionist at the surgery was typically abrupt.

"Is it urgent for today?"

"Well, yes, it is really. Her medication needs reviewing and…"

"And… is it urgent? Dr Parker has a pressing caseload today."

Maggie continued, "Something happened yesterday and I need to discuss it with the doctor… please, if you could just…" She was interrupted.

"Eleven fifteen… I've booked you in. Thank you, Mrs Chadwick." Then the dialling tone.

Why can't she just be nice, for once?

Maggie had to speed the morning routine up which was never easy.

Her mother was still in her nightie watching television. It was nine thirty.

"Mum, we have to go out. Come and have some breakfast, and then I'll help you to dress."

Gwen didn't move. She was watching a DVD playing 'The Sound of Music'.

"Mum, I've made you marmalade sandwiches."

The incident. It was marmalade that caused 'the incident' when everything changed.

*

Craig had been promoted to Managing Director of the property development company. They were able to purchase a brand new 3 bedroomed executive style house in keeping with their new-found affluence. Maggie had a good eye for soft furnishings and the overall effect was that of contemporary comfort with spacious open plan living; their desired dream house. But their swiftly gained asset was to be short lived.

Craig had taken out a large mortgage on the strength of his new-found career success, and for a while, they had enjoyed 'good times'. However, he was dismissed, and Maggie never did get to discover the truth behind this catastrophic life changer. He claimed it was a personality clash within the board of directors, but the punishment for simply a difference of opinion seemed harsh and unjust. They had enjoyed six ripe years. The challenges that followed left scars difficult to heal. They eventually had to sell their house, but they still owed the mortgage company a huge debt. They moved into rented accommodation.

The flat was at the top of a large mansion house, ironically, once a residential home. The hallway was spacious, leading to a sweeping staircase, the aorta supplying entry to many self-contained dwellings, the occupants of most invisible behind white hardwood doors.

At the top, a small landing led to two further doors. Hugh was given an independent room off this landing, and the other door opened into a one bedroom apartment, with a large lounge, kitchenette, and bathroom. Not a patch on their previous house. It was all that had been available at the time, as so many families were competing for accommodation. It was supposed to be a temporary measure.

Space deprived, they sold much of their furniture, and adapted to 'the compromise', Craig demonstrating irritation, and Maggie nursing a heavy heart. Hugh was content, managing to keep a healthy distance away from tense atmospheres, with a carpeted landing; a sanctuary drawbridge, separating himself when required.

Gwen lived close by, but her health deteriorated quickly. The close relationship between mother and daughter had been a constant throughout Maggie's life. Her mother had worked relentlessly to keep a warm and caring home for the two of them. A juggling act familiar to many single parents, but with help from friends, and initially a live-in job, with caring accommodating employers, and her church community, it was all just about possible. Maggie had been an 'easy' child, willing, cooperative, and largely content. She enjoyed school, but was no academic. Her work was beautifully written in meticulous handwriting, and she was good at creative studies. Science, maths and physics held no interest for her. Her exam grades were respectable, but not good enough for university. She worked in a farm kitchen, which developed into a popular eating venue, remaining there all through her twenties prior to meeting and marrying Craig. She had been encouraged to make some sellable articles such as aprons and quilted oven cloths, and eventually had her own section of the shop, reminiscent of a classroom craft corner at school. Her marketing skills would perish under close scrutiny, but this was of no concern to her. She enjoyed what she did, and that was what was important.

*

The 'incident' occurred one morning during breakfast. Craig was starting a new job after over half a decade of disappointment and rejection. A reluctance to pursue a character reference from his last employment had been a significant hindrance. He was nervous and had been sleeping badly. This was largely due to his bed doubling as the sofa, because Gwen was now living with them, after sustaining an injury which had happened a few months previously. There had been a phone call in the night.

"Maggie, it's somebody on the phone from the hospital. Your mum has had a fall."

Craig passed the phone to Maggie. She had been deeply asleep, and was disoriented.

"What? The hospital… which hospital?"

"The District General." He passed the phone to her. Serial incidents involving Gwen had proved difficult for Craig. He had become jaded with the constant dramas and Maggie treating her mother like a child.

Maggie became focused. "Hello… yes I'm Gwen Sanderson's daughter."

Her expression illustrated her fears. "Oh no! Has she fractured anything? I'll be there straightaway. She'll be fine when I'm there. Yes, she has been confused lately. I'm on my way now."

Craig groaned, and rolled over, snug in a huge chrysalis of white duvet.

"You could be a bit more sympathetic." Maggie dressed quickly, contemplating having a quick shower, then deciding not to. "She can't help it, Craig. She's getting old, she's frail…"

Craig muttered into the pillow. "She's unhinged, Maggie. She needs to go into a home. You just won't admit it."

Maggie resisted an argument, and closed the bedroom door quietly without saying goodbye.

*

Once in the car, her thoughts turned to childhood memories. She liked driving, especially with clear roads at unexpected times of the night. She drove safely, but exerting more speed than she would normally.

After leaving the house where Gwen had worked as a live in housekeeper, an appointment she had taken prior to Maggie being born, their next home had been small, just a two-up two-down amongst similar terraced houses. Theirs was second from the end. 'A good place to be,' her mum had said. 'It will keep the fuel costs down.' She was loving and 'mumsy', always wanting the best for Maggie, always feeling guilty for the absent father. She rarely spoke about him. Ted Clarke had not featured in Maggie's young life, and she knew little about him. The most her mother had ever revealed was that things hadn't worked out and she thought it best to make a clean break. No harm done, she would say... a statement with many possible connotations, but Maggie never did respond. She had always felt awkward, and preferred to let the subject pale into nothing, but she often thought about her father...

Weren't you intrigued to see how I turned out? I'm scared there could be a hidden callousness deep in my soul, inherited from you. I don't want to be like you... I will be my mother's daughter.

Maggie's thoughts turned to her seventh birthday. Her mum had made her a birthday cake. It had four layers and seemed huge, just like those pictured in story books. A red ribbon around white smooth perfect icing. Everyone had gasped when it was brought into the dining room with seven burning candles, her mum holding it so carefully balanced, smiling, smiling, willing her daughter to have a truly happy birthday. She had started singing 'Happy Birthday to you'... and everybody joined in. Maggie remembered that birthday beyond any other. There was nothing exceptional apart from that perfect cake, and her mum.

God, it was so bloody simple then.

*

She had to enter the hospital through the night entrance at the side of the main building. There was a doorman, security now so essential with so many angry people. She was aware of a faint smell of alcohol when approaching A&E. Maggie made her way straight to the reception.

"I've come to see Gwen Sanderson."

"Just a minute." Adept keyboard skills quickly sourced her mother's whereabouts on the screen. "She's in MAU, just go through those double doors and turn left," the receptionist smiled. Maggie analysed the smile. Was it sympathetic to the point her mother might be dead? Did the smiling receptionist know something she didn't?

She walked into MAU. Gwen was in the second bed, her eyes closed, her mouth slightly sagging at one side. *She's had a stroke.*

A nursing assistant was sitting next to her. She was writing, leaning on a clip board.

Maggie spoke first. "Hello… I'm Gwen's daughter."

"Hello." The nurse glanced across at her patient. "She's been very disturbed since her admission. They had to sedate her. Nothing heavy. I'm just doing her obs every half an hour. Blood pressure is up a bit. Is she usually so confused? It might be a UTI."

Maggie walked to the other side of the bed, bringing the chair up closer.

"A UTI?"

"Urine infection. The doctor wants to talk to you, he'll be here soon. This unit is manic, though. Even on a night shift." She carried on writing, glancing at the digital clock on the wall.

Maggie waited for the doctor. She watched her mother sleep, and felt disturbed by her frailty. Her hair looked different. She was out of familiar surroundings. The striped gown, so regimented. It was an uncomfortable image. Institutional.

Okay, so where do we go from here then, Mum?

The doctor was Spanish, his accent heavy.

"You are next of keen for Mrs Sanderson?" He was glancing through notes as he spoke.

"Yes, I'm her daughter. Her only child."

He smiled. "She has not broken anything. She had X-ray and scan, and nothing fractured."

"Well, that's a relief." Maggie waited for the next anticipated question.

"Does she have dementia?"

"Yes, she does. It's got a bit worse lately. She's getting mixed up with who people are and…" Maggie felt her voice break. She was tired, and could have easily cried.

"She may have urine infection. That will make her confused, but we have sent off specimen. I give her antibiotics. Is she on medication for her dementia?"

It was a matter-of-fact statement. This was nothing unusual for this overworked houseman. This patient was another senior, with mental capacity issues. Another box to tick. Another statistic. Another bed blocker.

"No. She won't take it anyway. She doesn't like tablets. Please doctor, is this going to set her back? I mean… she looks like she's had a stroke as well. I'm just worried about how she's going to cope at home. She lives on her own."

The doctor looked up at Maggie. "She can't live on her own anymore. This weel get worse. You need to see your Gee Pee. We will admit her to Martin ward overnight."

The bombshell had dropped. Her world was about to break… yet again.

*

Gwen remained at the hospital for a further four days, and then it was decided, largely due to bed shortages, that she would be discharged to live with Maggie, just until a more permanent arrangement could be found.

Craig tried so very hard to begin with. Their bedroom was large, and could accommodate an additional single divan bed. He suggested it would be more appropriate if he slept on the sofa, which did not help his already battered self-esteem, but it was a noble gesture.

"I can put a screen around her bed, Craig. You don't have to sleep in the living room." Maggie was desperate to try and make this impossible situation function as well as possible.

"I'll be fine in there. I can watch telly all night. Nothin' much to get up for anyway."

"You've got an interview soon, don't be so negative." Maggie always the supreme optimist.

Gwen's behaviour was irrational, bizarre, and challenging for those around her. Maggie was shocked at how, since the hospital admission, she had become so much worse.

Come on Mum, try a bit harder... please... this is becoming a living nightmare.

The 'incident' occurred at the beginning of their sixth month living as an extended family.

Gwen was sitting at the table in her nightie. She was singing 'Climb every mountain' and conducting an invisible orchestra.

Hugh had walked past the table and opened a jar of marmalade. He did not replace the lid, but left the jar on the table and walked away eating his toast on the move. There were some papers on the table. Maggie was in the kitchen making a pot of tea. Craig was also in the living room, trying to straighten his tie. He was fidgety and worried about being late. He had finally managed to find work, again in the building industry, albeit a massive drop in both salary and seniority but it was at least a job. He moved over to the table, and turned his back to Gwen to check his tie again in the mirror. He turned around. Gwen had smothered marmalade over the table, with both her hands and was now picking up the papers, sandwiching them with the aforementioned marmalade to each other.

Craig turned towards the table. "**What are you doing?**" he shouted, and lifted his right hand in desperation towards Gwen, but managed to raise his left hand, grasping his other, as if he were two people, the aggressor, and defender, and then pirouetting to the left, he hastily retreated from the breakfast carnage. Maggie was witness to this somewhat bizarre behaviour from the kitchen.

Craig walked to the window. His hands now behind his head. He stared ahead as he spoke.

"I can't do this, Maggie." He turned towards his wife. "I can't live like this. I nearly hit her. Damn it, I'm not aggressive, but it's all got out of control. This is a ludicrous situation. You're asking too much of me. I can't stay here."

Maggie was astonished by her initial thought.

Disastrous start to the first day you begin a new job; almost hitting your mother-in-law, and leaving your wife.

"Craig. You didn't actually strike her. You resisted, and turned away. It's only because you're nervous about today. It will be fine… I'll see the social worker soon."

Craig looked straight into Maggie's eyes, confirming his previous statement.

"I cannot live like this."

He left for work, and did not return home that evening,

or for the rest of that week, except once, to collect his things, which Maggie had dutifully packed into two suitcases and a large box, and left in the communal hall. They did not speak again for a very long time.

*

Hugh was brilliant with Gwen. He was young enough not to feel personally threatened that he may himself, one day, be stricken with this wicked debilitating illness. It would be a long time before advancing years flawed the functions his body took so much for granted. He was able to humour her sufficiently to avoid confrontational situations that otherwise might have got out of hand. He could escape, too. He was working now, following a seemingly endless college course that had resulted in him ditching the idea of ever becoming an electrician. He got a low-paid job working in a recording studio as a technician plus 'general help', which mostly meant he cleared up after everybody else. He didn't care about that. He loved the job because he had the facility to record his own music when possible. An absolute gem of a 'job perk'.

*

Back to Monday morning. It was now ten o'clock, and Gwen was still watching 'The Sound of Music'.

Maggie had managed to get herself washed and dressed and now she had to attempt to get her mum ready at speed. Ablutions could take the entire morning, so she had to exercise an 'Oscar' performance in powers of persuasion. Always kid gloves, as if dealing with a tempestuous toddler.

"Mum, look, the dress I have here is the one Maria

wears when she makes all the children clothes from curtains."

Gwen did not turn from the television, or speak.

Maggie continued with forced cheeriness. "Can you help me put it on then, Mum? I'm going to be late for school."

Gwen stood up. "Mustn't be late for school, dear."

Gwen walked into the shared bedroom. She fiddled with her pyjamas, but allowed Maggie to remove them without resistance. Thankfully, her pad was dry. There was no time to wash properly. Maggie managed to put the dress over Gwen's head and manoeuvre her stiff joints through the sleeves. Gwen's expression changed to irritation at this point.

Maggie intercepted, "Did you make me a packed lunch, Mum?" Diversion usually worked. She had to constantly think beyond the next step. She had become used to telling untruths to manipulate a situation, but at first, she had felt totally disloyal, as this was completely out of character. She had never lied to her mother, but now she had no choice.

*

With marmalade sandwich clasped in hand, Gwen followed Maggie down the stairs to the front tarmac drive, where an assortment of residents' cars were parked, Maggie's being the least enviable vehicle.

"If you sit in the front with me, we can get to school quickly." Gwen put the sandwich down on the seat, almost sitting on it.

Maggie retrieved the 'wet wipes' from her handbag. She had packets of these just about everywhere. She removed the sandwich, and wiped the seat.

Bloody marmalade.

The CD in the car played 'So Long, Farewell' and Gwen was content. Maggie drove with more haste than usual to the surgery.

*

Once in the waiting room, they both sat together on uniform plastic chairs. An assortment of books and magazines were scattered across a low table. One of the magazines was called 'How to knit farm animals'. There was a picture of a woollen sheep on the front. It reminded Maggie of the crafts she had made for the shop. It was incredulous to her that she had ever had the time to devote to making so many intricate items — all different, all unique to her. She would sew a label to each one. 'Crafted by Maggie'. She held her mum's hand. "We won't be long, Mum."

Gwen was trying to pick the pattern off her dress, her lips pursed, frowning forehead. She didn't speak. Maggie glanced around, aware that one or two eyes were fixed on them. This she was used to. Her mother had developed some characteristics which set her apart. Sometimes she would sing, or hum to herself, loud enough to draw attention to those around her. She often picked at her garments. Patterns on fabric worried her. Wandering off wasn't without its risks, but worst of all would be confrontational behaviour. Maggie had to tread very carefully to avoid such outbursts, so she usually let her mum sing, or wander around, without interrupting her, watching for warnings of her becoming disturbed. Gwen was quiet today but continuously picked away at her skirt, flicking the material, and then smoothing it down with the palm of her hand.

There were a number of people waiting to see the doctor. *Always running late. It's already eleven fifteen.*

15

Maybe those others are here to see the nurse. I reckon I've got about fifteen minutes before mum decides we have to leave. Come on... please let us be next.

Dr Parker appeared at the door between reception and the corridor.

"Jenny Miller."

A plump young woman, possibly early thirties, stood up, and followed the doctor through the door.

Gwen stood up.

Here we go...

"Mum. It's not our turn yet. Come and sit down."

Gwen preferred to remain standing up. She shuffled her feet, and moved towards the door, following Jenny Miller.

Maggie took her hand and walked around the reception area with her. Gwen had a firm grip, and was leading the way, with purpose, but no obvious direction. She led Maggie towards an elderly gentleman, and stood in front of him. "Hello." He had a kind smile. Gwen held out her hand to him, and he responded, repeating, "Hello. Very nice to meet you. You certainly have a firm handshake, my dear." Extracting his hand was proving difficult, but Maggie intervened, pulling her mum's ring finger up to release her grip. "She doesn't know her own strength." Maggie laughed, albeit nervously, and pulled her mum away. *Okay... we **have** to be next.*

Twenty-five laps of the waiting room later, Jenny Miller vacated the surgery and Dr Parker peered into the room gesticulating to Maggie to follow him.

Maggie sat next to his desk, and Gwen walked around tapping the walls, as if checking to see where she might perform some carpentry or hang a picture.

Maggie studied Dr Parker's profile. Probably in his forties, with good skin, grey hair touching his temple, darker towards the top and back. His eyes searching the

16

computer screen with beautiful GP hands on the mouse. Click. Click.

Marry me. I would be a devoted wife. I will love and care for you. Marry me. You are beautiful, steady, kind...

"The episode yesterday. Has this happened before?"

"No... it's very out of character. Susie is so good with her. It was completely unprovoked."

"I'm reluctant to give her sedation. It increases the risk of falls, but we could try her on something to help slow down the progression of the disease. She has deteriorated since I last saw her." His eyes continuously scanned the screen. Click, click on the mouse, and then he sat back in the swivel chair and looked at Maggie.

Your eyes can see my pain. Your beautifully trained eyes that are witness to so much.

"Are you coping?"

Do not dare make me cry. Go easy on the sympathy.

Maggie looked away, but then met his gaze. "Yes, it's tricky at times, but I'm okay."

"I know we have spoken about residential care before and you're reluctant."

Maggie could so easily give in. It had crossed her mind more than once lately, but she could not subject her mother to a life that would no longer be 'her' life.

"I've made a sort of promise to her. She sacrificed so much for me. I can't let her last years be spent in that kind of environment. I understand her."

Dr Parker smiled. "There are specialist homes. Some are very good."

Maggie responded quickly.

"Money is an issue. Mum hasn't any savings. I've discussed this with the social worker. We would need funding and the homes you're talking about won't accept her. Anyway, it's too soon. I'm not ruling it out completely, Dr Parker. Just not yet."

The printer warmed up, ready to dispatch the prescription. "These are not miracle cures, but it will slow things down a bit. She may lose her appetite, so keep an eye on her diet. Plenty of high carbohydrate foods. Call me, won't you, if you need a break? A bit of respite, even."

I would love to call you, but the respite you're offering is not the sort I desire.

"Thank you. Come on, Mum. Thank you, Dr Parker."

*

Maggie awoke during that night; her lips dry and her throat sore. She made her way to the kitchen and turned on the cold tap, letting it run for a short while, rinsing a tumbler out before filling it with the cool water. She swallowed and drank. She continued to drink the water and slowly wandered into the lounge. Sitting on the sofa, she stared into the night sky. Rarely closing the curtains, she preferred to watch the infinite stars. Only roof tops interrupted her view. The sea was there, in between the slates somewhere ahead, but indistinguishable by moonlight.

I wonder if Hugh is home. Maggie went out on to the landing to look for any tell-tale signs that her son may have arrived back earlier that night.

No sleeping noises could be heard from his room. Maggie slowly turned the handle, and then paused. *What if he has someone with him? You can't sneak into his room.*

Maggie did not investigate further. He was not there. She was almost certain. His coat was not on the hanger in the hall. *Oh, my boy... where do you go to?*

Her sense of loss seemed to be accelerated tonight. She felt so completely isolated.

Get a grip… some wine, I think.

This could almost be a textbook case of 'carer's disenchantment'.

Maggie sat in the lounge and nursed her glass of wine. It was three o'clock and so, so quiet.

She drank steadily until the glass was empty and then she refilled, enjoying the comfort.

This was her time, her space and right now, a simple pleasure that she knew could so easily transform into unease. *It's okay… just carry on a while longer.* And so she did.

*

The doorbell was ringing, and a harsh light shone through the open crack of the bedroom curtains. Maggie sat up in bed… quickly. Her head ached and the persistent distant doorbell would not cease. She heard Hugh's voice, and then a vaguely familiar deeper voice responded.

Please don't let it be… oh no, it is, it's Vicar Patrick. She groaned and glanced across the room to her mother's bed. She could see the familiar body shape curled under the duvet, fast asleep. It was nine thirty.

Hugh tapped against the bedroom door. "Mum, are you in there? The vicar's here to see you and Gran. Mum?" Hugh raised his voice slightly. "Mum!" and tapped against the door again.

Maggie waited. *Please Hugh, don't come in, and don't let Patrick in.*

Hugh walked away and Maggie heard a muffled conversation out in the hallway.

She stood up, and grabbed her dressing gown, her head seemingly departed from anything she was familiar with.

Waiting until the footsteps outside the lounge door

could be heard descending the staircase, and her son's bedroom door on the opposite side of the landing being firmly closed, she then ventured out into the lounge tentatively, but with huge relief that the coast seemed to be clear.

The empty bottle of wine was on the coffee table. *Did Hugh see that?*

There was a second bottle in the kitchen, thankfully with some of the contents still intact.

You absolute bloody idiot. Today has not started well.

*

With tea brewed, and post-shower, Maggie chose to avoid Hugh's room, but went to get her mother out of bed and, as predicted, given the extended lie in, had soaked through most of the bedding including the duvet and cover. *"My fault, Mum, not yours."*

She gently woke Gwen up, who would have continued to sleep had there been no interruption.

Compliant to trot to the bathroom with her daughter, the morning hygiene routine began with little said to each other until the toilet and washing duties had been completed.

*

They were both sitting at the table, eating toast and marmalade and drinking tea, when Hugh, smelling the familiar breakfast aroma, came into the lounge.

"Mm, toast... Hi, Gran. Mum, you were up late this morning. The vicar was here. Did you have a bad night with Gran?" Hugh sat at the table and poured tea into a mug, adding two sugars.

"Bad night with myself is more the truth. I wasn't sure

20

you had come home."

Maggie went into the kitchen to make more toast.

"I was late, but we had a good session with a new singer. Do you remember Clem from school? Clementine. You got on okay with her mum. She's written some stuff and we were trying it out last night. Gran... hey, that's my tea. Mum, get another mug."

Hugh wiped marmalade from Gwen's face.

Maggie brought fresh tea and toast to the table, and decided she was possibly still slightly drunk.

"Clementine... did she have long sort of gingery hair? Yes, I remember. Are they still around here?"

"Clem is. Not sure about her mum. I think her folks split up. She might be with her Dad."

"Oh..." Maggie faltered. She dreaded the subject of father access. The possibility that Hugh could one day choose the sanctuary his father might offer over the chaos of their flat would be understandable. He was completely brilliant with his gran, but it would surely only be a matter of time before his patience would tire.

"Dad called me. He's moving in with Amanda. He wanted you to know." Hugh glanced across the table. "He's fallen on his feet. She's minted!"

At this point, Maggie chose to return to the kitchen.

Hugh followed her. "Sorry, Mum. Completely tactless of me."

"Oh, it's alright. I'm not even sure I really care that much," she laughed. "Ha... why did he want me to know? So I can forward his post? He can have that pile over there for starters, now he's got access to another cheque book." *Change the subject right now...* "Oh, what did Vicar Patrick want so early today? I'll give him a call."

"Something about a fellowship meeting next week and wondering if you're okay?"

"There's no one to sit with your Gran… I'll have to cancel."

"So, where's Susie these days then?"

Maggie walked back to the table and stood between Gwen and her son.

"Your Gran… well, she…" spelling out the word, "h… i… t… her."

Hugh looked up. "Hit her?! Who? Gran? Susie hit Gran?"

"No. Your Gran, she h… i… t… Susie. Look, it's okay, we've been to the doctors. It's not her fault, Hugh. He's put her on some medication to help slow things down. I think it's sedated her, actually. She's really quiet today."

Gwen was sitting at the breakfast table, staring at the tablecloth with no expression. She fumbled with her fingers, her mind and eyes empty.

Maggie continued, "Susie is having a bit of a break. She'll be back soon. What are you doing today? No studio?"

Hugh pushed his chair back, and kissed his gran's forehead. "I'm heading over there now. I could be late again. Do you want me to bring anything home? Bottle of wine, maybe?" he smiled at his mum, and blew her a kiss, and he was gone.

Maggie headed for the bedroom to attack the offensive pile of laundry.

"What about 'My Fair Lady' today, Mum, for a change? If I have to listen to 'Doh a deer' one more time…" Gwen hobbled over to her chair in front of the television, and picked up the DVD of 'The Sound of Music'. Maggie pressed play. "Doh, a deer it is, then."

Chapter Two

This was how life was. This was how it was going to be for the foreseeable future. Her previous life had disintegrated and what was left was Groundhog Day.

When she and Craig were married, during the ripe years, they had spent their social time with a few select friends. There were many dinner party exchanges which had a tendency to become competitive and Maggie had always felt slightly at odds with the seemingly endless preparation that would eat up her time and make her nervous and edgy. She always lacked confidence, largely due to the fact she was in no way a professional equal with the female partners, in fact she didn't even think of herself as having a career. It was a part-time job she was good at, and enjoyed, but it would never be anything other than that. The dinner conversation often turned to job politics and she simply felt out of her depth, unable to participate with any conviction, so would consequently retire to the kitchen, preferring the company of dirty crockery and a comforting bottle of Chablis. It was during this period that it could be argued she developed an alcohol dependency of sorts. Craig would often make reference to this, making disapproving gestures to her as she returned to the post-dinner dining table.

Maggie tended to remain quiet at this point, aware that vocalising her thoughts could lead to scenes of embarrassment and would retire at the first opportunity, faking a headache or at worst, quickly heading to the bathroom to be sick.

Her marriage to Craig was uninspiring. Maggie couldn't remember at what point it was that their earlier days of cheerful playfulness mutated into a sort of humdrum bore. He worked long hours, and she was alone a great deal, but it didn't bother her at all, in fact she preferred it, but not admitting this to herself at the time. On reflection, Maggie considered the possibility that Craig may have had an affair, or at least a flirty relationship with someone at work, and that didn't bother her either. She concluded that maybe she had never really been in love, and that marrying Craig had just been an expected progression from dating regularly. Maggie had tried to remember when he proposed, but even that did not stand out as a magic life changing moment.

The friends vanished as swiftly as Craig's so-called promising career had. Fair weather friends, her mother would have called them.

Maggie opened the letter with reluctance, knowing its contents would provoke more anxiety. Another bill from the storage company holding Gwen's furniture and personal possessions. A final demand in fact, stating the next step would be debt collectors.

I'm going to have to deal with this, and soon. It's time to make a decision.

"Hello, can I speak to someone about house clearance? Well, the stuff isn't in a house anymore, so it's more a warehouse unit clearance, I suppose." Maggie held the phone into her neck, tilting her head whilst writing appropriate notes and keeping an eye on Gwen, who was marching with intent in and out of the kitchen. "It's mostly furniture but there are some lamps and rugs and quite a few ornaments too." She was listening to the response with difficulty as their signal was obviously poor in the office. "I'm sorry, I didn't catch that." Gwen had shuffled into the kitchen and not returned. "Oh... sorry, can you hold on a minute please?" Maggie rushed to where her mother was standing, emptying the best part of a carton of milk from the fridge onto the floor. "Oh, for goodness' sake, Mum." Maggie removed the carton, wiping her mother's hands on a tea towel, carefully avoiding the white pool underfoot and led her away from the kitchen into the lounge towards the phone. The line was dead.

"Mum, I have to sell your things. I can't keep them in storage anymore. We have to move forward." Gwen started to move forwards towards the kitchen again. "No, Mum, I don't mean move… Oh, Mum, sometimes I despair," but then Maggie laughed, some might have said with an air of hysteria.

Maggie was becoming exasperated. The constant mess, and challenging observations to keep one step ahead of whatever it was Gwen would do next was so often too much to bear. She didn't have any training for this. The decline in her mother's ability to do even the simplest of tasks was accelerating at such a speed she couldn't even begin to imagine how this was going to end. Where had 'her mother' gone? Alongside the sheer tedium of basic daily tasks, she was grieving for her loss, but without knowing exactly what she was losing because it changed every single day. She was losing her mother to this evil, soul destroying and debilitating illness without knowing what the outcome would be or when that would actually happen, and she couldn't even make a phone call without it turning into another catastrophe.

Gwen moved over to her chair. Maggie replaced the phone to the handset. She went into the kitchen to clear the mess. She walked towards the fridge and removed a bottle of Spanish house white. She poured her first glass. It was nine thirty in the morning.

*

She must have dozed off sitting in the armchair, her right wrist stiff under her chin and wet where she had dribbled. Attempting to get herself out of the chair, she checked the time. *Two fifteen, that can't be right?* Maggie walked into the kitchen and checked the oven clock. *Yep, two sixteen now.* With a mixture of guilt and panic she checked the bedroom. Gwen had made her own way on to her bed and was lying on top of the duvet. She wasn't asleep, and was quietly humming a tune. "Mum… I must have fallen asleep. We need lunch. What do you fancy? Cheese on toast?" Gwen's response was to move off the bed, and follow Maggie into the kitchen. The bottle of white was now empty. Checking the fridge, Maggie removed the opened pack of medium cheddar, butter and another bottle of Spanish white.

Soon they were both sitting at the table sharing cheese on toast and Maggie was drinking far more than she knew she should. "Fancy a glass, Mum? Cheese and wine go well together, you know… here, just half a glass, eh?" Gwen took the wine and drank the contents almost immediately. "Wow, steady, Mum… although I can hardly talk." She looked at Gwen's face. Her mum's familiar features had altered with her illness. She often looked lost and always so tired and her eyes no longer sparkled. It seemed to Maggie all expression had gone, replaced with hooded sad eyes. Her mum had always been so happy before all this.

She cleared the table, leaving her preferred beverage on the table. In a melancholy mood, she searched for appropriate music and chose a Janis Ian CD to play. Returning to the kitchen, she washed up greasy crockery, unaware that her mum was continuing to refill and devour the crisp white wine.

Gwen, fuelled by sugar and alcohol, began to move around the lounge in time with the music, humming and singing. She laughed out loud, and then began to chant over and over "Dare to be a Daniel… Dare to stand alone." Maggie heard her mother. "Wow, Mum, you're on good form." Gwen's new-found euphoria puzzled Maggie until she spotted the cause on the dining table. Two empty glasses and very little left in the bottle.

Horrified, Maggie checked the bottle several times and tried to recall her own consumption, concluding her mum had drunk just a little over half a bottle. She then checked the new drug bottle, reading 'avoid alcohol with this medication'. Gwen continued to shuffle around the lounge, trying to dance and almost shouting, "Dare to be a Daniel, dare to stand alone." Maggie gave her some water to drink and decided to let her mum enjoy the moment.

It's not going to kill you, is it? So, if it's a party you want, let's change the music.

Maggie searched for 'South Pacific', and increased the volume. One benefit of being on the top floor was that there was nobody upstairs to worry about, and the flat below she had never seen occupied, the so-called tenant, she didn't believe existed.

'I'm gonna wash that man right out of my hair' was met with great enthusiasm from Gwen and she laughed, attempting to sing along but unable to remember the words.

They danced together. They laughed and cried and hugged and just for a moment, there seemed to be recognition from Gwen. Their eye contact became fixed and the words that Gwen uttered were a bolt out of the blue.

"You look like Ted."

Somewhat taken aback at this completely random observation, Maggie was unsure whether to pursue the conversation or leave the unsaid hidden away, where it had always been.

"Goodness, Mum, where did that come from? You haven't mentioned his name for such a long time."

Maggie tilted her head to one side questioning her mother further.

"What happened to Ted, Mum, can you remember?"

Gwen became agitated, their eye contact broken, and she mumbled to herself incoherently, shuffling away towards the window.

"It's okay, Mum, don't worry, I'm sure Ted is fine, wherever he is."

The moment was lost. There was to be no further conversation. So many questions Maggie had harboured within herself for years were still unanswered, and as far as she was concerned, would always be simmering in her mind, with various probabilities. Depending on her mood when ruminating, she would express her anger and frustration verbally like a child role-playing, after which she would feel stupid. Almost as if she were a child. However, somewhere deep inside her that child was still there, unable to grow. There were times when she thought she could even be emotionally retarded. The self-destruct button pressed so often, needed removing. If her mother was broken, she was also splintered, and it wouldn't take much for her to shatter completely.

*

Maggie slept very little that night; her mind was disturbed and she had over-consumed the wine. Payback came in the form of palpitations, panic and nausea.

I cannot get my thoughts together. I think I might just die, and at least then this whole mess would end.

Chapter Three

The next morning, Susie arrived at the flat, clasping flowers and a packet of 'Indulgent' chocolate biscuits.

She turned towards Gwen sitting in the chair. "Hi, Gwen." Susie brought warmth and life into a dull and dismal lounge. "Hi, Maggie. I thought I would pop in, and sit with Gwen for a bit. Oh, Maggie, are you alright? You look a bit worn out... I'm really sorry about over-reacting the other week. I'd had a bit of a beef with my mum and wasn't dealing well with anything really. Gwen didn't mean to lash out at me, did you, Gwen?" Susie walked over to the familiarly positioned chair close enough to the television for enthusiastic viewing. She gave Gwen a kiss on her head.

"It's completely understandable how upset you were; however, you cannot imagine how thrilled I am to see you, Susie. Would you really sit with Mum for a while? I'm just tired and yes, I suppose completely worn out! I would love to get out in the fresh air and blow these cobwebs away."

"That's fine, Maggie. I've had withdrawal from 'The Sound of Music' and need my fix! Don't rush back. Have a break. Is Hugh here?"

"If I'm honest, I have no idea. We're like ships that pass in the night, but if he is, say hello from his mother and suggest to him we should share the dining table sometime."

Her relief in walking away from the flat was enormous. It was cloudy but not raining, with a welcome breeze, helping to clear the fog that consumed any rational thinking.

Joy, joy, joy. Susie, I love you. I have got to get a grip. Come on, Maggie. You cannot continue with this perpetual cycle of disillusionment.

She faced the pearl grey sky.

Lord, please give me the strength I need to continue.

Jumbled thoughts, hard to decipher. The previous night's events repeated themselves over and over again like an irritating tune from which there was no escape. She was consumed with guilt in allowing her mother to drink. *What kind of so-called caring daughter am I? If social services knew, they would take her away from me. God, please give me strength to care for her the way I should do. I mustn't crumble, I need to find control.*

*

The promenade café was a favourite of hers, with particularly good coffee. The shabby chic theme always inspired craft ideas in her head, but she had little inclination or time to be creative these days. Maggie tried to put things into perspective.

You're only human, and you've got your limits, just like anybody would have. Even the doctor thinks it's too much, he practically said so.

Maggie gazed out of the window, watching the grey seashore breathe in and out, covering the pebbles and retracting over and over; the tide eternal, just as her own life seemed to be at that moment. An eternal tide of frustration.

'This Woman's Work' by Kate Bush was playing in the background.

Blurred vision interrupted the scenic view… the lyrics too beautiful and so poignant.

Maggie soon headed out of the café as more people filtered in. Once outside, she managed to compose herself and she walked. Determined, hands deep inside her jacket pockets, she continued along the promenade until she could go no further, halted by a tumbling cliff, cornered off with hazard tape and a 'Nobody must go beyond this point Police Notice' abruptly interrupting what could have been a further few miles.

She turned around and retraced her steps, wondering how much time Susie really meant when she said 'don't rush back'. An hour or two, maybe. Three was taking advantage, probably.

There were things she had to do. Certainly, she needed to sort out the practicalities of keeping her mum at home and addressing the immediate problem of all her furniture in storage. There would be another bill soon, and she was pondering what to do, when it dawned on her that the storage warehouse wasn't too far from where she was at that moment. She had been away only about an hour or so.

*

The warehouse felt cold, with pallets stacked high at one end, and huge metal containers, numbered in white paint alongside the other two walls. Wooden steps led up to a reception office untidily adorned with files, random papers, more phones than Maggie could comprehend them needing, and several tarnished mugs with cold tea and coffee remains filling a stainless steel sink which didn't look like it had been acquainted with a spray cleaner or soapy water for some time.

How do people function in this mess?

"Gwen Sanderson. That's container number 15. She owes £260. Here's the invoice." Lacking a somewhat gracious approach, the storage supervisor passed a typed invoice, ink-stained and grubby, across the metal desk.

"Thank you. Can I see the contents and then decide what to keep?"

"You can do what you like love, so long as this

invoice gets paid." He sniggered, scratching his head. "People leave their stuff in 'ere for months sometimes… I reckon they forget about it until I give 'em a reminder 'ow much they owe me. Just makes you realise you don't need 'arf of what you've got, eh?"

"No, I suppose not, I'll have a quick look now, but I haven't got my car with me, so I'll come back with a cheque and take what I need. The rest can go to charity, or do you sell unwanted items?"

"You won't get much love. I'm tellin' yer. Kids these days, they want new. Ikea and all that Scandinavian crap."

They both walked to unit number 15, and with the expertise of a jailer, the inner door was opened to reveal Gwen Sanderson's previous life.

It was odd seeing familiar furniture completely divorced from its rightful place in such a hostile cold environment. Maggie couldn't decipher anything for a moment, and gazed around, unsure of what to say or what she should do.

Mr Storage Supervisor stood motionless next to her. "I'll give yer a couple of 'undred quid for them bits of furniture, but all this in boxes will 'ave to be cleared out of 'ere."

"Can I think about it?" *Bloody hell, what else can I do but just let it go?*

"If yer gonna leave it another week, then that's another fifty on top… Just sayin'."

Maggie inhaled, pursed her lips and replied. "I'll be back tomorrow with a cheque, and I'll take out these boxes. Have the furniture, and we'll settle the difference. I haven't anywhere to put it, and no means of transporting it either, so… you have it."

"Tell yer what love. Call it quits, and just clear them boxes."

At that point, Maggie knew she had been 'had', but nodded and said very politely, "Thank you."

*

She walked with purpose back home, aware of probably having exceeded her sitter's shift expectations, and also to avoid a predicted shower of rain.

Once indoors, Hugh and Susie were cross-legged on the floor, Hugh playing gentle acoustic rhythms on his guitar, and Susie absorbed in the moment.

Gwen was sitting with a cardboard box on her knee, her hands deep inside, revealing coloured pieces of material, foam, and wool.

"What have you got there, Mum?"

Susie looked up, and smiled. "It's a rummage box. A friend suggested it. She works at Primrose Lodge and they have all sorts of activity ideas. I think Gwen would enjoy some time there, Maggie. They are so well equipped."

Maggie knew about Primrose Lodge, and was aware of its merits, and she was also aware of their charges. "I've been thinking about somewhere like that, Susie, but…"

Hugh intervened, "Costs a bomb, I expect… eh, Mum?"

Maggie nodded and walked into the kitchen. "Anyone hungry?" Without waiting for a response, she started to prepare supper, hoping for once it could be a family occasion rather than the usual serve, eat, and clear up.

It became exactly as she had hoped, and the usual sombre mood of mealtimes was uplifted by youthful chatter, laughter, and delightful banter, which even Gwen seemed to pick up on, smiling as she divorced her food from her plate to the table, disregarding completely any kind of table etiquette.

"I don't suppose anyone has a van at your studio, do they, Hugh?"

"What do you need one for?"

"I have some boxes that need collecting from the warehouse where your Gran's things have been kept."

Hugh looked at his mum, and carried on eating. "I can do that for you, Mum. I'll get the van from work. When for?"

"Tomorrow?"

"Yeah, that's fine. No worries. I'm going up there tonight anyway, so I can bring it back here."

"What a wonderful son you have, Maggie." Susie was retrieving stray food from the surrounding surfaces and floor. She added, "Can't be an easy thing to do, sorting out all your mum's things. I'll help too, if you like, Hugh."

Sometimes Maggie was in awe of just how perceptive her son could be. She would cherish the time she had with him, knowing it would not last. He would fly the nest. That's how it should be, and that's how it would be, but just for now, he was here.

Chapter Four

It was late the following afternoon before Hugh was able to deliver the boxes retrieved from the warehouse. He and Susie between them had managed to carry all five up to the flat, giggling as one box came close to collapsing, the contents of which breaking free from the poorly taped cardboard case. "The bottom has gone soggy," Susie remarked. "It must have been damp in the warehouse."

"You are both heroes and deserve as much tea as you can drink... or what about a glass of wine?" Maggie was feeling relieved, knowing the storage issue was now resolved, and her mother's belongings, albeit precious few, were now safely at home, to be sorted out at leisure. "Sounds good, Mum. I'll stack this lot up in the corner of your bedroom, shall I?"

"There isn't anywhere else to put it, so yes, that's fine Hugh. Watch your backs, both of you."

Later, Maggie made sandwiches in the kitchen, glancing at her son and Susie in the lounge together, as they chatted whilst Hugh strummed nonchalantly on his guitar, and Susie hummed familiar tunes, encouraging Gwen to join in, but sadly with little response.

*

Later that night, nursing a warm glass of ruby comfort, Maggie sat close enough to the window to catch the night sky with stars staggered unevenly high, high above. An unknown quantity, an unknown world to most, and a visible means of escapism. *What goes on up there, I wonder? It cannot be, that there are more stars than grains of sand, surely? We know so little down here. Why do we fret over trivial things?*

Maggie made her way into the kitchen, and drained

the remains of the bottle of red into her glass. *No point keeping that wee drop for tomorrow.* Sighing and returning to her chair, she contemplated the day ahead. *So, another day tomorrow… but not another dollar, though… precious few dollars left for the rest of this week.* As she snuggled into her armchair, her thoughts turned to the mother and daughter impromptu party night. Looking sideways, she caught her reflection in the long mirror on the wall. *Hmmm, so, I look like my father, do I? Well that's something I've never even thought about before.*

When she eventually retired to her bedroom, needing to keep the room in darkness for fear of waking Gwen, she almost walked straight into the uneven stack of boxes. *Whoops, steady as you go there… better shift that lot soon before it's Mum who falls over it.*

Maybe that can be tomorrow's, or rather, today's mission.

*

The newly acquired rummage box donated by Susie was a success and enabled Maggie some time to clear her bedroom. Like a toddler with a new toy, Gwen seemed content to fondle the fabrics inside the brightly coloured box, picking them out and stroking fur and feathers and hanging pink netting up to the light, observing colour and shade changes.

Her daughter was also rummaging through her own recently acquired boxes but for different reasons and with much less enthusiasm.

I don't remember packing any of this in here. She had managed to sort the contents of three boxes into 'keepsakes' and 'discard ASAP' piles but a fourth box was unfamiliar. Then she remembered that Craig, prior to his departure from her life, had displayed an uncharacteristic random gesture of cooperation and offered to help her, when it became obvious her mother would be moving in with them. *He must have packed this box. It just looks like a heap of old Christmas cards and junk mail. How typical, not to even sort through it.*

Maggie glanced over at Gwen. She was still occupied with ribbons and fabrics.

I'll have to throw this lot out. Christmas cards from years ago, and birthday cards.

There were some old black and white photographs creased with age, with unfamiliar faces and places, although Maggie recognised the pictures of herself as a small child with a lopsided fringe, and one of her riding a tricycle. *It was blue, that bike, with a silver bell and a funny shaped basket on the front. It was never in the middle... always pushed to one side.* She had seen some of the photos before and decided to keep them all together, and at some point, make an album, and frame one or two for the wall.

There was a photo of a young Gwen standing close to the entrance of a church. Above the door, carved into the weather-stained stone lintel arch was the inscription 'Agnus Dei Have Mercy on Us'.

How old were you there, I wonder? Had you met Ted by then? Was that pre-me?

A loud crash interrupted her thoughts, and Maggie quickly rushed over to where calamity had struck, finding Gwen who had exhausted her rummage, and thrown the box plus contents at the television, knocking the DVD player to the ground. Fortunately, there was no permanent damage, apart from 'Sony' now reduced to 'Son' and in less than 2 minutes, the flat was once again alive with 'The Sound of Music', with a very young Julie Andrews embracing the Bavarian Alpine meadows. Maggie abandoned the photographs and embraced the kitchen to make soup.

Chapter Five

It was several days later when Maggie found the letter.

Creased from years of repeated folding and reading, the pages so delicate supporting beautiful handwriting shook as Maggie read over and over again, her hands trembling, and her eyes fixed on each sentence.

Courtyard Café
St John's C of E Church
Glimstone
February 1963

My Dearest Gwen.

It is with sadness and sorrow in my heart that I write to you, for my darling I would never wish this pain that I carry within me to be bestowed upon anyone. I wonder constantly how you are feeling and how you have been able to make this heartbreaking decision to end our friendship.

I know I have to accept your decision to move away and of course I understand why you have made up your mind to change the course of your life.

I cannot give you what you so deserve and it pains me to know that one day you will find someone to share your life and settle down and maybe even start a family with. That is completely selfish of me, but oh how I wish that person could be me. How I wish things could be different, but you and I both know why it can't be.

I will continue my life and work here within my Father's parish and I will continue to care for Maureen, but I have to admit to that being my duty rather than my passion.

I am a prisoner of guilt from which I cannot escape but my darling, despite that, I do not and never will regret the love we shared. Please think of me in a good way and remember I will always be with you in my heart and soul.

God bless you, Gwen. Goodbye my darling and I pray you will find happiness.

Your loving friend. Ted

Maggie searched the writing, making sure she had read and re-read every letter of each word. She looked at the date, which was hard to read as the ink had faded, but she was certain it was February 1963. She had been born in September 1963.

Mum was pregnant when he wrote this.

He didn't know about me... he couldn't have, otherwise why would have written 'you may even start a family'? If he knew she was pregnant, he would have surely made reference to it in this letter. And who the hell is Maureen?

Courtyard Café, Glimstone. That's where Mum was for a while. Glimstone, I remember her talking a bit about it and thinking it sounded like a landmark in Narnia.

Oh Mum. You never told him about me. He doesn't know he has a daughter.

And this Maureen, who is she? His mother? No, he would call her mother, surely.

Maureen... Maureen?

Sitting back on her knees, the obvious became clear. She placed the letter on the bedroom carpet. Maggie covered her face with her hands and then pulling her hands down to her mouth, she exhaled. Breathing calmly and slowly she confirmed with a sigh. Ted must have been married.

Chapter Six

Courtyard Café was as Maggie had imagined it to be. Within a walled garden, the grey stone building set aside from the church was a welcome for those who wanted to be close to God, without participating in a church ceremony. She sat at one of the wooden tables, nursing an anaemic coffee and pondered what to do.

It was now a couple of weeks after finding the letter. She had been mulling over the contents and weighing up the advantages of seeking out the place where her father had spent time with her mother, all along knowing perfectly well she would not be able to resist the temptation that blatant curiosity bestowed upon her. This very building could possibly have been home to the start of a forbidden love. Did they meet here? It would have been an acceptable place to share precious time without any hint of suspicion from others.

To say life had become an emotional rollercoaster was a major understatement. Maggie had read the letter with such frequency she was now able to recite word for word its contents, and had even spoken it aloud, with a hope of her mother recognising the narrative, possibly shedding some light on its contents to prevent Maggie from exploding with frustration, but of course, Gwen had not reacted with any recognition, and obviously, had she even shown a flicker of understanding, there was no way on this earth she would have been able to comprehensively explain the roots of Maggie's very existence.

Maggie observed her surroundings. Worn stone flooring with non-matching wooden tables and chairs softened with floral cushions tied on to the chair seats, and jam jars containing herbs passing as table decorations. Maggie thought it all looked rather dated but could see the effect they were trying to achieve. Various prints and watercolours hung from uneven walls, some with a small price tag, and in the background, just faintly, Maggie heard choral anthems, none of which she could put a name to, even though they sounded familiar.

So I wonder if this waitress knows the name Ted Clarke. I would say not, judging by her age, but it's worth a try. With optimism being her watchword, Maggie made an attempt to start a conversation when she was approached again by the accommodating member of staff.

"More coffee for you? We've just baked some rather scrummy scones too, served with fresh cream and jam," she smiled hopefully. "Can I tempt you?" Her manner was old for her young years. Maggie decided this enthusiastic supplier of unwanted calories had perhaps never travelled beyond Glimstone and was destined to remain exactly where she was for many years to come.

"No, thank you, although very tempting I must say… It's just," she hesitated, "I'm looking for a friend of my mother's. His name is Ted Clarke. Have you heard of him? Do you know anyone with that name?" *I have about as much chance of this being a yes, as finding out she is also a relative.*

"No, sorry. I don't know anyone of that name here. We've got banana bread, too and some gluten-free brownies if you're intolerant, you know… to gluten?" As hopeful to delight Maggie with Courtyard Café's baking extravaganzas as Maggie was to finding her parentage, it was clear that this encounter was in no way going to enlighten things further, so hastily settling the bill for the solitary coffee, Maggie made an exit and considered her next move.

It was of course, to venture into the church. Above the lintel, crowning the ancient east facing door were the words 'Agnus Dei'. She recalled the photograph and felt yet another stab of familiarity that had been present ever since she had arrived. It was not a familiarity in the sense that she was on familiar territory, but it was more a sense of belonging. The weight of anger and resentment ever present when she had pondered the need to know just who she was — her ancestry, her genetic makeup — had in some way been diluted in the knowledge that her father had not even known of her existence. He had not abandoned her or her mother. It had been her mother's decision, to go it alone, and although the reason for this was a revelation so completely out of character for her, Maggie couldn't help but feel an admiration for her mother's blatant dare-devil antics, and was, if anything, impressed by her forbidden fruit pickings. Rather than being the demure woman she had always considered her to be, there had been a fiery passion to which she had succumbed.

A bit of a dark horse, Mum. I wonder what other skeletons there are.

Once inside the church, her immediate need was to slip in between two pews, sit down, lower her head and pray. Her thoughts were so jumbled, it was hard to compose words to God without it becoming a frantic cry for help, but she reconciled that overall, God was used to that from many a poor wretch, and he would in no way judge her for simply begging for answers and clues as to where her father was and if he was, in fact, still alive. She also felt a need to ask forgiveness. *Father, forgive me for I have sinned, and continue to do so, but I can't find any escape, and I want it all to be different and yet not in the way that comes across. I don't want my mother gone. I want **her** back, and if I can't have the woman that loved me and was brave, and cared, and never ever seemed to tire from being so completely wonderful and altruistic and selfless... If she has to die... can at least the end for*

her be… be… a slip into sleep without her knowing… so
she can fade into her dreams, and not ever waken.

Maggie heard the inner church door open, and felt uncomfortable, preferring to pray alone, and wishing her inadequate conversation with God had been more concise and less garbled.

The intruder seemed to be familiar with the church, and was searching through a cupboard at the back by what would appear to be the choir vestry, judging by the long blue and white robes visibly hanging from a clothes rail.

Maggie seized her opportunity. The woman looked to be over sixty, maybe even seventy plus. Hard to tell, but just maybe…?

"Excuse me." The woman looked up and smiled.

"Yes, can I help you?"

"I'm trying to find out about someone called Ted Clarke. He was the son of a vicar here back in the sixties and… well, it's for my mother, really. She's not well, and she's unable to get about much now."

The lady smiled again. "I knew Edward. He used to have the café here. Courtyard Café.

Such a lovely man."

Maggie felt a little dizzy and grabbed hold of the nearby wooden pew.

"Do you know where he is now? Is he still local, I mean?"

"I'm sorry, I don't know exactly where he is now. The vicar, Godfrey, his father, died and Edward left this parish then. I do believe he moved abroad after his wife died."

Her light-headedness now extended to a dry mouth and a feeling of sheer desperation.

To be yearning for more information without appearing overly intrigued, was almost impossible. What should she say?

You see the thing is he's my Dad and I would just quite like to see him just once, if at all possible.

"Oh well, if he's abroad I suppose he could be anywhere. Maybe not even alive now.

My mother lost touch with him… with them both," she added hastily, "and she was just hoping, you know, to catch up with everything and see how things turned out for him… for them. I'll tell her he's not around anymore."

The woman was clearly thinking hard, and then she gave a little shriek.

"If you give me your telephone or mobile number, I think I know who might have some information, and I'll get them to phone you, or I can. What's your name? I'm Cathy."

"Maggie, Maggie Chadwick. I must be the only person not to have a mobile phone, but here's my home phone number." She rummaged in her shoulder bag and found a scrap of paper and a pen, scribbling the number with nervous fingers, and then passing it to Cathy. "Thank you so much. My mother will be so thrilled to know I've met someone who knew him, even if…"

Faltering, her voice trembling slightly, she paused, and turned away.

"Who is your mother?" Cathy asked.

"Gwen Sanderson."

Cathy showed no recognition and Maggie felt an element of relief but just why, she wasn't sure.

*

Maggie's thoughts were absorbed by her visit to St John's, and it was with a dull ache she drove back home. Mostly she was relishing having the freedom of driving, and to be somewhere else. Her mind was so preoccupied she almost drove through red lights, but pulled up sharply, receiving humiliating horn blowing from the vehicle behind.

Come on, concentrate. There's nothing you can do now. Maybe that warden woman will come up with something. But she knew in her heart that it was unlikely.

Home to Mum, and Susie, and Hugh, and I'll pick up a bottle or two en route.

*

Maggie arrived back to find an ambulance had parked outside the flats. Instinctively she knew it would be her mum who was in need of help from the medics. *Oh Lordy, what now?*

Hurrying up the staircase, she was breathless when she almost fell through the front door.

"Mum," Hugh greeted Maggie. "Gran has fallen. I'm so sorry, Mum." Hugh looked anxious and embraced his mum as she walked into the lounge.

"What happened?"

Susie was there too, holding Gwen's hand, kneeling next to her.

"She was watching TV, in her chair, and we both went into the kitchen to get supper ready, and the next thing… bang, and she was just down on the carpet by her chair. I don't know what she was trying to do, but she became kind of listless, and her eyes were rolling."

Hugh continued, "Maybe it was another stroke, or what was it she had before, a T-something?"

"It was a TIA, so the doctor at the hospital said. Oh, Mum." Maggie held her mother's hand. Two ambulance attendants, a man and a woman, were crouched over Gwen, who was lying on the stretcher on the floor. One held an oxygen mask over her face and the woman was attaching cardiac monitoring stickers to Gwen's chest.

They looked up and smiled at Maggie. It was the woman who spoke.

"We're just checking her heart and giving her some air, so her oxygen levels go up a bit. We don't think she's broken anything, but she needs to go to hospital just to be checked over. Don't worry, this kind of thing happens a lot with the elderly. We'll take her to The General to the MAU department."

"They know her at The General — she has a permanent reservation there." Maggie's light-hearted comment was merely an attempt to hide her anxiety.

*

She was tired after her previous long drive, but she followed the ambulance to the hospital, an all too familiar route.

As much as she needed to see some kind of end to her monotonous daily routine, and indeed a spell in hospital would free her of complete responsibility, she then became consumed with guilt at even contemplating her own benefits to this situation, when her mother was about to be put through yet more tests and demeaning medical intrusion.

If only she could just go to sleep, peacefully, and slip away into a beautiful dream and end this degrading decline.

MAU was always a manic playing field for just about all grades of medical and non-medical staff. Buzzing machines, continuous phones ringing, bleep, bleep, bleep, wherever you looked.

The nurses were attentive, and Maggie waited in the cupboard they described as the 'relatives' rest room'. She could see into the area where Gwen had been taken, and waited for the anticipated diagnosis. UTI, TIA, or some other disturbing abbreviation.

It was an hour before somebody came to see her.

He was a young doctor, who looked exhausted and malnourished. *Too many chocolate bars from the machine and nothing to sustain you, you poor love.*

"Hello Mrs Um…"

"Chadwick. Maggie Chadwick."

"Hello Mrs Chadwick, I'm Dr McPhearson. Sorry you have had to wait so long. We have taken some bloods from your mother and tomorrow we will do a brain scan to ascertain whether she has suffered a stroke, but it would seem she has a UTI so we will treat that with antibiotics and… He glanced at his notes, and coughed, seemingly embarrassed about the next question. "Have you thought about whether she should have a DNAR status, Mrs Sanderson?"

"Chadwick."

"I'm sorry, yes, Mrs Chadwick. She has, I understand, a progressive dementia."

Maggie looked up towards the young man in front of her. *You can't be more than twenty-seven or twenty-eight.*

"Yes. I have discussed this previously and she would not want to be resuscitated, in fact, she would see it as a blessing if she were to die. Maggie faltered "I'm sorry, I don't want to appear callous, but this is a living death, as I'm sure you are aware, Dr McPhearson."

He smiled in a kind and reassuring professional manner.

"We will ensure she gets the best care. Would you like to see her? She's very tired and…"

"Thank you." Maggie made her way out of the cupboard and walked towards the cubicle, now home for her mother for this, and possible several more nights.

Maggie sat by the bed for a short while, and then decided to go home, as Gwen was sleeping, and was completely oblivious to her daughter's presence.

"Goodnight, Mum. Sleep tight, and don't let the bed bugs get you." She kissed her forehead and then walked away.

*

Over the next few days, two things occurred which raised Maggie's spirits and gave her hope.

She had been tidying the whole of the flat, making the most of her mother's absence and attempting to add some homely touches, upgrading her living accommodation to something more pleasing to the eye than a rehabilitation unit for the elderly infirm.

A letter had arrived and immediately she recognised the handwriting on the envelope.

Goodness, Craig, to what do I owe this pleasure? Not like you to write even a shopping list, never mind an actual letter.

His note was brief.

'Maggie. Please accept these two cheques. The larger amount is for Hugh to help towards his studying or anything that might help his career, and the other is for you.

I am aware that I have not provided for you or my son financially lately and the enclosed is wholly inadequate, but it is an attempt to help out, albeit a one off.

I hope you will understand and you do not have a too harsh opinion of me.

Best Wishes
Craig.'

Hugh was to receive £10,000 and Maggie £2,000. Yes, there was no question that this would help. Should she have returned it, saying 'stick your money'? Maybe. However, she was in no position to refuse this good fortune, so without over-analysing or debating the ethics of this random gesture, she returned a note, simply saying, 'Thank you, yes this will help.'

The other bolt from the blue was a phone call. By now, Gwen had been in the MAU department for three days, shortly to be transferred to the ward where she had been a patient once before.

Her diagnosis had been suggestions of further TIAs and a CI (chest infection) and UTI (urinary tract infection). Maggie was becoming familiar with the jargon. She had been to the hospital every day, and had just returned to hear the phone ringing. *I'm not going to make that in time.* But she did. "Hello, Maggie speaking."

"Maggie, this is Cathy. You met me at St John's Church the other day."

The mention of this significant building made Maggie's heart race a little.

"Oh yes, hello Cathy. How nice of you to call back." *I can hardly bear to hear this.*

"Well, I have some news about Edward... Ted Clarke. You were asking about him for your mother."

He's alive.

"Oh yes, Ted Clarke. I'd almost forgotten." *So untrue.*

Cathy continued, "My friend has kept in touch with his ex-wife, and it would seem he is still alive and kicking so to speak, but now he lives in Spain."

Ex-wife? Spain?

Maggie cleared her throat, "Oh, so he married again after Maureen died, and umm, so he's living in Spain now... I mean is he living in Spain now, still?" *Keep your voice just a little less frantic.*

"Yes, it's all quite a saga, really. He moved over there shortly after Maureen died, and he married again to someone called Grace and they had two sons…"

I've got brothers? I think I'm going to be sick.

"But it would seem things didn't work out. He set up a sort of café or bistro over there and it's still a going concern. His sons run it now, of course, but anyway I'm rambling, and you don't want to know all this."

*You have no idea how much I **do** want to know all of this… and more.*

"Anyway, you can let your mother know of his whereabouts now."

Maggie was attempting to process all that had been said, but the knowledge that she had siblings was consuming her thoughts and she could barely reply but continued with, "Yes, I'll tell her, and Cathy, thank you for going to all that trouble, I mean you don't really know me, and I do appreciate it, but could I ask just one thing please? Where in Spain is he or where are they I should say?"

"Nerja. It's a resort on the Costa del Sol. He's escaped our dreary weather, Maggie. Ha! Can you blame him?"

"No, I can't… Thank you, Cathy. Maybe I'll see you at the church there sometime. It was nice and I would really like to meet up again. I owe you at least a coffee."

"I'm always around. I only live next door so come and knock when you're next over."

The conversation ended with several 'cheerios' and repeated 'thank yous' from Maggie, and she sat at the table, consumed with the fact her father was alive and she had two brothers.

*This is beyond believable. Dear Lord, thank you. **Thank you!** But what on earth do I do now?*

Chapter Seven

It was inevitable that Gwen would be destined for a transfer to Bridge House, suitably named, as it was built close to a disused railway bridge.

This decision by the hospital had not met with Maggie's approval of course, but she was in no position to argue.

She had pleaded with the doctors to allow her to manage her mother herself, knowing only too well this was a practical impossibility. Gwen could no longer walk any distance and was clearly not going to manage the staircase at the flat and was now in need of more personal care and associated equipment. So it was with reluctance she signed the necessary paperwork provided by the efficient assigned social worker, who seemed to think this was going to be just a temporary move where mobilisation and rehabilitation could be initiated, with a hopeful outcome. A glass more than half full approach was undeniably generous, but Maggie's pessimism was confirmed after her first visit where it was clear that the very idea of any kind of rehabilitation was beyond the capabilities of most of the depleted staff, a sad situation emphasised by the manager, whose opening sentence was, "I told them at the hospital not to bring her here today," permanent irritation seemingly her default setting. "Molly and Mabel are both off sick and these agency girls need to wake up and smell the coffee." She was searching her overloaded desk for Gwen's registration papers. Maggie hovered in the doorway, not sure whether to enter, or go unescorted to find her mother.

"Shall I...?"

The manager, whose name wasn't obvious, continued to rummage amongst various piles of documents and folders. "I'll get all her care plan written up when I have time, just sign the admission document, it's here somewhere… Oh, here it is," and she presented Maggie with multiple copies of consent forms for a variety of possible outcomes, none of which made a lot of sense, but she dutifully went along with this bizarre introduction to life in a care home.

It was Miriam who was attending to her mother when Maggie finally found the bedroom they had assigned for Gwen. She wondered if the criteria for working there was to have a name beginning with the letter M.

"Hello, Mum."

Miriam was a kindly soul, who punctuated most sentences with "Bless her."

"She's tired, bless her, it's a big upheaval for her, bless her, to be pushed from pillar to post and not really know what's going on… bless her."

Gwen seemed remarkably bright, considering this radical change to her domestic surroundings, and was enjoying the attention paid to her, firstly by the hospital ambulance drivers and now the motherly Miriam.

"I'll get her things put away, shall I?" Maggie was unsure of how much responsibility she was now allowed to have, wanting to fit in, without unintentionally interfering.

Miriam was pleased to receive some help. "I'll get you both a cuppa, shall I? While you put her bits and bobs away. Does she take sugar?"

"Yes, two please, but none for me. Thank you, erm, Miriam." A badge with Miriam's name on was clear to see.

"Aw, sweet tooth she's got then… bless her." Her large frame made an exit and Maggie perused these new surroundings, and this new situation.

"Well, Miriam seems nice, doesn't she, Mum?"

Gwen smiled and followed the pattern on the

upholstered chair with her finger, humming, seemingly quite content.

*

Once back at home, Maggie sat quietly and reflected on recent events.

This isn't what I wanted for you, Mum. None of it. Not the illness, or the outcome. It's all gone horribly wrong, and I don't know what to do to put it right, if putting it right is even an option anymore.

The picture she had envisaged for Gwen's twilight years was supposed to include pleasant trips to memorable destinations where they had enjoyed time together. Afternoon tea in beautiful gardens, and walks along the beach together. Going to musical events at the theatre and maybe even having holidays away, somewhere quiet and quaint, maybe in Cornwall.

Her mind drifted, and she began to think about the phone call from Cathy. Her father was alive and well and was living in Spain. Maggie searched for spiritual enlightenment. Had this revelation regarding her father been sent at this specific time to in some way guide her? Reading God's intentions was always a dilemma, trying to piece together the options he wants, against the stumbling blocks he inevitably puts in your way. Is this to test her reaction and commitment? It was a conundrum she had faced more than once in her life, and never more poignantly than now.

She knew what she must and wanted to do and Craig's money would give her this one-off chance.

*

Later that evening, as Hugh, Maggie and Susie consumed

macaroni cheese and two bottles of white plonk, the conversation became unusually animated.

"Mum, are you serious? How long have you known about all of this? You're going to Spain?" Hugh was shocked by Maggie's garbled account of recent revelations. She had tried to keep her own feelings as low key as possible, trying to be laid back, as if travelling fourteen hundred miles to find your father was a fairly average thing to do.

Susie was in awe of Maggie. "Wow, Maggie, this is so exciting! Your dad doesn't even know about you? All these years? You've got to go. Hugh, don't you see it's really important for your mum?"

Hugh was shaking his head in disbelief. "My Grandad lives in Spain?"

Put that way, Maggie found it difficult not to burst into tears. Hugh had a grandfather and uncles. She hadn't really explored in her own mind the implications discovering her father would have on her son. Hugh, although shocked, was warming to the idea of his mum travelling to Europe in such bizarre and unusual circumstances.

"Mum… this is mind blowing!" His usual cool laid back and calm persona exposing a raw edge was so out of character. "What about Gran? She's going to wonder where you've gone. How long will you be away?" Questions and disbelief all fired at Maggie, who was arming herself with multiple top ups.

"I don't know how long, Hugh. Not long, I suppose, just a few days and I don't think your Gran would know if I'd left her room, never mind the country, but if you and Susie could keep a watchful eye over things at Bridge House, I would feel a lot better about going. I'm doing this for your Gran as much as for me, Hugh."

Am I? Who am I really doing this for?

"I'm not sure what I'm hoping will come of it all, but if I don't do it now, I never ever will." Maggie drained her glass and went out to the kitchen for another bottle. She heard Hugh and Susie muttering quietly to each other, and waited a short while before returning to the table.

"One thing that has definitely got to happen, Mum, is you get a bloody mobile phone. I'll get you one now I've got some dosh to play with."

"That's for your education, Hugh."

"Mum, you're not going to Spain on your own without a mobile. Just leave it to me."

This sudden assertiveness from her son made her feel as if somehow roles had just slightly readjusted. She felt a sense of relief. This was all new territory, which seemed to be opening so many new avenues for them both. She couldn't quell her anticipation and excitement, but more than anything, apprehension. Now she had said what she was going to do, it had suddenly become a commitment.

Her list of 'to dos' was a deviation from the norm, usually consisting of 'pick up prescription' and 'do a food shop'.

Get Mum settled and take DVD player and S of M tape to Bridge House.
Pack 'the letter'
Passport
Sort out flight and accommodation
Meals for Hugh
Check if any doctor's appointments for Mum
Find suitcase or similar
Sort out some summer clothes
Learn how to use mobile

Book for plane
Phrase book

Maggie's excitement presented as an uncharacteristic lightness of mood, but she found herself frequently staring ahead, her mind deviating from the job in hand, losing focus and having to refer to her list, which was ever increasing.

She was also quite terrified and didn't really believe that this journey into the absolute unknown would become a reality.

However, it very soon became just that.

Chapter Eight

The plane was practically full. Maggie had commandeered a window seat towards the rear, bitterly regretting her choice when realising she would have to disturb her two neighbours if needing the toilet. She would abstain from any fluids and hopefully hold out 'til the Spanish airport.

It had been such a long time since she had flown anywhere, the entire procedure from booking in to boarding the plane had been fraught with self-doubt as to whether she was in the right place at the right time and what documents she needed to actually board successfully. They had been patient with her when she dropped her passport and then couldn't find her boarding pass, and she felt rather humiliated when a young competent passenger behind her produced all that was needed with such an air of confidence as if he were catching a bus, whilst she fumbled with her bag in an attempt to deposit her passport safely.

Maggie, you need to get out more.

She contemplated the last few days, wondering if her mother had absorbed anything she had said to her about being away. Her concerns about Bridge House escalated in her mind with every mile of separation. She was sure the carers would be kind, especially Miriam, who seemed to have taken a shine to Gwen, but it was the manager she had serious reservations about, mostly because of her lack of compassion and utter rudeness. Maggie had told her she had to be away for a few days, and she was worried Gwen would miss her, but this was met with a complete lack of sympathy, shrugging her shoulders saying, "She won't miss you and I doubt she even knows who you are anymore. Just go and enjoy some time off," and that last remark compounded her guilt even more.

Why is she even in the caring industry? She ought to be a remand officer or something. Bloody woman.

Maggie was gazing at her newly acquired phone, which was presently on 'flight mode,' not that she knew what that meant, but she had been instructed and helped by the air stewardess. She was trying to familiarise herself with the small keyboard and address book holding only one telephone number. There was no internet facility, which had been her choice when Hugh explained her various options, all of which baffled her, relying totally on his sound judgment.

Her thoughts then turned to why she was on this plane and what was the likelihood of actually finding Ted, as she didn't even know the name of his bistro, except it *was* a bistro, so maybe that would be a clue. She had two half brothers whom she supposed would be so integrated into Spanish life they could well have become Spanish citizens.

And what of her father? Maggie had tried to work out what sort of age he would be, and estimated late seventies. She thought about Maureen, his first wife, and wondered what was the reason he needed to 'care' for her. Was she ill? Maybe she had been involved in an accident. No matter what the reason, she couldn't help but think that for Ted to turn his attentions to another woman could have been considered callous at best. Her mum would not have encouraged him, she was certain. Would she ever be able to find out what the truth was behind their 'fling', or had it been more than that? Well, clearly, it had ended up a bit more than that. He had married again and that had also ended badly. Maybe he was incapable of being faithful to one person.

What if I don't like him? What if he doesn't like me? What if he doesn't even want to know what happened after Mum left? What if I can't even find him? What if, what if... Her mind was too busy a place, and she tried to close her eyes and keep calm. She remembered her prayer at St John's and took great comfort thinking her mother would have prayed facing that very same altar.

Have faith… just keep that in your head.

*

Málaga airport was busy, loud and confusing. Most signs were written in both Spanish and English, which gave Maggie a clue as to where she should go to reclaim her luggage, but she decided her best option was to follow the people in front of her who had been on the same plane. *Good grief! It's so noisy!*

The Spaniard's reputation for loud chatter was amplified manyfold because of the airport acoustics.

Everyone jostled along, all seemingly competent in knowing exactly where to go, and Maggie simply followed, trying to quell her anxiety that was now all consuming as it dawned on her she was here, in a strange place, with absolutely no knowledge of the area, or where she was going. *Just put one foot in front of the other and keep going. It's that simple.*

Once she was finally outside in the glaring sunshine, her spirits lifted when she spotted a row of gleaming white taxis, and she could feel the intense heat on her shoulders, prompting an enormous sense of relief that she had arrived safely, with all luggage and herself intact.

Upwards and onwards then. What a lot of taxis!

Maggie made her way to the first available white Mercedes and was welcomed enthusiastically by the attentive Spaniard driver taking her bags and case and beckoning her into the back seat.

"Nerja, please," she said, assuming he understood.

She needn't have worried as his command of English

was impressive. He reminded her of the doctor at the hospital when Gwen had been admitted into the MAU.

"Where in Nerja you go?"

"It's a hostel, or a hotel I'm not sure."

"Plis tell me name of 'otel"

"The Hostal del Sol, I have the address written somewhere, um just a minute."

They won't score points for name originality.

"It's okay, I know. Plis… sit belt."

Once strapped in, he drove off at speed. Although tired from travelling, she observed the huge buildings around the airport, many of them appearing to be long term parking, and then more roads all merging together, followed by a mass of high-rise apartments on either side of the highway. A building resembling a space station appeared to her left, and the sea to her right was a beautiful bright blue, and as they drove away from the outskirts of the city, Maggie was overwhelmed by the rocky mountains and hills, something she hadn't expected at all and found them to be profoundly majestic and humbling. There were unfamiliar Mediterranean trees dotted here and there, and villas and apartments built haphazardly amongst the neighbouring hills, with cranes where the work was still in progress all alongside the fast highway. She was transfixed and excited and unsure of just how long this journey would be, and probably she should have checked the cost.

"Is it far?" Maggie asked.

"Fourtee minutes or samthing," was the reply.

Just as estimated, around forty-five minutes later they were heading off the highway towards the town of Nerja. They continued down to the coastal road and soon the taxi pulled up beside a 'pedestrian only' walkway, where the hostel was situated, right in the centre of this buzzing vibrant Costa holiday resort.

"Thank you." Maggie paid the driver after he arranged her luggage on the pavement and pointed to the nearby Hostal del Sol.

Maggie dragged her suitcase and bags along to the entrance, which was only a few steps away, and found the reception area, attended by a young woman behind the desk, checking her computer whilst engaging in a phone conversation.

After the necessary passport check and key exchange, Maggie was soon entering room number three, which was basic but functional. There was a small balcony overlooking the pedestrian street below opposite a heladeria displaying a magnificent array of technicolour ice cream, with tables outside under a canopy.

Maggie familiarised herself with her temporary home, impressed by the fully tiled sparkling bathroom, home to a shower, toilet, bidet and sink, and a bedroom with two single beds pushed so tightly together, she was afraid she would rip the sheets trying to get under the covers. The small kitchenette and dining area contained facilities adequate for a microwave meal, a kettle for hot drinks, and a small double hob, handy for a fry up.

Putting her few clothes away in the wardrobe, she decided to fill the kettle and then realised the two essential ingredients for a cup of tea were sadly lacking.

Idiot. You should have stopped off at a shop to get some groceries. Obviously, they're not going to provide fresh milk and PG Tips.

The central location of her holiday accommodation was within easy access to just about everything. The road where she had been dropped off by the taxi contained many shops, cafés, and a small supermarket, which Maggie went to soon after unpacking, hoping to find some familiar items necessary for the next couple of days.

Tea, milk, some bread, butter, marmalade, no chance of that, so jam will do, some fruit… ah yes, a couple of bottles of that, too.

She returned to the apartment and decided to give Hugh a call from her mobile.

"I'm here, Hugh. It's a really a lovely place and so busy with, from what I can hear from this balcony, an awful lot of English."

"Well done, Mum. You made it okay. How was your flight?"

"Absolutely fine, about three hours, maybe less, but pretty straightforward. Oh, Hugh, I can't believe I'm here."

"Enjoy the rest, Mum. You deserve a proper holiday and shouldn't really be scouting around trying to find your Dad." His words took her by surprise. She was unable to get used to even hearing the word Dad in context with her own life. To hear Hugh referring to her own father was almost surreal — alien, completely unfamiliar vocabulary.

"I had no idea how large a town this is. I'm not sure I'm ever going to be able to find even the bistro, there are so many places to eat here. Well, I have a few days in front of me. Hugh, have you seen your Gran today?"

"She's fine, Mum. Miriam is making sure she's well and truly looked after, so don't worry."

Guilt, guilt, guilt, and why do I feel like my role has been stolen? I should be happy for Mum.

"That's good, Hugh. Okay love, well, I'll have a walk around and see the sights, but an early night is definitely on the cards. I'll call tomorrow. Say hi to Susie."

"Bye, Mum, have fun and take care, eh?"

Maggie opened the wine, relieved to find a corkscrew amongst the mismatched cutlery.

She sat on the small balcony and observed the groups

of people passing by; some with small children, babies, dogs, young couples arm in arm, many of them holidaymakers, but also the local Spaniards walking with purpose, chattering with each other, almost sounding as if they were having some kind of argument, with raised voices and exaggerated gestures.

They're a noisy lot, these Spanish.

The noise was to increase as the night wore on, but Maggie was too tired to even hear any of the Nerja nightlife, deciding to have a much earlier night than anticipated, and was sound asleep by 9.30pm.

*

She was completely disorientated when she woke during the night. *Where in God's name...?*

She fumbled for the light switch in the bathroom and then blinked as the stark bulb invaded her sleepy eyes.

Unable to get back to sleep, she sat on the balcony. Even at this early hour in the morning there were signs of life from either the previous night's shenanigans or from locals rising early for shifts at work.

Maggie felt at peace and thought about all she had discovered in recent weeks. It was overwhelming and yet now she was here, in a place where she could possibly meet up with her own father, she did not feel afraid, but once again, as she did in the church at Glimstone, a sense of contentment and a possible connection. She nursed a small glass of wine, just allowing herself enough to enhance her feeling of well-being. Just enough to take the edge off any anxieties that might suddenly decide to spoil this serene and beautiful moment. She was here. She would find her father. She would close the unknown shutters forever, and open a door of hope.

Chapter Nine

Later that morning, when the town's vibrant colourful charm emerged with all its Spanish sounds and smells, Maggie, fully refreshed from more sleep than she can ever remember having during one night, inhaled the warm sweet air as she strolled through the narrow streets, soon widening towards the famous Balcon de Europa. There was a beautiful white church and orange trees with stone seats and walls, where cheerful sun-kissed bodies sat watching passers-by, taking pictures with their phones, cameras now a thing of the past for most.

The Balcon extended out with a small beach below on one side and restaurants and a hotel along the other side, but at the end, the expanse of blue ocean was breathtaking. Maggie felt as if she were walking onto a film set. Beyond the small beach, there was a coastal path and beyond that, further beaches with the rocks and cliffs rising higher, further the eye could see. It was all so beautiful and although Maggie was no stranger to sea views, this was beyond anything she had hoped for. *Wow! Imagine living here! It certainly beats my run-down crumbling corner of England.*

She was tempted to sit at one of the cafés and devour the sights and also some local refreshment, but she was keen to carry on and explore the less populated nooks and crannies of this delightful town.

Row upon row of colourful shops with as many of their tempting trinkets displayed outside as well as inside. *Well, if I need a handbag, I know where to come.*

Leather goods seemed to be in abundance, with bags and belts and all manner of other creamy caramel coloured accessories adorning the pavements, and jewellery and dress retailers with the mandatory Spanish flamenco frocks hanging from rails, gaudy and brash, but it would seem, in demand. Ice cream parlours similar to the one across from the hostel seemed to be on every street corner. The cafés spilled out onto the pavements too, all advertising variations of a theme, essentially paella, fish, steaks and pizza, mostly served with chips, but there were also the more exclusive dining establishments, where the food seemed to be cooked outside, presented as Gastro Theatre, the Spanish waiters and chefs clearly performing their art with music playing and customers embracing over-indulgence, clinking glasses, toasting life as it should be.

Maggie was transfixed, inhaling the mood, her love for life unfolding like a feathered bird breaking from its nest, wings spanning taking off in flight. She felt alive and free, inspired and enthusiastic. She smiled and walked, and smiled and sang to herself, and smiled craving life, happy and carefree and then… she stopped.

She had walked away from the heaving heartbeat of the town and was now in another square, although much smaller than the one in the centre. There was a café, and across from that there was another church. An Anglican church.

Maggie continued to walk towards the black railings surrounding the white building, less ornate than the Catholic church. Once inside, she gazed at the huge wooden cross at the altar and sat for a while on one of the wooden pews. *An Anglican Church in Nerja?*

She was completely alone, and felt able to kneel and pray and give thanks, not just for arriving safely and having the courage to explore foreign territories, but for feeling something more than just existing. For feeling as if there was life and purpose. This optimism hadn't been in Maggie's life for quite some time. *This is all going to your head. What makes you think just being away somewhere else is going to miraculously change your life?*

But despite her own cynicism, she could not deny something had changed. She could not ignore the joy in her heart. She was almost afraid to acknowledge the sheer delight of just feeling different, just in case it was snatched away. It had been absent for so long.

On a notice board outside, the weekly events at the church were displayed. The following day was a Sunday and there was a service at eleven o'clock. *Well, I might just go to that. Better try and retrace my steps so I don't forget where to come.*

Maggie made her way back into the hub of the town, observing landmarks so she would be able to find the church in the morning.

She was hungry and chose a small café back towards the Balcon, thankful the menu was written in both Spanish and English. The town catered especially well for English tourists, for obvious reasons; there were a lot of them.

Maggie was enjoying the sights and indulged in a jug of sangria, unaware that a combination of spirits had been liberally combined with the wine with only a hint of lemonade.

It wasn't until she had finished her main course, awaiting coffee in an attempt to counteract the effects of the sangria, that the realisation dawned, that there was a good chance Ted Clarke could be a member of the church she had just been to visit.

What if…? What if…? But I can't stand outside as if I were at the airport with a name board just seeing if by chance he was there. No… don't be ridiculous.

She became mentally transfixed yet again, wondering if this search would actually reveal anything at all. Was she meant to be doing this? Always questioning, and always unable to answer but still, almost convinced, deep down, that she was doing the right thing.

*

Maggie decided to walk further and see if there was a café or bistro in the centre of town that could possibly be the place Cathy had spoken about on the phone, in what now seemed an age ago.

Despite walking for well over two hours, stopping from time to time to look inside the various shops, Maggie could not confidently pick out anywhere that might be home to her recently discovered family. She decided to venture down to one of the small beaches not far from her hostel.

The weather was so warm. It was June and the Mediterranean temperature soared.

The beach, although secluded, was clearly well known to many. Maggie sat close to a rock and shed one or two items of clothing, but she had omitted to wear her swimming costume under her clothes. She lay on the shingle sand close to the water's edge, resting her head on her bag, listening to the ripples of the sea and surrounding people, the sounds of holiday and carefree hours.

She awoke feeling damp. The sea had gradually seeped towards her, creeping at first, and then an unexpected wave kissed her feet and legs, just trailing back before engulfing her entire body.

And no towel, of course. Maybe I'll head back to the hostel.

She was able to dry off in the sun, but still decided to make her way back, feeling tired, probably due to the sun, change of air, and without doubt an entire jug of sangria earlier.

Once back at the hostel. Maggie changed, and then sat on the balcony with a glass of wine, and phoned Bridge House.

"Bridge House, Meredith Mathews speaking. How can I help?"

Who? Meredith Mathews?

"Oh, hello, this is Maggie Chadwick. I'm Gwen Sanderson's daughter. I was just phoning to see how she is."

"Now, erm… let me see. I'm new today. I'm the stand-in manager. I'm going to have to ask one of the girls, just a moment please."

Stand-in manager? What's happened to battle axe remand officer then?

Maggie had to wait some time before Meredith returned to the phone.

"Hello it's Meredith again. I can't seem to find anyone at the moment but if you call back, maybe tomorrow?"

Maggie felt uneasy. Surely there was someone around.

"Where is the other manager? I didn't know her well, but has she left?"

"I'm only allowed to say she has been temporarily removed… possibly for good… so not so temporary really."

Maggie cleared her throat, "I'm quite anxious to know if Mum is alright. Isn't Miriam there?"

"Just a minute. I'll find Mary… Miriam, I mean Miriam."

This is the most bizarre place, the M recruitment theory reaffirmed. The other manager was bad enough but this one is completely barking mad.

It was Miriam who came to the phone.

"Oh, hello, Maggie. Your mum is fine. She's had cheese on toast for tea and we took her into the garden in her wheelchair earlier. She's absolutely fabulous, bless her. You're not to worry. Just enjoy your holiday. Bless you."

I think I'm reassured.

"Thank you, Miriam. I'm sure Hugh will be in tomorrow, later in the day."

"Alright my dear. I think I saw him earlier on. I'd better go — we're very short staffed."

"Okay, bye for now, and thank you, Miriam," but Miriam had gone.

Why do I feel so completely hopeless when it comes to my mother's care?

She phoned Hugh.

"Have you met this new manager, Hugh?"

"Hi, Mum. She's mad as a box of frogs, honestly. I stayed with Gran for a while earlier today, but the staff were all up in arms about this new woman being sent in. Not sure what the other one has done to blot her copy book."

"But your Gran was alright?"

"Yeah, don't worry, she's okay. Any luck with finding Ted or the bistro?"

"No, nothing as yet, except there's a church here. It's an Anglican church, so I'm going to the service tomorrow. It might be possible that he's a regular... you never know."

"Hey, Mum, that seems like a good start. Good luck, and let me know how you get on."

"Will do. Bye for now, then."

Maggie regained her former brighter spirits, content that Hugh had been to visit Gwen again that day. She counted her blessings, Hugh being top of the list.

*

The following morning was Sunday, and Maggie, intent on getting to the church, awoke early, and enjoyed her new bathroom facilities. She sang as she showered, afterwards indulging in the complimentary body moisturiser.

Shall I make my own breakfast or have I time to sit at one of the Balcon cafes?

Deciding to settle for home prepared jam on toast and tea, she checked her watch, and set off towards the Balcon area and then started to retrace her steps from the previous day. The big Catholic church in the centre square chimed, the bells ringing loudly, one, two, three, up to eleven. Maggie checked her watch again. *They want to get that fixed, it's an hour ahead. Oh Lordy, it is an hour ahead. Spain is an hour ahead. I'm never going to make this service now.*

She hastened her step and figured if she hurried, she might just make it for the last half an hour. The heat was already spiking, and she began to sweat, and wished she had taken a bottle of water with her.

She adjusted her watch and made it to the church by eleven thirty. The doors were closed, and Maggie was unsure about entering. Deciding on a coffee at the café opposite, she sat and waited for the service to end, which it did, approximately half an hour later.

Maggie scrutinised the people leaving. Mostly middle-aged women and a few men filtered out on to the area in front of the church. She beckoned the waiter for the bill, paid, and stood up slowly, then made her way towards the few of the congregation lingering outside. Not wanting to appear lost, she decided to go into the church to see who was left. The vicar was at the door shaking hands, exchanging a few words with each parishioner.

He smiled at Maggie.

"I'm sorry," she smiled apologetically. "My watch

was still on UK time, and I've missed the service."

"An easy mistake to make, but thank you for attempting to come, and maybe if you're staying for a while here in Nerja, you could attend next week."

"Well, it's a flying visit actually, pardon the pun, but I only have a few days. Erm, I'm actually looking for someone who might be a member of this church."

"Well, maybe I can help you… who are you looking for?"

Okay, so prepare yourself…

"His name is Ted. Ted Clarke. I understand he lives in Nerja and has a café here somewhere, but I don't know the name, apart from it's a bistro, I think."

The vicar revealed a broad smile.

"Oh yes, Ted is a regular here, but sadly not this morning. He does get quite busy on a Sunday as I do believe they serve an excellent traditional Sunday roast at The Courtyard Bistro. Are you alright, my dear? You look a little unsteady."

Maggie struggled to comprehend all that the vicar was saying, but it was the words Courtyard Bistro that made her realise beyond doubt, that this had to be her father the vicar was talking about.

"I'm fine, thank you. It's the heat, I think, I'm not used to this kind of temperature. So, The Courtyard Bistro, is that quite local?"

"Now, let me think how to explain this to you. You need to go back into the main part of the town and then venture out towards the other side, to where there are a row of cafés, just down by the coastal path. There is a supermarket there too, called Día. If you find that, then the café you're wanting is just along from there. It's quite a walk from here, and I'm afraid I have some post-service business to attend to, so I can't escort you there."

"I wouldn't hear of it. Thank you so much for your

help. I can't quite believe it's been so straightforward finding where he is. He's a friend of my mother's and I told her I would look him up if I came to Nerja, and well, here I am, and so, erm... I guess I'll pop along there and... well... you know... say hi."

Stop rambling!

"Well, I hope you find him. Maybe you will venture back here again one day."

This prophecy held more truth than she could have ever imagined.

Maggie began to walk away, feeling so many mixed emotions, it was hard to get anything straight in her head.

What shall I do? Just go along there now? I think I'm actually terrified.

When an idea, a dream, or even just a curious thirst for a piece of personal knowledge comes close to being identified, there can be an element of doubt as to what the reasons were in the first place for needing to know this new truth, and what the consequences could be, should this new truth not be what one was wholly expecting, or even should be expecting. The doubt that sets into one's mind could be in danger of overwhelming the previous enthusiasm for discovery.

These were the thoughts splintering Maggie's mind as she cautiously wandered back towards the main centre of the town. She looked around at the many people walking without intent, simply wandering aimlessly to find the best deal for a Sunday lunch, or just a drink with their companions, either friends or family together on holiday.

Do I want to do this? Why am I doubting whether this is the right thing? I could just leave and go back knowing he's here and knowing that at any time I could return. Maybe bring Hugh. Maybe not return. This is ridiculous, I'm losing my nerve. It was easier when it was all just a possibility, but now it's becoming more like a probability, and I am truly bloody scared.

Maggie decided a little Dutch courage might be a good idea.

She found a bar on the roadside leading out towards the other side of the town just as the vicar had indicated. There wasn't a supermarket of any kind nearby, so she knew she hadn't missed the bistro, or was close to it yet.

I'll call Hugh.

"Mum. How's everything?" Hugh sounded very high spirited, and Maggie decided he was enjoying his own company, coming and going without the watchful eye of his mother or the unintentional dramas of his gran.

"I know where he is, Hugh. Ted is definitely here in Nerja, and I've been told more or less where to find him, but I'm not going to lie, I'm actually quite nervous now, and I'm tempted to just let the unknown remain simply that."

"No, Mum, you must carry this through now. Hey, look, it's not as if he's going to be playing a big part in your life. He's in the wrong country for that. You just wanted to get to meet him. You said it was for Gran, Mum, don't you remember?"

"I think I was using that as an excuse, Hugh. Trying to make out it was for her not me, but it isn't... It's for me. I just wanted to know who he was, I mean is."

"Mum, you're bound to be pensive at this stage, but it's like you said, he doesn't even know you exist. I think he would want to know that he had a daughter."

Put that way, Maggie could see there was another perspective. She hadn't even thought how it would be for Ted. Some men would rather not know, but she had a feeling that he wouldn't be that kind of man. She hoped he wouldn't be that kind of man. She wasn't sure just what she hoped for. Probably some kind of Disney fairy tale ending.

"I know, you're right, Hugh. I wish you were here too. You sound in good spirits. What are you up to?"

"Just having a chilled day so far, Mum. Susie is here, we're getting ready to go and see Gran."

It was those words that made Maggie determined to carry this through. Her son was holding the fort. He was putting himself out for her, so she could find the person she had romanticised about for most of her life.

"Hugh, thank you. Give Susie my love. I'll let you know what happens."

"Go on, Mum. You're made of strong stuff. That's what you used to say to me when I was a nipper."

Maggie smiled and ended the call.

Chapter Ten

Ted glanced at his watch. Ten thirty. There was no possibility of getting to the service that Sunday morning. He was irritated with Will, his youngest son. Will, aged thirty-three, was responsible for the running of the bar at The Courtyard Bistro. Ted ruminated frequently as to whether this was an appropriate position within the business for his son, whose capacity for the alcohol he served often matched that of the entire group of regulars who would sit at the bar. Despite Ted's reservations, he also knew that Will was liked by just about everyone. Will was never happier than after several pints into the day, making cheerful conversation, and familiar banter with the locals he knew so well, and also the stream of holidaymakers that the bistro was so popular with. He was good at his job, but was not reliable for getting up in the morning. This day was no exception. Ted cleared away stray glasses from the previous night and early hours of that morning, placing them in the glass washer with an expertise acquired over years of practice. He wiped the tables situated in the bar area and checked to see if Bruce, his eldest son, was on track with the lunch prep.

Needless to say, he was. "No sign of Will yet then, Dad?"

Ted shook his head, and continued to resurrect the bar into some kind of order, ready for the busy session about to commence that lunchtime.

"Did that delivery arrive for the dining room? The new tablecloths and serviettes and so on? I put quite a few things on the list but can't remember half of it now." Ted tried to find the order amongst various pieces of paper by the till.

"Yes, Dad, I've put them over in the cupboard, and we

can use them today. Marta said she would come in and give us a hand, so I'll leave that all to her."

Marta was Bruce's girlfriend. They had been together for over a year now, and Ted was pensively waiting for Bruce to announce he would be moving out of the apartment above, knowing they would certainly be wanting their own place together before long.

All three men had been living in the apartment for years, which was large, but not ideal, especially for Ted, who desperately needed his own space now he was approaching his octogenarian decade.

Will made his entrance into the bar.

"Leave that, Dad, I'll do it."

Ted observed his youngest, amazed at just how he seemed to be able to function day after day, despite abusing his body relentlessly night after night. The takings in the till were testament to the full house of happy customers the previous night, and because of this, he didn't feel he could chastise his son for being somewhat cavalier about time discipline.

"Looks like that crate of San Miguel needs topping up, Will."

"I'm on it, Dad… leave it to me. You going to church?"

"It's too late now. I'm going to pop upstairs and then I might head out for half an hour."

Ted decided to take a walk down towards the sea, taking Ralph, his adopted crossbreed four-legged loyal companion, and have a coffee at a small café just along a lower promenade running adjacent to the beach.

He could leave the boys to it now. They were more than capable of getting things ready for the enthusiastic Brits longing for a Sunday roast, something Ted found extraordinary, as one of the things he always loved about his own previous holidays was experimenting with local cuisine, and trying out something new. The bistro was successful in creating the right kind of atmosphere with delicious traditional English meals served with generous portions, at a set price with no hidden extras. At first, back in those early days, it had been a gamble to try and emulate a British style restaurant in a town where there were more places to eat than parasols on the beach, but after the first couple of years experimenting with ways to make the whole idea financially viable, it began to thrive beyond anything Ted could have imagined. It was popular and successful and for that, Ted was grateful.

The sun was hot. Ted placed his cap on his head, covering his thinning white hair, and he carefully negotiated the steps alongside Ralph, down towards the lower promenade. He had a copy of The Times, albeit the previous day's, and was content to sit for a while in the shade, with a café con leche and skim over the news. Ted wasn't sure just what effect this Brexit business was going to have when the UK would finally leave the European Union.

He tried to find an update but there was nothing relevant to Spanish businesses. He wasn't convinced Theresa May was the right person to lead negotiations. She seemed weak in character to him, unable to carry things through.

Ted found himself to be thinking about his own business and what the future would hold. He would soon be eighty. Most would have retired a couple of decades ago, but he still enjoyed overseeing the daily routine, keeping his eye on Will, feeling relieved Bruce didn't need to be monitored in quite the same way. He wondered what would happen if they decided not to carry things on. Businesses had been selling well, but with this uncertainty about trade deals and goodness knows what else on the horizon, it was having an adverse effect on the local economy. Those who had been lucky enough to have a holiday home in this area were now worried as to how their lives would be affected, if the UK would no longer be part of the EU, with their existing rights to freedom of movement potentially devastated. It was a worrying time, and many decided to sell, which of course, was never good if the market was suddenly flooded. It wasn't the English who were buying these bargain holiday homes now; it was other nationalities remaining in the EU whose rights would be unaffected. Without the English, the Sunday roast would die a death. There was always the constant stream of tourists, though. Ted concluded he was worrying unduly, and arose from his chair and after paying the bill, he and Ralph made their way back.

In front of the bistro on the pavement, there were three small square tables with seating for two, maybe three, if the third person was content to be deprived of any kind of view other than the wall in front. Once inside, the bar area had a few scattered tables and chairs but the most popular area for enjoying a meal was to the rear, where the courtyard was situated. This particular part was open to the sun and sky and most tables had parasols for protection. Arched, pretty brick walls to the side, adorned with an array of bright red geraniums, and palms, pretty hibiscus, clematis and trailing sweet peas provided an immediate feelgood factor. Not only did the courtyard look stunning with so many vibrant colours, but the aroma was delightful, all enhanced by a water feature at the back. This relaxing environment, combined with excellent cuisine, provided the key ingredients to the success The Courtyard Bistro could confidently advertise, rewarded by loyal customers often needing to make reservations, especially at the weekend, due to its popularity.

Ted had installed an electric overhead canvas covering, in preparation for inclement weather, but these hot June days usually meant the area could be kept open, providing a bright and airy ambiance. He was proud knowing he was responsible for creating somewhere a little special, despite there being a plethora of competition locally.

Will was on his second San Miguel, mostly to quell the symptoms of the previous night's indulgences. Saturday nights were reputed to be heavy sessions.

Bruce was discussing the 'specials' with the chef, and already, even though it wasn't even midday, folks were making their way to the rear courtyard, eager to peruse the menu, the regular drinkers preferring the bar area, where they could easily sneak outside for a smoke.

Ted chatted to new faces, offering pre-meal drinks, along with the menu and small plates of salted almonds. He gave Marta a hug as she squeezed by him. This was a typical Sunday, and it was going to be busy. It was also going to be a day Ted would never forget.

*

Maggie stopped outside Día, the small supermarket, fully aware the next building would be the end of her search. She walked across the road to view the bistro from a slight distance and to stall for time. Her heart was pounding, and she was still hesitant, pacing one way and another, unsure whether to walk straight in, or hover outside. Walking this way and that, she was aware her behaviour was probably looking somewhat suspect from anyone observing her. She felt inside her shoulder bag to check for the umpteenth time that she had the letter, and of course, it was still there. *Just go across and bite the bullet.* There was a large dog sleeping outside by one of the tables on the pavement. She decided this would be a good spot to sit, and have the dog as a distraction if need be.

Ted noticed a customer approaching from across the road. He was inside, polishing a wine glass with a linen serviette. He watched her as she sat down.

Maggie sat at the table and looked up to see a white-haired bronze-skinned gentleman around late seventies, walk towards her. She felt her lip tremble, and rummaged again in her bag pretending to search for something, except there was nothing she needed, and her hands clumsily knocked the bag to the floor, the contents of which spilled on to the pavement.

She started to panic, and felt utterly stupid.

Ted walked up to Maggie's table.

"Can I help you?" He stooped down and gathered a few stray items that had rolled across the pavement. Fortunately, there was nothing embarrassing, like spare underwear. He passed the items to Maggie, and she gathered everything together, pushing it all back into her bag.

"Can I get you anything? Are you dining? Or just wanting a drink?"

I have never needed a drink more. This isn't how I planned this at all.

"Thank you, just a drink for now, please. A glass of house white would be lovely."

Ted retired inside, and Maggie tried to compose herself, figuring out in her head what she would say. She had rehearsed this conversation more times than good for her mental health. She held the letter, keeping it on her lap.

It's him I know it's him, I can tell, and I want to cry, I'm so nervous.

Ted returned with a glass of crisp, cool white wine,

placing it down on the table.

He looked at Maggie, tilting his head to one side.

"Do I know you?" A poignant question indeed.

"Why do you ask?"

Ted replied, "You remind me of someone."

Without further hesitation, Maggie asked, "Is your name Ted Clarke?" The words she had rehearsed in her mind over and over again, now spoken out loud.

Ted moved closer to the table and nodded.

"Yes, that's who I am, christened Edward but everybody calls me Ted." He smiled, revealing kind creases by his eyes and around his mouth.

Maggie reached for her glass. "You knew my mother. Her name is Gwen. Gwen Sanderson."

Ted's expression changed and he gripped the table becoming visibly shaken.

"Gwen Sanderson... she's your mother? Is she here with you?"

"No, she's in England. She's unwell. She's in a care home at the moment."

Ted had to sit down. "Do you mind if I just sit for a moment?"

"No, of course. I know this must be quite a shock for you."

Ted looked up at Maggie. "I didn't know whether she was alive still. We lost touch completely."

Will was hovering by the entrance. Ted beckoned him over.

"Will, can you get me a large whisky please?"

"Are you alright, Dad? Is something wrong?" He looked at Maggie quizzically, wondering who she was.

"I'm a bit shaken up but it's alright, I just need to talk to this lady for a while. Maybe bring some more wine too."

Maggie, on hearing this person was Ted's son,

couldn't help but feel anxious, not wanting to create a bad first impression. He was after all, her half brother. She smiled but received no similar gesture in return other than a blank stare. Will retraced his steps inside, and Ted continued to shake, his hands gripping the table to steady them.

"I'm sorry for appearing so emotional. This has come as quite a shock."

"I know, it must be quite hard to take in. You see, I found a letter, and it's quite clear just how fond of her you were."

Will had returned with the requested drinks, plus a jug of iced water. Again, his expression towards Maggie was veering towards hostile. He was keen to know just who this woman was who was clearly upsetting his father.

"Thank you, Will." Ted reached for his whisky, swallowing a large mouthful. He breathed in deeply. "It's alright, Will. You can carry on in the bar. I'm fine, and I'm just going to have a chat with... I'm so sorry, I haven't even asked your name."

"It's Maggie. Maggie Chadwick."

Maggie hesitated before saying anything more. She felt for the letter on her lap, and put it on the table. "I found this. It was amongst Mum's personal belongings when I had to sort everything out. It's such a beautiful letter."

Maggie passed the creased envelope to Ted and watched him closely as he opened the contents and read each line. Tears welled up in his eyes, and he reached in his pocket for a handkerchief. Maggie was also close to tears but tried to keep composed. She wanted to see his reaction and talk to him about his relationship with her mother before pursuing things further.

Ted coughed and wiped his eyes, and nose. He passed the letter back to Maggie.

"I can remember writing every word of that. I can remember everything so clearly, Maggie."

Maggie spoke. "Would you mind telling me about you and Mum? You see, she doesn't remember anything these days and she has never really told me what happened."

Ted stood up. "Just one moment, Maggie, I'll be back in a second."

Ted went inside the bistro, returning with another whisky, and some bread and almonds in a basket. "I don't know if you're hungry. Please stay and have something to eat.

I doubt I could eat a single thing right now.

"Thank you. I'm fine for the moment, but maybe later."

Ted began his story.

"My father was the vicar of St John's Church in Glimstone on the south coast. He was an excellent vicar, but as a father, I have to say, I have my reservations. He was a disciplinarian and had fixed ideas about his children. I had a sister too, and she ended up moving abroad to work as a missionary in Kenya. She died, sadly, from malaria. He wanted me to follow in his footsteps. It was drummed into me from as early as I can remember... 'When you're a vicar, Edward...' and I was never even allowed to express an opinion. Well, as far as I remember, that's how it seemed to be. My mother was also completely devoted to the church and her work as a vicar's wife. The vicarage was constantly busy with people coming and going, coffee mornings, meetings, parish councillors, other vicars from the diocese; it was a busy place, and in those days, Maggie, children were not given the kind of understanding and freedom of speech they have today. Oh, my goodness, you were definitely seen and not heard. Don't get me wrong though, I was happy enough with my Eagle books, and Meccano, and we had endless time outside in the enormous garden, so I can hardly say I was deprived. Anyway, to cut a long story short, it became quite clear, to me anyway, that I was never going to become a vicar. I wasn't cut out for it, and the idea of going to college to study theology just wasn't something I wanted to do. Anyway, you probably get the picture. I became a disappointment. And that has stayed with me for most of my life, I suppose."

Ted paused and drank the rest of his whisky, pouring Maggie another glass of wine.

Maggie was listening, watching her father's mannerisms, mesmerised by every word uttered. Ted continued, "There was a café within the church grounds, and it was run by an elderly couple who eventually died, and I just took it over really, not expecting it to be my job or career, but you know, Maggie, I really enjoyed doing it. I made a lot of changes to the décor, painting and adding a bit of colour, and then I took an interest in catering… self-taught, although at home we did have a cook. She was a lovely woman. My surrogate mum, I used to call her. She gave me so many ideas, and showed me as a boy how to make pies and puddings. Our Yorkshire puddings here are her recipe. So it just sort of happened.

"And that goes for my relationship with me and Maureen. That just sort of happened too. She was my first wife. She was the daughter of some friends of my parents, and she was always at the vicarage, and we got on alright. As she entered her early twenties she was diagnosed with rheumatoid arthritis. To be honest, I didn't really know what that was, but everyone was upset about it, and I could see Maureen was too. She changed after that diagnosis. My mother sat me down one day, and suggested I married Maureen. She said she would need someone to care for her, and as we were good friends, it seemed the obvious next step… that was how she put it. So that's what happened. I married Maureen, and we lived close by in a small house near to the vicarage, and I carried on at Courtyard Café. I was fond of Maureen, but I was never in love with her." Ted looked at Maggie. "Are you sure you want to hear all this?"

You have no idea just how much I do.

"Yes, really, please go on."

"Your mother came into the café one day. She ordered a coffee and a slice of Bakewell tart. I can remember it as if it were yesterday. I always had some music playing. I loved classical music… I still do, and she asked what it was. It was Albinoni and she smiled, saying how much she liked that piece. She started coming in quite often after that, and we would chat about this and that. She was working at the time, in a material shop that did alterations to clothes and suchlike. She was good with her hands and was always making clothes for herself. Her pride and joy was her Singer sewing machine. She was also a regular at the church, but we had never spoken before she came into the café. I realised before long that I was looking forward to her visits. I sang in the choir at church, and I started to look out for her in the congregation. We became good friends, your mum and me. That's how it all started. She became more active in the church, and helped with the tapestry when the kneelers needed restitching. One day after a morning service, the girl who helped me in the café was ill and it was particularly busy. Your mum offered to help, and I was so grateful to her. She wouldn't accept any money, either. Your mum was kind and fun, Maggie. She was so good to be around. Always helping, and caring for people. She would go the extra mile, if you know what I mean."

Maggie was desperate to hear more, and nodded, not wanting to interrupt Ted's flow. He seemed to need to offload his story. Maybe he had never had the opportunity to talk freely about this time in his life. He continued, "All this time, Maureen was getting worse with her illness. We had to get a nurse in to help her get up in the mornings, her legs stiffened up, especially in the cold. She also became acutely depressed, and her moods were hard to judge. I tried with her, Maggie, really I did, but she was indifferent to me, somehow. It was as if it was all my fault. I'll be honest with you. I started to dread going home and worked longer and longer hours. That was wrong of me, I know that. I wasn't very old, only in my early twenties. It seemed as if I was doomed to have a miserable life with her, and I wasn't ready for that. So you see, Gwen was a breath of fresh air. She knew I was married, and she always respected that in the way she was with me, keeping it strictly as friends. Mind you, I found that hard and I would manipulate situations so she would be able to work at the café sometimes. And then once, I remember there was a group outing from the church to the theatre. I asked if she'd like to go, as Maureen wasn't up to it, and as it was a group outing, it seemed in order for her to join in. We went to see a stage musical of 'The Sound of Music'. We sat next to each other in the theatre, and I felt as happy as anybody could be." Ted replenished his glass with some wine, and topped up Maggie, who was trying desperately hard to control how much she drank, feeling like polishing off the entire bottle and then asking for more, but didn't.

"Anyway that must have been… now, let me see, I think it was the end of 1962, and life just carried on as usual until the Christmas. I'm not sure how much I should tell you, Maggie, but let's just say we became closer, and we both knew it was a forbidden love. Christmas Eve, I was working in the café, and it was always busy that time of year. We used to have a service for the children in the afternoon and most of them came into the café afterwards for hot chocolate and mince pies or chocolate biscuits. Gwen was off work that day, and she helped me. We had carols playing, and even though we were rushed off our feet, it was just being together that made us both happy. I think we pretended we were a couple without saying as much.

"Once everybody left, we closed up, but there was a lot of clearing up to do. We had a wood burner fire there, which was blazing away, and we were both tired and hot. I opened a bottle of sherry. I said to her, 'let's have our own Christmas celebration, come on, we deserve it'. Gwen didn't usually drink at all, but she had a sherry, and then we had another. We sat by the fire. The door was locked and the carols continued to play. One thing led to another, Maggie, that's all I'll say. I knew it was wrong, but we loved each other, and I told her so. Christmas came and went, and Gwen became busy at her work and I wasn't able to see her as much as I'd wanted to, then one day in February, she came to see me and told me she was leaving the area, and moving away. Maggie, it broke my heart. I was devastated, but I understood why she was going. We had become too close. I couldn't divorce Maureen. I had already bitterly disappointed my parents, and maybe you're thinking I should have just upped and gone with her, but it wasn't that easy. For a member of the clergy to have a divorced son would have had implications I couldn't live with, but my heart was broken. I wrote that letter and took it to her house, but I didn't go in. I pushed it through the letter box, and I sobbed like a child most of the way home." Ted's voice faltered, and he stopped speaking.

Maggie touched his hand.

"Thank you for telling me all that. I hope you don't think I'm prying. I wanted to know, you see... I..."

Maggie paused. *Do I tell him? Shall I just add to his heartbreak? I can't do that... not right now.*

"I don't even know where she went. I knew why she'd gone. She had integrity and pride, and she knew, I suppose, that our affection was deep but would never be able to flourish. Oh, how I loved her. When Maureen died in 1975, I did think about trying to find her. It would have been difficult, because we didn't have the technology like this social media we've got now, but it occurred to me she had probably settled down with someone and was happy. The last thing I wanted to do was upset her life again. I lived with the guilt, and have done most of my life, but you know, Maggie, I don't regret what happened between your mum and me. It was wrong, but it was honest between us both. Where did she go to? She obviously met someone else... because there's you."

Maggie chose her words carefully.

"She moved up north and got a job as a live-in housekeeper, and they were good people who looked after her when I was born. She was able to carry on with her job, and she did for a number of years. After that, we moved south again into a terraced house and she worked in a material shop like before, and I would go there after school, and watch her make clothes and curtains. She was a talented seamstress. She was a wonderful Mum, and I miss her because now she isn't the person she was." Ted was looking confused. He reached out for the wine, and poured fresh glasses for them both.

"What about your father, Maggie? What happened to him?"

This was it. She had to tell him. He had opened his heart out to her. She couldn't hide the obvious truth any longer. She could tell by the expression on his face he was already putting the pieces together in his mind.

"My father? Well, he moved to Nerja, and opened up a restaurant."

Nothing else was said. Their hands reached out and they held on to the lost years with tears, and an understanding that this was their moment, not to be shared, but to hold on to each other, recognising that a whole lifetime had passed them by. Time that they could never get back, which brought a feeling of desperation for them both and yet also a recognition of the fact that even though so much had been lost, an instinctive bond was bringing them together, even in this short period of time. The need for them both to hold on to whatever time they had left would be imperative because they had both lost the woman whom they had loved most in the world... and because of that, they must never lose each other.

Timeless silence, and then Ted spoke. "Maggie, I will need some time to talk to my boys about this. I can barely believe what has happened here today, and I need to be able to digest everything, and we also need our time together to get to know one another. How long are you here for, Maggie? I do love that name. Were you christened Margaret?"

"No, I've always been Maggie. I'm only here for a few days. I must get back to Mum. Listening to you talk today about your life together so long ago has made me miss her so much. I wish with all my heart she could be here too. I wish she didn't have this godawful illness which eats away at her soul." Maggie was feeling the effects of the wine, which compounded with nothing eaten since early morning, could have easily resulted in emotional tears.

She poured herself a glass of water. "I'm feeling a little woozy actually, maybe I had better have something to eat, please." *I don't know what to call this man. He is my father, but I simply can't call him that... not yet.*

"We shall dine together, Maggie. Come inside and let me show you the bistro. There is a lovely area at the back and we can sit in there. Come on, just follow me, and you can hold on to me if you feel unsteady."

They both walked carefully into the rear courtyard, where many were sitting enjoying Sunday lunch. Maggie's head was trying to decipher all that had been said to her, whilst simultaneously trying to take in all that was around her. The courtyard was beautiful with so many sweet aromatic flowers, and serene music playing in the background. They both sat at a table at the back, and it wasn't long before platefuls of olives, crisps, roasted nuts, and bread were all laid before them, shortly to be followed by two large servings of meat, roast potatoes, the infamous Yorkshire puddings and vegetables. Maggie ate enthusiastically, drinking water as opposed to her usual tipple. "I have a son, Ted. His name is Hugh. He's twenty-three. He's amazing and so caring towards Mum. He's visiting her at the care home every day, and making sure she has her DVD playing. You won't believe the film she watches constantly. It's 'The Sound of Music'. I'm surprised it's not worn out; it's been played relentlessly. You said you both went to see a live production together."

"We did, Maggie, we did!" Ted was becoming excited, his eyes meeting hers every time he spoke. "It was a live performance of the musical at our local theatre. Everybody was talking about it. I don't think the film came out for another couple of years. We both loved it, but I think we would have enjoyed seeing anything… it was the being together we loved the most. Do you have a photo of her, Maggie?"

"No, I was so stupid not to bring any with me. Your letter was my priority, and I didn't really believe I would ever find you."

Ted spoke. "So I have a grandson, too. Hugh. What is he doing, does he work?"

"He's very happy working at a recording studio. He loves music and plays the guitar. I think he rather hopes to make a living from performing one day. His father and I split up. I don't see him anymore. No love lost there on either part. Hugh sees him occasionally."

Ted shook his head. "So many marriages end. I'm no exception. I have two failed marriages behind me. Maureen died but it was still a failed marriage. I met Grace, the boys' mother, when I came here on holiday, back in the late seventies."

"Tell me about Grace, Ted. What was she like?"

"Grace was a fun-loving party girl. She was happiest when surrounded by friends with music and dancing. She was a good dancer, actually. It was a holiday romance, I suppose, but we carried on seeing each other in England and got married in 1980. My parents had both died by this point, and I had nothing keeping me in England, and she loved the sun and sea, so it was an easy decision. We came here and I managed to buy the bistro, which at the time was cheap as chips, as they say. The apartment at the top gave us living accommodation and so we just cracked on with trying to make a success of things. To begin with, she was full of enthusiasm and we both enjoyed doing the place up. It was a horror show when we bought it, Maggie, but with some structural alterations and new furnishings, it soon became operational. Business was slow to begin with but every year we seemed to increase trade, and I was proud, you know, of starting something from scratch and making it a success. Goodness me, I'd felt I'd failed at everything else!" Ted laughed, and continued.

"Bruce was born in 1982 and I was a very happy man. For the first time in many years, I really thought I was getting somewhere. Both the boys have remained here in Spain from when they were born. They're Spanish citizens, and have no desire to live in England. They've visited a few times with me, but it holds nothing for them. Things became a bit rocky between Grace and myself though, after Bruce was born. I can't put my finger on why. She became discontented with the business, and felt tied down with that and a baby, oh and me, of course! Anyway, erm, we had Will, born in 1985, and we just carried on, me with this place to manage and she helped when she could, but to be honest, her heart wasn't in it, and I could see she was drifting away. When the boys were about, ooh, let me see, they must have been in their early twenties, Grace moved up to Valencia, with someone she'd met. The boys decided to stay here with me because by this time they were an important part of this little gold mine and I needed them. I still do. They are good lads and they work hard." Ted lowered his voice, "Will can be a bit of a liability sometimes, and he likes a drink. The thing is, the customers love him, so it's no good me lecturing him because he does do a good job… well most of the time. Bruce is the more steady of the two. He and Marta have been together for over a year now. I'm sure they'll want a place of their own soon. I just hope he doesn't want to move away to somewhere different. But you know, Maggie, you can't dictate what your children do. I can remember what that feels like, and it's not good. All I want for them both is to fulfil their own potential. It's not about money, although of course that helps, but it's about being who you want to be, and being true to yourself. So many people these days are only concerned about making money, but there has to be something more to life than that. Feeling you've given something back, and not just taking. That's what I think is important, but goodness, listen to me rambling on here."

Maggie smiled, saying, "You can ramble on all you like. I love listening to you. There's a lot to catch up on. It's where do we go from here that's the burning question, isn't it? I will have to go home in a couple of days, and do I tell Mum I've found you? I doubt she would even comprehend it, if I did tell her. I'm unsure of just how confident I feel about where she is at the moment. The staff seem sweet enough, but from a point of view of professionalism, they fall short. The sad thing is, she can't come home to me now. She needs so much more help than before, often needing two people. It was only supposed to be a temporary measure, but I can't see it continuing to be temporary. It's not the right place for her, but what can I do? I'm not sure even how much longer she's got left to live. It's all unknown territory."

They had both finished eating and were now enjoying coffee, and Ted also a brandy. Maggie was abstaining from more alcohol, not wanting to let the drinking get out of hand and spoil this momentous occasion. This was too important. The emotions she was feeling were so mixed, but overall, her joy and gratitude outweighed anything negative that was niggling away, as always.

"I'm unable to fly anymore Maggie. I had a couple of blood clots in my legs, and I have to take blood thinners. They advised me against flying, so I really am stuck here but I have to say it's no hardship. It a wonderful part of the world to be. I count my blessings each and every day, I really do. What about Gwen coming here?"

Maggie sat back in her chair and almost laughed. "Oh, that would be utterly impossible, Ted. I'm not sure she would even be able to get in a car, never mind an aeroplane. She's almost housebound although they are taking her into the garden in a wheelchair. If only I had found you just a year ago, even. She was so much better then. Her dementia seems to plummet and then plateau, but the nose dives down are becoming more frequent. It's a tragic illness, and it breaks my heart to see her reduced to the person she is now." Maggie's voice faltered. Ted held her hand.

"Maggie, I want to help. I'll try and think of something. I've no idea right now, but there must be some way her twilight years can be improved upon. I can see how distressing this all is. Let me help you somehow."

I doubt she's got years.

Maggie revealed a truth. "Sometimes, Ted, I wish she would die. That's just awful isn't it, because I love her so much, but I can't bear how this is going to end. I've seen patients in the hospital, at later stages of the disease she has, and it's beyond cruel. Some are like animals. It can't be right for people to have to suffer like that. My faith in God keeps me going but I have prayed that he will find a peaceful end for her. I've never said any of this to anybody and forgive me if it sounds callous, but I hope you understand. You wouldn't want it for yourself or anyone, would you?"

"I completely understand why you feel that way. I'm afraid the same thoughts crossed my mind when Maureen was in the later stages of her life. She wasn't afflicted mentally but she was in tremendous physical pain. You do ask yourself why God would allow that to happen. It's the big conundrum about faith and belief, isn't it? It's the one trump card that non-believers will always pull out. Why does God allow people, especially children, to suffer?"

"None of us can answer that easily. Suffering always brings us closer to God, and he in his infinite wisdom sees the bigger picture with everything, but it's hard to accept... so hard to accept and understand."

Will had been hovering in and out of the dining area, periodically glancing across at his father and his newly acquainted friend, Maggie. Who was she? He felt unnerved by the intensity of their conversation together. His dad rarely ate in the restaurant, especially during the busiest time of the week, but he had been intent on sitting with this stranger and talking for so long. It was all rather atypical and disconcerting. Bruce had been contained in the kitchen for most of the lunchtime session, but was now sitting at the bar with Marta and Will, and they were enjoying a post 'Sunday lunch shift frenzy' aperitif before they ate. All three looked over to where Ted and Maggie were sitting. Maggie was aware of their glances.

"What will you tell your sons? They have been looking over here and I think they're trying to figure out who I am."

"For now, you're the daughter of a friend. Are you happy for me to say that? I would rather pave the way for a more intense explanation when the time is right."

"Of course. I probably should go, and let you carry on with your Sunday."

"Where are you staying?"

"Hostal del Sol... Not the most original name, is it? But it's okay, and very central."

"Yes, I know where you are. I would like to walk you back there, if you're heading off now."

"I would love that. Thank you."

Their goodbyes to inquisitive faces were brief. Ted and Maggie walked together through the baking hot streets, she holding his arm at his request, talking further about life in general, their likes and dislikes, their political stance, although Maggie was not up to scratch with much of what was going on in the Houses of Parliament, but Ted explained the effects Brexit could present, particularly when it came to running a business.

Once at the hostel, Ted hugged Maggie, asking if they could meet up again the following day. "I don't want to take up all your holiday, but I would love to see you again."

"Yes, of course. Shall I go to the bistro in the afternoon, **after** the lunch session this time?"

"Mondays are never as busy, but yes, please do that. I will look out for you."

They parted, and Maggie walked up to her apartment. She filled the kettle, and found her phone, pressing the last number called. "Hugh... Hugh, I have found my father."

*

Ted wandered back home, his mind occupied with the last few hours spent. He had no doubt that somehow, he had to find a way to recover the lost years. Gwen had never left him spiritually. She had been ever present, even when times had been good with Grace. He did not feel any disloyalty because of that. It was impossible to erase a person from your mind, even with the strongest will. Gwen's face, her smile, her ability to cherish the moment and live in the present were attributes he treasured and admired. Grace had been completely the opposite. Always looking for more. Always wanting the next gadget, dress, pair of shoes, and later searching for ways to escape, booking trips away, holidays, anything except an acceptance of what she already had.

By the time he reached the bistro, he felt emotionally exhausted, and physically tired from having walked across the town twice. However, he knew it was unlikely he would be having a peaceful evening. Once upstairs in the apartment, it was minutes before he was joined by Bruce and Will. Marta was holding the fort downstairs, the rush now over, with just a couple of tables displaying the aftermath of lunch, the occupants having pushed their chairs back, content with life, nursing full bellies, in a relaxed frame of mind.

"Come on then, Dad, who is this Maggie you've been so intensely talking to? We're intrigued." Will grabbed another beer from their well-stocked domestic fridge.

Bruce, showing a degree of sympathy, aware his father looked worn out, said, "Here, Dad, sit down, I'll get a cuppa for you, or are you after another whisky?"

"Cup of tea, Bruce. That will do nicely, thank you."

Ted retreated to the sofa, and sat down with a sigh. "Maggie. Well she certainly has sprung a surprise on me, that's for sure. She's the daughter of someone I used to know a very long time ago. Right back when I had Courtyard Café at St John's. Unfortunately, her mother isn't too well, and it doesn't sound as if she's going to get better, but it was one of those blast from the past moments, you know. We just chatted about the old place and people her mother knew." Aware he was not recalling an entirely accurate picture of their conversation, he changed the subject. "The chicken was exceptionally good today, Bruce, and those potatoes… lovely and crunchy."

Dissatisfied with his answer, Will challenged his father further. "So why were you so upset? I mean you looked really distressed, Dad, come on, you're not telling us the whole story, are you?"

"Leave it, Will. Dad's tired. Here you are, Dad." He placed the tea in easy reach for Ted. "I'm going back downstairs, come on mate, leave Dad to rest up now."

Reluctantly, Will joined his brother and they departed downstairs to continue with their evening's work. Ted felt relief at seeing them go. He was too tired to explain the situation in a diplomatic way and didn't want to feel under pressure. He had much to think about, but already a plan was formulating, and he began to feel a tingle of excitement again as he reached for the phone. There were a couple of people he needed to talk to, and there was precious little time left to act.

Chapter Eleven

Maggie ended her phone call to Hugh. She had been almost delirious, and Hugh had asked her to speak more slowly and calm down several times as she unravelled the day's conversations and events. Her head was buzzing with further questions she wanted to ask Ted, only too aware that her return flight was in a couple of days. She needed to call Bridge House. Hugh had expressed some concerns about his Gran because of the upset in the care routine, largely due to the sudden change of management and fragmented staff.

"Hello, Meredith Mathews speaking."

Why does that sound so ridiculous?

"Hello, it's Maggie here, Gwen Sanderson's daughter."

"Oh, hello. I'm so glad you've called."

Now I'm worried.

"She's had a bit of a blip today. We had to get the community nurse in."

"Why, what's happened?" Maggie reached for the bottle of wine in the fridge.

"She had some tummy pains. Your son mentioned it to us before he left today. He's a nice boy isn't he, your son? I never did have a boy, just girls. My eldest is almost thirty now…"

Please get to the point.

"Anyway, the nurse came and said she was in retention. Hadn't been to the loo most of the day, I don't think. We're not entirely sure how long because Mabel doesn't usually look after your mum, it's usually Mary… no erm Martha… no, Miriam, that's who she likes, isn't it?"

Dear God, this is painful… just be patient.

Maggie interjected, "It must be difficult remembering

all the names, especially when they all begin with the same letter."

"Oh yes, I hadn't thought of that."

How could you not?

"So, my Mum, is she alright? She hasn't had to go into hospital because of this retention problem, has she?"

"Oh no, the nurse was very good. She's used to this happening. She popped in a catheter. So no more wet pads for Gwen now. All a lot easier in many ways."

For some reason, Maggie felt uneasy by this last statement.

"Oh, well yes, I suppose it saves her having to be taken to the toilet. Will you give her a hug from me? I'm missing her. Thank you, Meredith. I'll be back in a couple of days."

Maggie finished the call abruptly, and burst into tears. She wasn't sure why she felt so upset. Worse things than this had happened with her mum. She had been so elated just a moment ago, when talking to Hugh.

What's wrong with me? I'm an emotional wreck.

Maggie took her wine on to the balcony and thought about her day, and her father, and the two brothers, wondering just when Ted would break the news to them. It wasn't long before sleep beckoned, and she retired to the bedroom, and drifted into oblivion.

*

Monday morning and the mandatory sunshine for this time of year inspired Maggie to take her first swim in the sea. The water was glorious, if a little chilly to begin with, but she soon became accustomed to it; she swam for quite a while before returning to the beach. The sun was so warm, and she soon dried off, and discarded the towel from around her shoulders. She would go back to the hostel and shower before meeting Ted again at the bistro. She hoped she wouldn't have to speak with the brothers. For some reason, she wasn't sure about Ted's youngest and could foresee difficulties if it was to become a forced relationship.

Ted didn't give Maggie chance to even step inside the bistro. When she arrived, he was outside with his dog Ralph, but walked quickly towards her, greeting her warmly.

"You've caught the sun this morning. Have you been sitting on the balcony?"

"No, I've been on the beach, actually. And I went in the sea. It was glorious. It's some time since I swam in a sea of any sort. Where I live it's usually too cold until about August."

"Ah yes, I certainly don't miss the British climate. This suits me better. The sun, the outdoors, good food, and a merry heart are my priorities for living."

"Well, you're thriving on it. You're certainly looking good."

Ted beckoned Maggie towards him. "Come on, I've got somewhere to show you. I've been very busy last night and this morning."

They walked in the opposite direction from the town with the sea to their left, down various steps and intricate narrow walkways. Ted was clearly familiar with short cuts, and soon he halted in front of a row of white houses, each with a front terrace, with only a pavement separating them from the beach. On producing a set of keys from his pocket, he opened a large black gate and stepped back, allowing Maggie to walk through towards the house. He opened some wide patio doors to reveal a large living room with a gleaming tiled floor typical of Spanish properties. There was a kitchenette at the far end of the room and two other rooms leading off to the side, and a staircase. Ted was enthusiastic for Maggie to look around, ushering her into the bedroom.

"Look, it has a wide door, and it's en-suite with so much room, Maggie."

Why is he showing me this?

"Yes, Ted, it's lovely. Oh, here's another bedroom next to that big one."

Ted proceeded up the tiled staircase and once at the top, after catching his breath, opened the two doors to reveal yet more bedrooms with a balcony overlooking the beach opposite.

"What do you think, Maggie? It's a very nice beach house. I've seen this advertised to rent for a while and I know the chap at the estate agents. He's English and comes into the bistro a lot. I'm fairly well known in this town now, and sometimes it's handy to have a bit of 'clout', if you know what I mean."

"Is this for Bruce and Marta?" Ted didn't reply. He led her back downstairs. He seemed intent on showing Maggie the larger of the two ground floor bedrooms again. "It's been designed for wheelchair access. You see you can wheel a chair all around this area and get outside on to the terrace easy enough, and there's no steps at all to get to that little promenade at the front."

I'm not sure where this conversation is going.

"Don't you see, Maggie? It's perfect for Gwen. And you too, of course. It's just right for someone in a wheelchair. I've talked to Keith, the agent. They want to sell it but it's up for rent until that happens."

Maggie was speechless. There were so many obvious stumbling blocks catapulting into her mind, but she didn't want to burst this ridiculously creative bubble her father had been brewing since she last saw him the previous day.

"Ted, it's…"

Reading her thoughts, "It's doable, Maggie. I've thought it all through."

Have you? You clearly haven't.

Maggie took Ted's hand as she spoke. "Even if I thought there was a remote chance of this becoming a reality, I would never be able to get her here, Ted. She's frail and would never be able to get on a plane and…"

"I've got another friend." Ted touched the side of his nose, and gave her a wink. "He's based in England at the moment, but he brings motorhomes over here for people who want to buy or hire them. Sometimes they only want to travel one way through Spain and France, so he brings them here for them to drive back."

Maggie was beyond confused at this point. "I'm sorry Ted, I don't follow you. What's that got to do with Mum, and being here?"

Ted beamed as he spoke. "She could be driven down. With you, of course. They're big, these motorhomes with fixed beds and toilet facilities, and he's so used to doing it, he could have you here in a couple of days."

Again, speechless, Maggie looked at Ted, not sure if he had actually gone mad, and yesterday was just an act he had been able to carry off when introduced to her. She could hide her bemusement no longer. "Ted, that is the most insane idea I think I've ever heard. You want me to bring Mum over here in a camper van!" Ted interrupted quickly, "Motorhome, not a camper van."

"Oh, well, that makes all the difference!" She laughed as she spoke, not wanting to appear rude. "Are you honestly serious?"

Ted looked deep into Maggie's eyes. He held her shoulders. She knew what he was going to say before he uttered another word.

"I have never been more serious about anything. I haven't been a part of your life 'til now. I haven't contributed anything for your upbringing, or your son's. Can you imagine how I feel, knowing how your mum must have struggled all these years, and now she's ill and frail, and you both need a helping hand, and Maggie, I want to make this all up to you. I want to at least give Gwen a chance at having some joy in her twilight years, listening to the sea and feeling the warmth of the sun on her face, and being with you here in this beautiful little beach house... Maggie, don't cry."

The tears were flowing helplessly. "I'm sorry, I'm so emotional. I keep crying and it's because this is all such a revelation and I didn't even know anything about you, until I found that letter just a few weeks ago, and suddenly my life is now completely upside down, but not in a bad way, just all topsy turvy, and looking after Mum and guiding Hugh in his young adult years by myself has been so utterly dispiriting and difficult at times. There were even moments when I thought I was going mad, and you're... you're..." She was sobbing whilst trying to talk. "You're so unbelievably kind, and I don't know how to deal with it, Ted."

Ted held her as she cried, and was humbled by the sheer despairing situation she had been subject to these last few years.

"Let's see if we can give this a go, Maggie. Never give up... we've too much to lose and little time left, it would appear. You can come here for as long as you want, and if you like it, well, you can stay."

"So fairy tales can still happen, Ted?"

"Aye, lass. They can."

Chapter Twelve

Maggie's return to England was imminent, and despite desperately needing to see her mother, it was with a heavy heart she packed her suitcase, and made her way to the reception lobby to wait for her taxi to the airport. She loved the vibrancy of this colourful Spanish coastal resort, and was desperate to return.

The prompt arrival of her driver ensured she would be at the airport in plenty of time to enjoy a coffee and savour her last hours in Spain.

Once in the taxi, her thoughts reflected on the last few days, and how her world had been transformed. It was almost as if this whole episode of her brief time in Nerja had been a dream, and she had to continuously reassure herself that not only had she found her father, but she had also been offered an opportunity that would reshape her immediate future. The discussions she and Ted had entered into since his proud announcement of a 'solution' with the beach house, had been vast and complicated, trying to figure out endless practicalities, and with every stumbling block, Maggie would shake her head insisting this was an impossible task and could never be arranged with any fortuitous outcome. Ted, the ever faithful supreme optimist, would reassure her, saying she must have courage, and should seize this opportunity, not just for Gwen but also for herself.

His words echoed in her mind as the taxi drew closer and closer to the airport. 'I can't believe you have come all this way to find me, and now that you have, I don't want to let you go. Am I being selfish? Probably... yes, but I can't help feeling this has all happened for a reason, Maggie. I feel such a strong connection with you, and I know that's because I loved your mother so much, and here you are, the daughter of the most inspiring woman I have ever known, and I'm lucky enough to have met you when it could have been that our paths might never have crossed. Keep how you feel **now** close to your heart, my dear. Don't go back and forget the magic.'

Ted had been right. It was as if some kind of divine experience had occurred. She couldn't put her finger on exactly what it was, but ever since her arrival, and finding the Anglican Church, she had felt a strong spiritual presence. She was scared that it would disappear, like a child gripping hold of a companion comfort blanket, clutched reassuringly since birth. She didn't want this newly discovered path to a different, more hopeful life to dissipate into nothing more than a crumbling pipe dream.

Keep this in your head. Keep this feeling of the now, the present, the anticipation... don't let it go... please God, let this happen.

*

The atmosphere inside the airport was the same as it had been on her arrival. One entered a period of time paralysis, the only recognition of day or night being the reminder on the departure display board.

More confident than she had been before with the security checks and passport control, Maggie was soon amongst the hubbub of duty-free sales and the associated buzzing frenzy of travellers.

She people-watched as she nursed the most enormous cup of coffee presented to her at one of the airport cafes. *If I drink all this, I'll be forever on the loo during the flight.*

She observed a young mother walking closer to her, juggling baggage with tray, whilst attempting to pacify a fraught toddler intent on removing both shoes. She precariously placed the tray on her table, avoiding disturbing a newborn snuggled close to her chest in a papoose. Maggie reached across to help, bringing out a chair for the small child. The woman smiled gratefully, manoeuvring herself into a confined space not designed for a nursing mother.

So many of us women have to struggle to cope with just day to day tasks... She deserves a medal, travelling alone, coping with such small children. Maggie smiled, saying, "You've got your hands full. Let me help."

The mother spoke with a heavy accent, "You are kind, but I think I can manage. We will be boarding soon, and 'opefully, this little one will sleep," she gestured towards the toddler.

Maggie replied, "I find it hard enough coping with just myself, never mind dependent little ones too." The realisation that she would soon be travelling with her mother who could be more challenging than any tempestuous toddler gave her momentary palpitations, and she decided to leave the rest of her coffee, and make her way to the departure lounge. "Bye bye, and I hope you get some rest on the plane." She waved to the small child, and made her exit, heading for area C in departures.

*

It wasn't long before she and the other passengers were being ushered through yet more security and began filing towards the plane. Maggie looked outside one last time before embarking, wistfully capturing the view and savouring the moment. *See you again soon.*

Minutes later, the cramped jostling of bodies claiming seats and cramming bags into the overhead storage was a jolt back to reality. She was going home. Her brief interlude away from the humdrum that her life had become was over.

Hugh and Susie were waiting at 'Arrivals', arms outstretched as she rushed towards them. Her bags and duty-free treats were divided between helpful hands, and they greeted each other with hugs and smiles, remarking on how well Maggie looked and the difference just a few days away had made. She had deliberately not mentioned any of the imminent plans to Hugh on the phone. She wanted to reveal this next phase in her life face to face, to visibly assess his reaction. They made their way into the airport car park, squirming at the cost of a brief stay, Maggie coming to the conclusion that the ticket had cost more than her car was actually worth.

"Happy for me to drive, Mum?"

"Yes, my head is in too much of a whirl to navigate our way home."

The roads were busy but before long they were heading away from the heavy traffic to calmer B roads towards the Sussex coast.

It was clear to Maggie that Hugh and Susie had become 'an item' in her absence, observing their tactile gestures and knowing looks they were giving each other. *No wonder you sounded so cheerful whilst I was away.*

Susie was desperate to hear all about Ted and asked many questions, all of which Maggie gave an honest answer to. "Was he how you expected him to be, Maggie? Can you see yourself in him?"

"Yes, we have a few shared mannerisms, I was so fascinated to watch the way he spoke and moved his hands. He's given me a few recent pictures." Maggie hastily rummaged inside her handbag to reveal a handful of photos of Ted and the boys, passing them to Susie, Hugh glancing across, trying to see the images of his uncles and grandfather.

"He does look a bit like you, Maggie, or you look like

him, I should say. You've got the same shaped mouth. He looks so suntanned and rather handsome for an older chap, don't you think?"

Maggie laughed. "He has a kind face and a twinkle in his eye most of the time. Bruce is the taller of the two sons and Will is the darker one. I didn't really talk to them much. Ted hasn't told them of my relationship to him, and to them, yet. He wanted to wait and gradually spill the beans. I think there's some kind of issue with the younger one, Will. Ted hinted that he was a big drinker. Must run in the family…" Maggie laughed, and continued, "There's something I need to discuss with you, Hugh, well… with you both, and I suppose now is as good a time as any."

"Sounds intriguing, Mum. You're becoming quite the dark horse lately with all these skeletons falling out of the closet."

"Pull over at this pub here. We can have a drink and I can talk to you properly and show you the photos, Hugh."

Maggie was still in holiday mood, feeling frivolous, wanting to delay her return to the pressures of home.

They all sat in the large airy conservatory of the gastro pub with a bottle of wine and three glasses, Hugh adding just a small measure to his sparkling water. Maggie was already halfway through her first glass, clearing her throat suddenly feeling nervous.

"Okay, here goes. You will probably find this impossible to take in, because I certainly did when Ted first broached the subject, but I have thought it through and arrangements are already under way, and I'm sure with a bit of jiggery pokery…"

Hugh interjected, "Come on, Mum, spill the beans."

Maggie drank some more Dutch courage.

"I'm taking your Gran to Nerja."

She watched Hugh's face as she spoke. His reaction

was important to her. She realised this would have an impact on his life too.

"Ted has a friend who has a motorhome business, and he is prepared to drive me and your Gran down through France and Spain, and Ted has already got a beach house which I've seen... and it's perfect for wheelchair access, and..."

Say something! Are you horrified or do you think I've gone mad, or both? Say something, Hugh.

Hugh looked at Susie, and then at his mother, saying nothing, but then sitting back in his chair he began to laugh, rubbing his hands through his dishevelled hair. He sat forward again and looked at Maggie with what can only be described as admiration.

"Mum, I don't know what to say. This was the last thing I was expecting. I don't know what I **was** expecting but taking Gran in a campervan..."

Maggie interrupted, "Motorhome, not camper," smiling as she recollected a mirrored response only days previously.

Hugh continued, "Okay, so you're going to take Gran in a motorhome about one and a half thousand miles to stay in a beach hut on the Costa del Sol? Well, bloody hats off to you! It's an insane idea, but bloody hell, Mum, if that's what you want to do, then go for it."

At that point, Maggie suddenly felt anxious. This crazy plan was now becoming a reality. She had said what was going to happen, and now she had to carry it through, much the same as when she first announced she was going to Nerja. The possibility becoming a probability, changing her whole perception of how she was actually going to tackle this delicate yet enormous operation.

"Come with me! Both of you, come with me. This motorhome is huge and can sleep six people, so I'm told.

111

There's a fixed bed for your Gran. I'm thinking aloud now, but it would be so much easier to do this if you could come along and give me a hand, too. This is all being arranged, and, I should add, paid for by Ted. He was so insistent, and the beach house is easily big enough for us all. It's not a hut, you idiot, it's quite a large house, right by the beach."

Hugh and Susie were both trying to compute what was being said, Susie visibly in awe, her mind racing with ideas and possibilities.

"We could go, Hugh, couldn't we? This is so exciting! Maggie, what's happened to you? I've never known you so adventurous. It's as if you've had some kind of epiphany."

"I think that's exactly what has happened, Susie." Maggie finished her wine, dividing the remains left in the bottle between two glasses, acknowledging Hugh was driving.

Hugh spoke. "I'll give this some thought, Mum, but I'll have to clear things at work. When exactly are you thinking of doing this random road trip?"

Maggie cleared her throat again. "This weekend."

Silence is often described as golden, but on this occasion, it was more of a shocking pink.

Chapter Thirteen

It wasn't until the following day that Maggie was able to get to Bridge House. Once she had got back home, there seemed to be so much to do, resurrecting the flat and getting the laundry pile cleared, plus she was tired from travelling and had almost a PTSD reaction presenting as complete exhaustion to which she succumbed, climbing between familiar bed covers by nine o'clock that night.

Prior to going to see Gwen, Maggie had to sift her way through one of the many boxes still gathering dust in her bedroom to find her mother's passport. She knew she had seen it recently, knowing it had been used only a few years ago for a church visit to the impressive cathedral in Amiens, northern France. *Impossible to think you were capable of venturing away like that with friends from the church only a short time ago.*

It was hidden amongst an assortment of official papers and an old building society bank book.

Good. One less thing to worry about but several more coming to mind, though.

She glanced around the flat before leaving to visit Gwen. *I've got one hell of a lot to do here in such a short time. Anyway... first things first... time to see Mum.*

*

There was nobody in the entrance hall at Bridge House, so Maggie made her own way straight upstairs to her mother's room.

"Mum... oh, Mum, I'm here now. How are you?" Removing her jacket as she spoke, Maggie kissed her mother and sat beside her holding her hands. She scanned her face. Her hooded eyes appeared sad. "How are you, Mum? I've really missed seeing you. I had to go away for a few days, but I'm back now all safe and sound, see?"

Gwen looked up at Maggie, showing a flicker of recognition. "I'm withered blue."

Maggie smiled. Sometimes her mother's choice of expressions were unusual to say the least, but nonetheless, accurately descriptive.

Maggie responded, "Withered blue, Mum, well let's see if I can make you feel sunshine orange instead. I've got a surprise, Mum. We're going to go on holiday. You and me and Hugh and Susie. You remember Susie, don't you? She sits with you sometimes, and she's Hugh's girlfriend now. We're going to have an adventure, Mum, just like in 'The Sound of Music'." Gwen removed her hands from Maggie's grasp and started to clap them together just as a child would when receiving a treat. Maggie felt her spirits lift. She continued to tell Gwen where they were going, but of course, none of this registered in any way, but the excitement in Maggie's voice transferred over to Gwen, who was clearly participating in their mutual anticipation of what was going to happen.

Maggie's eye was caught by the transparent bag containing dark copper coloured fluid hanging from a stand by her mum's chair. "That will be your catheter then, Mum. Doesn't look like you've had much to drink today." Maggie poured some of the tepid water from a plastic jug into some orange squash and held it to Gwen's mouth, who drank the entire contents almost at once. "Oh, Mum you haven't even been given a drink. I'm so sorry to have left you here like this. I don't know where Miriam is or any of the other 'Ms', come to that. It's deserted downstairs so there's no one to ask what's been happening. This is only for a short while longer. There's someone who wants to see you, Mum."

Should I tell her? Will she understand anything?

"Mum, I've found Ted. I've found Dad, and I'm taking you to see him."

Gwen continued to appear engaged by Maggie's conversation, but there was no recognition of Ted's name, which came as no surprise.

Maggie stayed for some time, fuelling her mother with more juice, and some biscuits she had brought back from Spain. "Remember when we used to go to the seaside, Mum? You and me together when I was little. All those sand castles we made, and then our treat getting ice creams. You always had raspberry ripple, and you called it your raspberry tipple. Do you remember, Mum?" Gwen was more interested in devouring today's treat, crunching the biscuits, holding her hand out for more. "Didn't you get any lunch at all today?"

Eventually, Maggie had to leave but was determined to find a member of staff somewhere in the building. Making sure the DVD player was working, she made her exit to the opening chorus of 'How do you solve a problem like Maria,' and searched for someone to talk to.

Meredith was sitting at her desk in the office with the door open. Maggie tentatively knocked as she approached her.

Meredith looked up, grinning. "You're back from your holiday. You don't seem to have been gone very long. Just a short trip, was it? It's been all go here. We've had such fun out in the garden and the children from the school came to sing yesterday… well I think it was yesterday… the days get so mixed up. I'm already thinking about Christmas, and I've asked the children if they will come and sing then too. I love Christmas with all the carols and festive fun."

Maggie interrupted, "Meredith, I want to let you know that I'm going to be going away again this weekend and

I'm… well I'm actually going to take my mum with me for a little break."

Meredith screeched with delight at this prospect. "Oh, a jolly holiday, that will be such fun for Gwineth, she will just love to be out in the fresh air, just like in the garden here. We always put a straw hat on her, and she looks quite the gardener."

You are definitely a weeny bit crazy.

Meredith continued, "Where will you be going to?"

Thinking it best to avoid presenting the absolute truth Maggie chose not to answer this with any accuracy. "It's Gwen… my mum is Gwen, and we're just going to travel here and there and see the sights, taking in the sea air. As you say she is a lover of the great outdoors. I'll be bringing the… erm… transport on Saturday morning, so just a couple of days to get things organised. Will it be a problem with the catheter, Meredith? Is there something I need to do with it?"

"Oh no, not really, just hope it stays in." She laughed. "I'll get one of the girls to talk it through with you. Not really my field of expertise. Would you like some tea? I'm going to have a cup myself, and I might indulge in a chocolate cup cake. You're very welcome to join me, Margaret." Despite her blatant eccentricities, Maggie couldn't help but like Meredith, even though she had little confidence in her ability to fully grasp the basic essentials for running a residential establishment. She declined the offer of tea and headed back home to attack the 'to do' list.

*

Driving home, Maggie was working things out in her head. *Wheelchair! Damn! Where the hell do I get a wheelchair from?*

Fortunately, some of Craig's recent generosity was still in the plus figures, but not by much.

Maggie diverted the car away from her usual route home, and headed to the town hoping to source the necessary wheelchair. *This town is full of older folks. There must be some kind of shop or loan scheme.*

As it turned out the local charity shop put her in touch with a supplier of used wheelchairs and she was able to get one for less than fifty pounds.

Eventually she arrived home, suppressing the gloom that always loomed over her when opening the door to the flat. She wasn't sure why that was, unless it was something to do with bad karma with everything that had happened over the last few years since living there.

She had only two and a half days to make arrangements and pack. The clock was ticking.

Chapter Fourteen

Ted was in an equal state of nervous apprehension. For him, it was more to do with the fact he hadn't broached the subject with his sons, of having Gwen and Maggie to stay in his newly acquired beach house. He needed help with replacing one of the existing beds with something more suitable for Gwen. He had no idea where to get this from but decided to take a trip to the hospital to find out. These random comings and goings were causing suspicion from his family.

Bruce was with Marta in the bistro's kitchen. "He's preoccupied, Marta. Ever since that woman... Maggie was with him." Despite Bruce being completely fluent in Spanish his conversations with Marta tended to be in English, as she was also bilingual, and enjoyed the challenge of speaking English.

"Don't worry, Bruce. He seems happy enough. In fact, I think he seems more cheerful than ever. It is his nature to be a happy man." Marta was cleaning work surfaces as she spoke.

"Yeah, I know, it's all a bit weird, that's all. I'll talk to him later and see what he's up to."

*

Ted arrived back from the hospital, having found a way to get a clinical bed installed and was relieved it would be in place by the weekend. He wasn't sure exactly how long it would take Alfred to drive down from England, but it was best to get everything in place first. He would have to buy some groceries too, but not yet. The house had been used as a holiday let for quite some time, so all the essentials such as linen, towels and kitchen items were already there. At least that was something he didn't have to think about.

*

Later that afternoon, once the lunch session was almost petering out, Ted sat at one of the tables in the bar area and beckoned both boys to sit down with him. He had to say something soon, and putting this off was only making his anxiety worse.

With a large whisky for support, Ted said, "I need to talk to you both. Come and sit with me here."

Bruce and Will dutifully sat down, knowing what this would be about.

Ted continued, "Maggie, the lady that was here with me… Her mother was more than just a friend."

Ted cleared his throat, realising he would have to own up to his infidelity when married to Maureen, which made him feel uncomfortable.

"I've told you how things were with me and Maureen, and I think you know our marriage had not been a happy one. Well, the thing is, I became very friendly with Gwen, Maggie's mother and…"

Will interjected at this point. "Dad, I think it's fairly obvious what you're going to say. Maggie is your daughter, right?" His words a statement of fact.

"Well since you put it like that, yes, she is. I didn't know anything about her mother expecting a child when we went our separate ways. It was a difficult situation and I'm not proud of what happened, but the thing is, it did, and well, yes, Maggie is my daughter."

Bruce was silent, allowing Will to speak.

"So how do you know she is *your* daughter? I mean, she could be anyone. Just someone claiming to be related to you."

Ted shook his head and put his hand on Will's

119

shoulder. "Will, could you not see how obvious it was that we are related? Do you think I didn't feel a connection with her when we were talking? Don't be so cynical. There's no question, she's definitely mine. It's what I do about it all that's the next matter in hand."

Will got up and walked behind the bar, helping himself to a San Miguel. "Want one, Bruce?"

"Not right now, thanks." Bruce continued to speak, "Wow, Dad, that's quite a revelation, isn't it? No wonder you looked shell-shocked. We have all been wondering what's been going on. So, we have a sister. Well whaddayaknow? Why didn't you introduce us to her properly?"

"I will be doing, very soon. The thing is, Gwen is unwell and she's in a care home and I've made arrangements for her to come here with Maggie. They will be here early next week if all goes to plan, and I've found somewhere for them to stay."

Will was pacing by this point, clearly unsettled by the conversation.

"Dad, why can't she just stay in England, and you go over there to see your long-lost love?"

Ted responded, his voice showing irritation. "Why are you always on the defensive? I know this is a bolt out of the blue."

"You can say that again, Dad. Suddenly our lives are going to be turned upside down by a sick old flame and her offspring. Too right it's a bolt out of the blue. And who's paying for all this? Don't tell me… our business is. The business that we all slave away at, day after day. No, Dad, I'm not happy about this at all. Why should I be?"

Ted finished his whisky. "Let's get one thing straight. I have my own money too, you know, and yes, I'm paying for it because I want to. She didn't ask. In fact she did everything to try and put me off."

"Oh, did she?" Will's sarcasm turning into blatant rage by now. "So, what will it be next, Dad? She gets a third of the business? Or even a quarter, now Marta is one of the family?"

This forced Bruce to speak up. "Will, mate, bloody calm down. What's wrong with you? Why are you talking like this? Why so threatened?"

Will, helping himself to another beer, said nothing.

Ted stood up. "Don't just make this an excuse to get drunk, Will. Look I've no idea what arrangements will be made, if any, for future financial considerations. I'm shocked that all you can think about right now is money. It doesn't become you, lad, to be so blinkered from the real issue here which is... I've discovered I have a daughter. You both have got a sister you didn't know about, and I think the thing is, we just need a bit of time to..."

Will interrupted, "Except she's not **my** sister, is she, Dad? Let's face some more truths, shall we? This blatant elephant in the room. She won't be **my** biological sister, will she? If someone's got to get the trump card here it's **not** going to be me, is it?" Will stared at both Ted and Bruce, and then he stormed out of the bistro.

Silence.

Ted turned towards Bruce. "This has all gone so horribly wrong. Dear God, I've been a good father to him, haven't I? Tell me I've been fair and treated him just as I have you."

"Don't upset yourself, Dad. Of course you have been a good father to him. That's the whole point."

Ted interrupted. "I didn't want to discuss it, Bruce. We all knew about your mother's indiscretion, and I thought, naively I suppose, if we just pretended nothing was different, that you were both my sons, that it would all be… well, just normal. He knew I wasn't his biological father. I did talk to him about it, many years ago, and he didn't want to know. He was in denial. We both were. The whole family was. It **was** the elephant in the room, and it still is." Ted looked wearily at Bruce, who put both his hands on his father's shoulders.

"This is not your fault, Dad. It was Mum who chose to have the affair, and you have always been decent about it to the point where I can honestly say I was in awe of the fact you never ever made judgement or even brought it up in conversation, especially when you and Mum were arguing about stuff before you split up."

Ted took a deep breath before speaking. "Well, now you know why. I would have been the biggest hypocrite going, don't you think, if I had judged Grace and condemned her for what happened? I knew all about it even before Will was born, and when she told me she was pregnant, I somehow felt it was poetic justice. This has all become such a mess now. What can I do to put it all right, Bruce?"

"He'll come round, Dad. I'll talk to him. He's feeling threatened because of Maggie's arrival on the scene, and I suppose you can understand it really. Don't beat yourself up. You didn't even know about Maggie, and now you're giving her, and her mum, a chance for a different life, if that's what the plan is. How long will they be staying, do you think?"

"I said she could stay as long as she liked. Bruce, you must understand I was so in love with Gwen. Your mum and me… well, we had a good life, and I did have love for her, don't think I didn't, and we had happy times, and anyway, look… I've got you, a son I'm so proud of, and of course I'm proud of Will too, and I can't see the point in harbouring grievances and being all sanctimonious about having done the 'right thing'! I treated Will as if he was my own flesh and blood, and I always will do. That's what he needs to get into his head. Now then. Come on. Let's crack on with some work. Goodness knows where your brother has gone."

"I know where he will be, Dad. I'll go and find him, if you can finish clearing the kitchen for me. I'll go and counsel the wayward one." Bruce hugged his Dad. "Hey, I love you."

Ted quickly retired to the kitchen, not wanting to make a public display of his fragmented emotional state. "This is a week I won't forget in a hurry."

Chapter Fifteen

Hugh sat at the kitchen table with Maggie. It was just the two of them, and they were going through the checklist.

"They've been pretty decent at work. I skirted around the reason why it was all happening so quickly. By the way, have you heard anything yet from the driver fella? What's his name again?"

"Alfred. No. He's supposed to be calling me before Saturday to give me an idea when he'll be getting here. We'll pack stuff from here and then we can go straight to Bridge House and get your Gran. Good grief, Hugh, I hope this is all going to work out okay. I've hardly slept a wink since I've been back, with 'what ifs' going through my head all the time."

Hugh nodded. "Yeah, I've been a bit like that myself. I'm worried about Susie. She's intent on coming but her mum is being very sceptical about it all and giving her a hard time."

"Shall I go and talk to her mum? Would that help?" Maggie looked at Hugh as she spoke.

"Let's see what she says when she gets here later." Hugh looked down and fiddled with his phone before speaking again. "Mum, erm, are you okay about erm… if Susie stays over, I mean, will you be okay if she's in my room?"

"Goodness me, I wouldn't expect her to sleep anywhere else." Maggie laughed. "She wouldn't want to sleep with me. I grind my teeth…so I'm told."

Hugh felt relief and phoned Susie whilst Maggie went discreetly into the kitchen.

*

Over the next couple of days, things were divided into piles and the flat started to look more like a boot fair than a family dwelling. Alfred had called Maggie to offer advice about things to take, and things definitely not to take. He was an old hand at long road trips and spoke with some authority. He had a charming northern accent, and didn't mince his words. "There's a right big boot we can put most o' big stuff in. The wheelchair fer one thing will 'ave to go in there, and all food except stuff for fridge. Don't be bringin' ten pairs o' shoes wi' yer."

Maggie had felt better after speaking with him on the phone. She had spoken to Ted several times too, their relationship seeming to flourish with every conversation. He had told the boys about her. As predicted, Bruce seemed quite taken with the prospect of having a half sister come into the family, but Will had not received the information with quite the same enthusiasm. Ted had omitted to explain just why Will had been so anti this change to their lives. That he felt was a conversation for later when they knew each other better.

*

Saturday arrived. All three were at the flat, having had a combined ten hours sleep between them. However, the adrenaline kicked in, and after a quick breakfast, the kitchen had to be cleared and the food packed, and then the clothes stacked ready to be transferred to the motorhome cupboards, although Alfred had warned of limited space, and to be 'economical wi' choices of what to put on'.

Maggie had phoned Bridge House at least twice that morning, remembering last minute details. She was apprehensive, worried that Gwen wouldn't even be dressed, never mind packed up and ready to go by the time they arrived to pick her up. Around mid-morning, the sound of a large vehicle was heard pulling up outside the flat.

"Mum, he's here!" Hugh ran down the stairs two at a time to assess the interior of the motorhome and meet Alfred. A larger than life character with a shining bald head the colour of golden syrup heaved himself down from the driving seat and shook Hugh's hand with a firm manly grip. "Eh up, you must be Hugh. We'd better crack on and get stuff down from yer flat. There's a few stairs to manage, so I were told."

"Yeah, come this way, Alfred." Hugh led the way and before long, a procession of four bodies like working ants, traipsed up and down the staircase with various parcels, boxes, small cases, and an assortment of necessities, being told quite categorically by the authoritative Alfred if something was 'not 'appenin'.'

It was about two hours later when Maggie finally closed the door, locking up and unlocking three times to re-enter, checking she really had unplugged all electric cables and switched the boiler to 'off'. *Everything's done and what isn't, won't matter. Just leave. Dear Lord, keep us safe on this incredible journey. Goodbye, my wee home. For now, anyway.*

*

Maggie had wished a film crew could have captured their entrance into Bridge House drive, as all the Ms rushed outside to see this huge vehicle negotiate the rather tight entrance and pull up outside the front of the home.

Meredith was not to be denied this spectacle and clapped in glee when she saw Gwen's impressive transport. "Oh, my goodness gracious me, this is just hysterical! What an adventure for Gwen!"

There were more faces peering from many of the windows, looking aghast, never having seen quite such an impressive mode of transport turn up at Bridge House before.

Arthur took control, asking if Gwen could be brought down as soon as possible.

"Wiv got to get a move on if we're going to get that three o'clock crossin' through tunnel."

When Gwen was wheeled down, Maggie felt a rush of tears, swiftly brushing them away, deciding this was not the time for over-sentimentality. Hugh and Susie rushed up towards Gwen with excitable greetings and worked out the best way to get her in through the door at the side of the van, which was a tight squeeze, but there was no other way of entry into the main living space. Maggie made her way up to Gwen's bedroom to check that the essential DVD had been packed and nothing of any importance left behind. *I don't think any of us will miss this place, although right now I've got collywobbles, and I'm wondering should we have considered bringing Miriam too.*

Once back downstairs, she witnessed Alfred and Hugh helping to push Gwen's rear end into the van, with Susie inside, mouthing encouragement to Gwen as she seemed intent on stepping in completely the wrong direction.

"Forwards, Gwen, just another step. Come on, you can do it."

Oh my goodness, how on earth are we going to cope?

Gwen finally followed basic instructions, and after interlocking with Susie in an intimate dancing position, was able to be swung to one side, establishing herself firmly on to one of the seats ready to be strapped in.

"Hey, you've done it!" There was a raucous round of applause from the onlookers, with Miriam frantically banging on the window nearest where Gwen was sitting, waving furiously, shedding a tear too.

"Oh bless her, just look at her sitting there. Have a lovely holiday, Gwen. Send us a postcard."

Maggie was beckoned into Meredith's office to sign various consent papers and was given a bag of clinical necessities which seemed ridiculously large and would not be appreciated by Alfred. "Give it us 'ere and I'll put it in boot. There's nowt yer need right now from it, is there?" And before long, they were off. With waves and whoopees, it was quite the royal send off, and Maggie wondered if she had been a little hasty in her condemnation of Bridge House.

"Have you got your iPad with you Susie, with you know what on it? Oh, and let's do a quick passport check." Maggie was sitting in the front seat next to Alfred, with Hugh and Susie in the back seats, Hugh opposite his Gran and Susie next to her. There was a table in between the seats which was useful for keeping Gwen in a safe position. Towards the back was the bathroom with shower, loo and sink, and opposite that, a kitchen area with just about everything needed, including a microwave oven, and an impressive fridge. Right at the back across the whole width was the fixed bed, although there were a couple of difficult steps, Maggie noticed, for access. She would worry about those when she needed to.

It was better for Gwen to remain seated rather than lying in her bed when going through security, so that their passports could be shown, and passengers counted easily.

Susie was sorting out her iPad so Gwen could watch Maria and the Von Trapps happily and Hugh was busy texting on his phone. Maggie kept looking back at her mother and wondering just how this had all come together, and what exactly the next couple of days had in store for them. Alfred had reassured her he had made this journey 'more times than he'd 'ad 'ot dinners', and didn't need much in the way of sleep. His bed, should he need it, could be pulled down from above the driving area at the front, like a secret pod. He was a big chap and Maggie hoped this facility would contain his huge body without him cascading into the centre part of the van.

She would rest with her mum in the double back bed, and Hugh and Susie could sleep in the bed that had to be made up from the middle seats and table that they were currently sitting at. The whole interior was of impeccable design, and very clean and spacious. Maggie decided she could happily live in it, and spend her life exploring all of Europe, but probably after many hours of travel, she may not have quite such a romantic vision of life on the road.

"We're off then... Anyone want a peppermint?"

Chapter Sixteen

The only person familiar with the Eurotunnel Port was Alfred. For the rest of them this was completely new territory. He navigated his way without hesitation through the various checkpoints with the ease of a regular European commuter, and soon they were queuing with a variety of other vehicles ready to enter into the huge mouth of the cargo container. The trains had large grey forbidding carriages and Maggie shuddered on seeing this ominous-looking mode of transfer to France, finding it reminiscent of disturbing war images of hordes of captured Jews being sent to horrific camps without any means of escape.

To Maggie's delight, it only took them about forty minutes to reach Calais, and once they were through the tunnel, it was plain sailing.

Alfred announced they would drive for an hour or so and then stop at a service station on the autoroute. This was met with cheery smiles from everyone.

Enjoying new and unfamiliar scenery, Maggie was mesmerised by the huge expanses of land, and the glorious display of bright yellow fields, awash with hundreds of sunflowers in bloom. It was a heavenly sight, enhancing her feeling of exhilaration with every kilometre driven.

Taking into account the extra hour, it was approaching seven o'clock when they pulled into the service station recommended by Alfred. For Gwen, this was already becoming a late night, having been subject to a care home regimen for the last few weeks.

Manoeuvring Gwen from the table seat and out of the van was not without its challenges.

"I'm sure she'll get used to this in time," said Maggie, as she attempted to persuade Gwen to disembark rather than sit down on the steps. The catheter was also proving problematic, now attached to a leg bag which kept slipping down towards Gwen's ankles, needing some adjustment of the flimsy velcro straps unfortunately *not* holding it in place.

Finally, all five of them, with Gwen snug in her wheelchair, made their way into the bustling cafeteria, home to many truck drivers, it would seem.

"Always choose places that lorry drivers go to," announced Alfred, happily wheeling Gwen towards a large table. "Now, I've strict instructions, and I want no arguments, that you've to 'ave what you want to eat and drink, and it's all included in 'price of yer van rental. I've sorted this all out wi' Ted, so go and 'elp yourselves to buffet," comically pronouncing the silent T.

Needing no further encouragement, as lunch had been a rushed sandwich, their first French meal was without doubt a fine feast chosen from a vast array of fresh salads, meats, cheeses, lasagne, fried chicken and a number of other dishes difficult to distinguish but nonetheless equally tempting. Much to the delight of them all, next to the water dispenser were two further taps, one for red and the other for white house wine, all complimentary with the meal.

"Never ever have I seen wine on tap like this before. The French certainly know how to prioritise," laughed Maggie.

Alfred seemed amused at Gwen's insistence on abandoning the need for a knife and fork, preferring to use her fingers to eat with, but he demonstrated a gentle and kindly approach towards her, which Maggie found endearing.

"Mi Gran 'ad dementia so don't worry, I'm used to dealin' wi' this kind o' thing. It breaks yer 'eart, it does."

Gwen appeared uncharacteristically compliant as

Alfred helped her with her meal, enjoying the attention from this giant of a man.

He departed from the table to go outside for a cigarette and left the four of them to finish eating, and enjoy the free top ups of wine so readily available.

"This is a bit of alright, eh, Mum? Gran seems to be okay at the moment, too. What's going to happen about sleeping tonight? Any idea what the plan is?"

"I think Alfred is keen to just keep driving. He's hoping to cross the border into Spain tomorrow, so we've a fair few hundred miles to go. I'll get Mum into the bed now and I'll lie with her in case she's worried. She would have probably been asleep a couple of hours ago by now back at Bridge House. I don't think you can make *your* beds up unless we actually stop for the night."

"I'm far too excited to sleep, Maggie!" Susie was glowing and clearly enjoying the start of their adventure. "We can both doze in the seats. That'll be fine, won't it, Hugh?"

Hugh nodded in agreement, still munching his way through an enormous plateful of chicken, chips, salad and couscous.

As predicted, Maggie's concerns for getting Gwen up into the double bed were confirmed. After multiple attempts, it was decided the only way up would be to carry her somehow.

"I could give her a piggyback and climb up with her," declared Hugh, realising almost immediately that was to be a non-starter. Eventually, Maggie got up onto the bed as the receiver, and with a combined effort between the two men and Susie, Gwen was safely delivered without suffering too much distress. At the far side of the bed there was a deep pocket designed to hold books, but it doubled very well as a catheter night nest. "Look at that," said Maggie as she deposited the bag into its hold.

"Perfect, Mum. Now let's get your pillows sorted out and I think you'll be away with the fairies before much longer. I'll be right here beside you, and we can tell each other stories like we used to."

There was no response from Gwen, who already had her eyes closed and was humming herself to sleep.

*

It was five thirty in the morning. Maggie awoke to unfamiliar surroundings and sat up abruptly.

I must have slept for ages. I don't remember us stopping. Where on earth are we and where are Hugh and Susie?

She could see through the window at the bottom end of the bed. It was just beginning to get light. The sun was blood orange, highlighting wispy mushroom clouds. Everything so still. There was a faint mist and dew on the ground, and she could see woodland not far in the distance, and by a small field, she spotted Hugh and Susie embracing and kissing as they walked slowly towards the van. *My boy is in love.*

Maggie imagined how it must have been for Gwen and Ted at a similar age.

Her mother was asleep.

Maggie moved closer to the window. She was in a timeless zone, completely unaware of exactly where she was, and yet she felt a sense of supreme inner calm and peace… a tranquillity so real, so tangible, she could smell, hear and feel it, as if her senses had been given new life. This was a moment to hold on to. A wild calm, capturing all that felt good, her peace at its peak.

Treasure this. All is beautiful. Never let this moment go. Never forget.

*

Shortly afterwards, the day progressed with essentials such as cups of tea, toast and eggs, and bacon too for Alfred, who was partial to a full cooked breakfast, not forgetting the mandatory marmalade for Gwen. A fold-up table was erected outside and with an 'all hands on deck' approach, soon to be laden with all of the above.

Gwen had to be carried out of the bed, Maggie remembering the attached catheter just in time before 'it' and Gwen parted company. Maggie had mastered the emptying technique and had also adjusted the entire contraption to allow freedom of movement for Gwen's legs.

"We'll get the hang of things, won't we, Mum?"

"Hang it, hang it," was Gwen's response.

Eating outside always stimulates the appetite, and all of them managed to devour most of the morning goods. Gwen was taken for a short stroll along the grass verge.

Alfred had pulled over into the 'aire' in the early hours of the morning. He hadn't bothered about getting his bed into position, preferring to doze in the driver's seat, as had Hugh and Susie also, so Maggie and Gwen were the only two privileged enough to enjoy a decent sleep in a bed.

"These errs they 'ave in France are champion. You don't get 'owt like that in England. Over there they put them 'ite restrictions anywhere that's nice to stop over but over 'ere, they make yer feel welcome. There's toilets over there too look, if yer want to freshen up like, and save our cassette in t'van's loo."

"I'll volunteer to empty that, Alfred, I'm not squeamish." Maggie began to clear the table making it her job to wash up. "So, whereabouts are we now?"

"We made good time travellin' thru night. We're just

134

north of Bordeaux so we'll get t'Spain in about 4 hours or so, but I want to get a move on today and get as far down as we can. Yer might find yerselves gettin' a bit fed up in van, but I've got to get this to mi customers in Málaga after I've dropped yer all off, and I've got to give it a spruce up first."

"We'll be fine, Alfred," said Susie. "I think I'll sleep most of today, but I don't want to miss the scenery. It's amazing here. Those woods there are just beautiful."

"Aye, well get a shifty on. What are we doin' wi' mother? Is she sittin' in seat or up on top?"

"Maybe let her be in the seat for a bit and see if she gets restless. Hugh has taken her for a bit of a walk, so she might be happy to sit for a while."

She wasn't keen to be sat down at all. It took some cajoling to get Gwen into the safest seat by the window, but eventually she relented, and like the previous day, was content with the Von Trapps via iPad.

It wasn't even eight o'clock when they drove out of the aire and on to the main road, shortly to join the autoroute once more.

Maggie sat with Alfred in the front and decided to use the text facility on her phone. This would take her some time, as her skills with this were still in their infancy, but after about a quarter of an hour, she had successfully delivered a message to Ted, explaining where they were and that all was well.

*

All wasn't quite so well in the Ted household. After the proverbial cards had been laid well and truly on the table, Will had failed to return to the bistro, leaving Ted to manage the bar, whilst Bruce and Marta between them and the chef, worked in the kitchen and at the tables.

Most days in June were inclined to be busy and Ted was beginning to feel fractious coping single handed, when he had other things to organise for his imminent arrivals.

After the argument, Bruce had found Will at an English bar called The Cavern, but had not been able to persuade him to return home. He was in a bad place mentally and demanded he was given some space, so Bruce left him where they often frequented together when not working.

Will was pushing the self-destruct button in a menacing way, and Bruce was concerned just how long this binge would last, and what the outcome would be. One thing was for certain, it was unlikely to end well.

"He makes me nervous when he's like this, Bruce." Ted had escaped from the bar for a few minutes to grab a bowl of soup for himself from the kitchen.

"It was the same when your mother and I split up. Never knowing where he was from one day to the next, and Lord knows what trouble he's getting himself into."

"Don't worry, Dad. After lunch is done here, I'll nip over to The Cavern, and see how he is. Maybe he should go away for a bit and have some time out. We can hire some help here — there's always people looking for work in Nerja. In fact, I've got the names of a few written down somewhere by the till."

"I could do with some help, that's for sure. I still need to get the beach house ready for Gwen and Maggie, and they're bringing Hugh, her son, and his girlfriend, too. This was supposed to be a happy reunion but I'm pensive now, especially if Will's going to turn up and make a spectacle of himself."

"Try not to fret, Dad. I don't think he'll do that."

"I'm nervous at meeting Gwen, too. I know she won't recognise me, but it's going to be emotional meeting up again. I think I might go and see Colin at the church.

136

Goodness, to think it's only just over a week since all this happened."

Ted returned to the bar to continue serving those less mentally burdened, whose only concern was having a good time on holiday.

*

Meanwhile, the road trippers were making good headway.

Gwen had been content in the seat next to Maggie, which enabled Hugh and Susie to commandeer the fixed bed at the back and catch up on some sleep, albeit under protest from Susie, who was afraid of missing out on crossing the border.

"It's nowt spectacular when yer cross from Biarritz end. One minute yer in France and next yer in Spain, and if yer blink yu'd miss it anyroad." Alfred was keeping focussed on driving, using boiled sweets to keep up his energy levels.

"Well, wake me anyway if I'm asleep, won't you?"

Maggie answered, "If I don't drop off myself, I'll give you the heads up when we're getting close."

Hugh had already fallen into a deep sleep, oblivious to any of the changes in landscape and the architecture which Maggie had become transfixed by.

As they approached the border, she noticed how many of the houses seemed to look almost Swiss-like, with red roofs and chalet style exteriors. The rolling green hills merged into a more rugged landscape, and as they crossed into Spain, with a sleepy Susie insistent on witnessing this event, the Pyrenees could be seen in the far distance, marking a striking natural border all of their own.

The motorways, known as autovias in Spain, were

much less busy than the roads leaving France, allowing for straightforward driving, much to Alfred's delight. He occasionally commented on how 'bloody 'ighways department in England could learn a few tricks from these Spaniards.'

Maggie was dozing on and off and Gwen, also seemingly hypnotised by the constant driving, said very little, but happily tapped the window, as if wanting to alert the attention of other drivers in the cars passing by.

They stopped for lunch in another highway café, again choosing one frequented by lorry drivers, but this time there did not appear to be wine 'on tap' as there had been in France.

Once again, Maggie noticed how much louder the Spaniards were compared to the French and English, verbalising their opinions with exaggerated arm movements, so expressive with their language, speaking with such alarming speed and volume.

Alfred knew a few words in Spanish, so he assisted everyone in making themselves understood, settling for the menu del día, including a vegetarian option, which both Susie and Maggie opted for, as the meatballs in the onion-heavy tomato sauce looked a bit too rich for their liking.

Alfred ate his lunch in the time it took Maggie to cut up Gwen's food for her, and he vacated his seat, saying, "I'm off to 'ave forty winks in van, so stretch yer legs a bit after this and we'll be off in about three quarters of an 'our, alright?" and he made his way out of the restaurant whilst searching for his cigarettes.

"I don't know how he keeps going," Maggie commented, as she gingerly cajoled Gwen into eating, unrewarded with any success. "Come on, Mum, you've hardly had anything today. Are you feeling alright?" Maggie felt Gwen's forehead. "Hmmm, you feel a bit warm."

Hugh poured her some water. "Maybe she needs a drink. Here you are, Gran, have a swig of Spanish mineral water." He had to almost shout above the background noise of their fellow diners. Gwen managed to drink some water, but showed little interest in any of the food offered, content to play chess with the condiment bottles of olive oil, salt, and pepper.

"I'll grab one of those sandwiches to take with us, and maybe she'll have it later." Maggie made her way up to the counter, turning round to Hugh and Susie, pulling a quizzical face, as she had no idea how to ask for a sandwich in Spanish.

Once they had finished eating, they made their way outside, and pushed the wheelchair around an enclosed exercise area, probably intended for people with dogs, but it was an adequate place to stretch legs and digest lunch before returning to their home on wheels. Alfred was still snoring when they reached the van, but was grateful for being woken as 'time was pressin' on', and they needed to 'get crackin''.

With the now well practised art of getting Gwen into the fixed bed, the general consensus was that Gwen should try and sleep through the next part of the journey until their next stopover, which was to be just south of Burgos at a motel Alfred was familiar with.

Gwen was obviously tired, falling asleep almost immediately, and the other three passengers were able to have a game of cards to pass the time, sitting at the table together whilst Alfred drove steadily on, his radio tuned into a Spanish music station and his mouth devouring more boiled sweets.

It was almost seven o'clock when they pulled into the impressive-looking motel which looked like a Moorish castle alongside a huge car park and various outbuildings, plus an adjoining petrol station.

Alfred was content to remain in the van, as that way, he said he would sleep better, knowing he was on guard, should anyone try to break in. Maggie was to have a room with Gwen, and Hugh and Susie had a separate room to themselves. They all collected overnight necessities and made their way to the motel rooms, which were set apart from the more flamboyant hotel rooms within the bigger Moorish building. It was all fairly basic, but a welcome bed and shower was a joy after almost thirty-six hours of being in the motorhome.

Gwen had become agitated after her sleep during the drive, and Maggie wondered just what sort of a night she was likely to have with her, in a strange room with unfamiliar surroundings, but she then considered how well her mother had adapted to travelling, and hoped perhaps, with the use of Susie's iPad, she may keep her calm enough to get through this one night in the motel.

Gwen's face was flushed and she felt warm to touch, so Maggie gave her two paracetamol tablets that she had crushed up, disguised in a chocolate desert, which seemed to be acceptable to Gwen, who had eaten very little all day, and was partial to anything sweet. "Let's hope that might stave off anything you've got brewing, Mum." Maggie noticed the catheter bag contents seemed to be quite dark and cloudy.

"You need to drink more, Mum. We can't have you getting another urine infection, not here, not now." Maggie remembered the huge bag she had received from Meredith at Bridge House and thought she should look inside to see what the contents were.

Susie sat with Gwen whilst Maggie went to the van to get the bag from the boot area. Alfred managed to locate it, and she returned rummaging through the contents. There was an assortment of tubes and additional catheter bags, some large incontinence pads, and also some pouches with nozzles.

"Susie, what are these? It says bladder irrigation. What on earth am I supposed to do with them?" Susie was searching on her phone for the answer.

"Oh, it's to wash out the bladder through the catheter tube. Look, there's a video to show you what to do. Maybe that's what we should do to prevent another infection, Maggie."

"I'm sorry? Watch a video so I can perform a bladder irrigation? Seriously? You'd think they might have talked me through this at Bridge House. Surely this is something a trained nurse should do. I don't suppose there's a nurse here in the motel."

Susie giggled. "Trying to explain all this to somebody English would be bad enough, Maggie, never mind to someone Spanish."

"Yes, you're right. Let's just hope this passes quickly, whatever it is she might have."

But Maggie's optimism was short-lived. During the night, Gwen became restless, continually trying to get out of bed and making unusual unfamiliar noises.

"Mum, what's wrong? Come on, try and sleep a bit."

The night seemed endless, and Maggie wasn't sure what she could do. She felt inadequate and she began to question whether this had been the right thing to do, bringing her mother all this way, removing her from a network of support so essential when things go wrong. She had been given an assortment of medication, including some sleeping tablets, which so far, she hadn't needed to use, but she was desperate to get her mum to rest and decided it might be her only option. Using the same technique as with the paracetamol, she attempted to spoon chocolate mousse, offering it to Gwen with the small tablet hidden amongst the sticky substance and by the third spoonful, she succeeded with the correct dose to hopefully help achieve a better night for all. It also occurred to her that there had been no evidence of bowel movements since they began their journey. She opened a bottle of Lactulose, also supplied by the care home, and after trying some herself to ascertain whether this also needed to be disguised, decided its sweet taste would be appealing to her mum, which in fact it was, and a good hefty dose was swallowed without hesitation. Maggie was wishing she had some wine to mellow the night away, but there was nothing so grand as a drinks fridge in this rather basic accommodation.

Gwen still struggled, fighting against Maggie when she tried to position her head on the pillow and cover her with the sheet and thin blanket. It was warm in the room and Maggie opened the window to let in some air, but the outside air was, if anything, warmer than inside. She heard a faint tap at the door. It was Susie, making sure Maggie was alright, having heard the disturbance.

"She's not having the best night, to be honest, Susie. I've just given her a sleeping tablet, so hopefully that will kick in soon. I think she has got another infection and that means sourcing some antibiotics for her. Not sure where exactly we go to get some of those though, here in the middle of nowhere."

"Aren't there any in that bag of stuff from Bridge House?"

"No, just mostly catheter and toilet essentials in there. What time is it?"

"About half two. I couldn't really sleep anyway because I slept so long in the van today. Do you want me to sit by her and you get back to bed?"

"No, Susie, don't worry. She looks as if she might be drifting off a bit now. You go back to Hugh."

They said goodnight, and Maggie sat by Gwen and

stroked her hair, soothing her by humming lullabies, just as her mum had done for her as a small child.

"We didn't see this scenario coming, Mum, did we? No wonder you're confused and wondering what's going on. It will be alright. I'm taking you to see Ted. Close your eyes and dream of long ago when you were so young and in love. Calm your mind, Mum. All will be well. That's what you used to say to me. All will be well."

They both eventually slept. The problem a few hours later was the night situation in reverse. The sleeping pill was making it impossible to wake Gwen up and Maggie envisaged them having to carry her into the van whilst she slept. Taking it in turns to venture into the restaurant for breakfast, to allow for 'Gwen sitting' duty, it was almost eleven o'clock before they were even packing up to continue their journey south. Alfred was getting agitated, having presumed they would have been on the road an hour or two by now. Eventually, they transferred Gwen into the wheelchair and made it to the van with her still dozing, but had to wake her fully when physically hoisting her up into the fixed bed. It wasn't the most dignified operation, but eventually she was made comfortable and continued to sleep off the night sedation and hopefully recover from whatever it was that had unsettled her.

Alfred was trying to make up for lost time with his foot pressed down hard on the accelerator. It was going to be a long drive today, but by supper time, with a bit of luck they would all arrive at Nerja. Unfortunately, due to the additional medication given through the night, it wasn't long before they had to pull over into a roadside parking area to allow Gwen to use the van's toilet facilities, which caused quite a commotion with the limited space available but after approximately half an hour, things in the nether regions had progressed well, and Maggie attempting to wash her mother using the small sink mastered immense skill in maximising the limited facilities.

"There we are, Mum, now that must feel an awful lot better." Maggie noticed Alfred pacing outside smoking a cigarette whilst speaking on his mobile. "Oh dear, I hope we haven't lost too much time. Come on, let's get you settled into the seat here." Hugh and Susie made encouraging gestures towards Gwen to speed up proceedings. Susie also produced her makeup and some hair styling products.

"I think we need to give you a bit of a makeover, Gwen. Before long, you're going to be meeting someone very special. How about a bit of powder and blusher, and I'll try and style your hair and give it a bit of body."

Gwen seemed to enjoy the pampering and was clearly feeling much better following the necessary ablutions. She began humming to herself whilst playing with some of the items from the makeup bag.

Alfred returned and seemed less agitated. "I've made a couple o' calls and we'll be alright. I reckon we should be getting to Nerja about sevenish. I'm takin' van to Málaga tomorer now, so pressure's off a bit."

They all readjusted seat belts, and Susie, ever prepared as always, arranged some crayons and paper in front of Gwen and assisted her with drawing trees and flowers. Hugh was engrossed in music on his phone and Maggie helped with the craft session.

They were back on track, albeit a couple of hours later than planned, but spirits were up, and the overall mood was that of cheerful anticipation, in the hope of reaching their destination in a few hours.

*

Back at The Courtyard Bistro, cheerful anticipation was sadly lacking, as preparations for another busy lunch session were under way. Ted had made sure the bar was ready for action early that morning, and after a hurried breakfast, he decided to head off to the church in an attempt to calm his anxiety and refresh his soul, and hopefully bump into Colin.

Bruce and Marta were talking through the various basics of setting and clearing tables to Mike, a young traveller who was spending time in Nerja, and happy to have been in the right place at the right time when it came to getting temporary cash in hand employment.

Will was still noticeably absent, and it was unclear to anyone exactly where he was.

"Let's hope he doesn't turn up here today, Marta, especially after an extended drinking binge. Frankly, that's all we need right now." Even Bruce was becoming uncharacteristically agitated, wondering how the day would progress with the arrival of a new member of staff and a new family. It wasn't going to be your average weekday, that's for sure.

Ted arrived at the church just as a choir practice was about to begin. He also felt on edge with the added guilt of leaving the bistro to self-indulge in some spiritual guidance when they were already at a disadvantage with staff.

He sat at the rear of the building and immediately lowered himself down to pray. His conversation with God combined a request for forgiveness, with pleading for help and asking for a minor miracle. The choir had reached the final verse of 'Fight the good fight' before Ted raised himself up on to the pew, concluding *that* particular hymn was indeed very apt.

He sat waiting for the choir practice to finish, and was then able to have a chat outside with Colin, his vicar and very good friend.

"Life seems to have become somewhat complicated, Colin. I have to thank you actually, for directing a very important person my way."

"Would that be the lady I spoke to last week, Ted? She was asking about you and seemed visibly shaken when I said I knew who she was looking for."

"Her name is Maggie. She's my daughter — a daughter I didn't know I had, Colin."

Vicars are well practised in disguising knee-jerk reactions when receiving unexpected and sometimes alarming information, and Colin was no exception. He simply tilted his head to one side, and put a reassuring arm around Ted's shoulders. "God certainly moves in mysterious ways, Ted. This must have come as quite a shock, to say the least."

"A shock, yes, but I have to say I am completely overwhelmed. I was very much in love with her mother. However, it was a forbidden love, I'm ashamed to say. I have asked for forgiveness more times than I can count throughout my life, but I cannot and won't deny that Maggie is now a part of my family and not only that, her mother is alive and arriving here later today with her, and Maggie's son and his girlfriend. But Gwen is unwell, and I've been wondering whether or not she would want me to see her the way she is now, if she were able to make this decision for herself. Have I been too hasty in wanting to make amends for my misdemeanours and thinking of myself and not her? She has dementia, and I suppose if I had dementia, would I want someone I loved many years ago seeing me in a regressive state? Oh Colin, I'm all over the place and I was just wanting to do the best, but I think I might actually be doing quite the reverse, and to put the tin hat on everything, Will disappeared in a fit of pique when I told him about Maggie and Gwen, and Lord only knows where he is and what state he's in."

Colin guided Ted away from a group of sightseers that were gathering close by.

"Ted. There is a reason that God has presented Maggie to you. If you loved her mother the way you say, then just because her mind and body are not as they once were, doesn't mean to say that your presence in her life now won't make a difference to her time left here on this earth. She will need all the love and support she can get, and I cannot think of anyone more equipped than you to help create a calm and peaceful end of life pathway for her... as Isaiah proclaimed in chapter forty, verse thirty-one, 'but those who hope in the LORD will renew their strength. They will soar on wings like eagles; they will run and not grow weary; they will walk and not be faint.' Ted, you must take a leap of faith, and remember God is always looking out for you. Whatever happens, if love and kindness are at the forefront of your intentions then there is nothing that can't be achieved. I'm glad you came here today, and I'll pop by this week to see how you're getting along and meet the rest of your newfound family. God bless you, Ted. Oh, and don't worry about Will. We'll have a look for him today and if we find him, I'll let you know."

"You're a good friend, Colin. Thank you. I had better dash off as we've got a full house this lunch time. Ha, and a full house later, too."

Ted walked back towards the bistro feeling uplifted and ready to embrace all that God had bestowed upon him.

Chapter Seventeen

The carpet of olive trees that reached as far as the eye could see was a more appealing view than the somewhat bland region below Madrid known as La Mancha, which seemed to be very flat and nondescript in comparison. Maggie observed the countryside, aware they were now in Andalucía, which although vast, was the region Nerja was a part of. Opposite, Hugh and Susie were interlocked, dozing sporadically. Gwen was content with the iPad and a bag of sweets, preferring to remove all the wrappers, then replacing them in the bag rather than eating them. Maggie watched her, imagining how Ted would be feeling, now that their arrival was imminent. There were considerations about this trip that Maggie had given very little attention to, and she would periodically scribble her thoughts down on a memo pad as a reminder. Informing Bridge House that it was unlikely Gwen would be returning any time soon was the main thought preoccupying her, and knowing if she gave notice, then this was without doubt going to be a one-way trip for Gwen, at least. What about the flat, too? She assumed Hugh and Susie would return there themselves and maybe live together, but the rent would be too expensive for them on their own, long term. Her financial support benefits would continue, but for how long? *Best not to overthink all of this if you want to keep your sanity. One day at a time, and jump each hurdle as and when you've got to. I think a glass of wine might be beckoning.* The fridge was easily accessible from where she was sitting, and Maggie grabbed the open bottle of white, pouring herself a tumblerful before replacing it back in the fridge.

The outside temperature was exceeding thirty degrees but fortunately, the van's air conditioning was efficient in keeping the interior cool and comfortable. The late afternoon dissolved into early evening and Alfred suggested a quick stop over for a 'brew' and leg stretch. They pulled over into what seemed to be a disused railway station now converted into a restaurant and campervan parking area. They all spilled out onto the simmering gravel embracing the heat, stretching arms and legs before helping Gwen down the van's few steps as she clutched the bag of sweets she was reluctant to part with.

Alfred walked over towards the restaurant, checking out what was available, whilst taking the opportunity to have a quick cigarette. "We can sit out 'ere instead of goin' inside. If yer feelin' peckish, wiv got time for a snack. I'll 'ave a look inside and see what's what."

Gwen was able to walk a little, with help from Susie and Hugh guiding her carefully, holding her from each side. They found a table shaded by trees, and waited for Alfred to emerge from the restaurant. "'Ow's about chips and pizza? They can 'ave that ready in a minute or two."

"Sounds great, Alfred." And as promised, a huge platter of chips and several pizzas cut into manageable slices was placed before them, hot with sizzling cheese spilling over the sides.

"This looks sensational." Hugh was the first to help himself, unable to hold back as he devoured huge mouthfuls, whilst cutting up a portion for Gwen.

Maggie was enjoying another glass of wine with her food, enchanted by this new way of living that was so completely opposite to how life was back at home. She was amazed at how her mum had adapted to such an intense change of routine, seemingly undisturbed by it. Familiarity was something she had been told was all important for dementia sufferers, but there was nothing familiar about the last couple of days they had all just spent together.

"This is a pretty area, Alfred. Do you come this way all the time?"

"Aye. If I can, I like to keep to mi usual route. That way I can work out times a bit better, and I've been doin' this a fair while now. We should be there in about two hours, I reckon. Ted said to take yer straight t'ouse. I know where it is. Door'll be left open so we can just go straight in."

Maggie's stomach did a flip at the mention of being back in Nerja with her father. What would Hugh and Susie make of the place? And Ted and her half brothers, and ultimately how will her mum cope, and how will Ted react when he sees her?

I need another bottle of wine, I think. Probably it was a good thing that they returned to the van shortly afterwards, without additional alcohol.

Proceeding further south, the Sierra Nevada became visible ahead, so breathtakingly beautiful, emphasising the diversity of Spain's landscape. Shortly after, as the olive trees petered out to a more rugged rocky landscape with huge bright blue lakes, the views changed yet again, with white dwellings built higher into the hillsides, and clusters of rooftops noticeable down in the valleys. There was an air of increased activity on the roads and before long, as they approached the coastline, the twinkling shimmering turquoise sea prompted a resounding clapping of hands and shouts of "We're here!" with Gwen entering into the spirit of euphoria, clapping happily and smiling.

"Not long now," announced Alfred. All eyes were taking in the scenery and even though it was eight o'clock, the sun was still warm and red, projecting a romantic glow against the hills.

"It's beautiful, Maggie." Susie was mesmerised. Maggie held Gwen's hand. "We're nearly there, Mum.

It's been a long drive but we're almost there."

Once they approached the town, Maggie started to recognise the area, and soon they were driving along the same road she had walked along when trying to find the bistro just over a week ago. Alfred manoeuvred the van through narrow streets and difficult corners, but before long, they were parked in a small road close to where the beach house was situated. It was still light, but the sun was beginning to set behind the mountains, casting a ruby glow across the landscape, creating a beautiful balmy evening.

All were desperate to disembark, Hugh and Susie keen to see their holiday home for the first time. With Gwen comfortably established in her wheelchair, they hastened around the corner and along the promenade path towards the house. There were keen sun worshippers straggled along the beach opposite, savouring the evening sunset, with a few setting up barbecues, not ready to leave their happy place until much later on.

Maggie opened the front door, and everyone piled in, pushing Gwen across the threshold into the large open plan living area.

"Hey, this is okay Mum, isn't it?" Hugh was observing the décor, exploring the ground floor with Susie, both clearly delighted with the size and position of the house with the beach just a few steps from their front door. "Just a bit more upmarket than a beach hut." He winked at his mum and proceeded up the stairs with haste.

Alfred announced he would return to the van and start to bring the luggage in and maybe they could '*put kettle on.*'

Maggie checked the fridge for milk, smiling with gratitude on finding a plethora of cheeses, butter, fresh milk, two bottles of white wine, and several small bottles of the Spanish beer. There was a basket of fruit and a box of vegetables, with bread and even cakes amongst the groceries.

Well, Ted, you have certainly done us proud. Maggie filled the kettle and called up to Hugh.

"Can you go and give Alfred a hand, Hugh? And I'll settle your Gran. She's looking quite tired."

Gwen was almost asleep in the wheelchair. Maggie pushed her into the larger bedroom, thinking she might have to sleep in the same bed as her for that first night, but quickly saw that the bed was only a single, and it was a hospital bed with a mechanical aid to raise the bed up and down to enable Gwen to get in and out more easily. There were flowers in a vase by the window, and a card reading 'Welcome home my dear Gwen' which brought tears to Maggie's eyes. "Oh, Mum, this is like a dream. Please be happy here. I want this to have been the right decision, I want to have done the right thing and I so need it to work out."

It wasn't long before all of their bags and other paraphernalia were spread across the living area floor and Alfred, after finishing two mugs of tea, decided he would bid them farewell.

"It's bin a pleasure bringin' yer all down 'ere. I 'ope you all 'ave a right good time, and all goes well wi' mother and Ted. I think she'll 'ave a luverly time sunnin' 'erself and 'avin' you all around 'ere... all 'er family together. Proper champion, it is."

Alfred appeared visibly touched as they all hugged his huge frame and said goodbye, thrusting bags of sweets and chocolate into his hands as a gesture of thanks for all he had done. He returned to the motorhome to spend the night in a nearby campervan park, before heading to Málaga the next morning.

Susie helped Maggie get Gwen ready for a night's

sleep. They moved the hospital bed close to the wall so there was only one accessible side and less chance of her falling out. "I think I should be in the same room with her, Susie. I'll see if I can get the other bed in here, too."

It wasn't too difficult to sort the room out so Maggie was able to sleep alongside her mum.

The now 'spare' room downstairs was soon put to use as they transferred suitcases and bags and the wheelchair, allowing a spacious free living area. A little later, the three of them sat outside, exhausted from travelling and unpacking. The air was still so warm, even though it was now nighttime. They ate cheese, bread and fruit, and drank the wine Ted had left chilling in the fridge for them.

"So, when is Ted coming over, Mum?"

"He said he would leave us to settle in and then head over tomorrow morning, rather than coming tonight. I'm sure I won't sleep a wink." Maggie gazed across at the ink black sea. "I can't believe we're here, and this is actually happening."

Hugh opened another beer. "I've got to hand it to you, Mum. This is all down to you coming over and finding Ted. It's all a bit insane, isn't it?" He gestured towards Susie. "And you're in a dream, aren't you, Suze? It's all happened so quickly. Getting down here wasn't nearly as difficult as I thought it would be. It's a long way but Alfred's like a bionic truck driver. How does he keep on going through the night like that?"

"A constant sugar drip from boiled sweets helps… I'm going to miss him." Maggie drank more wine and reflected on the last couple of days. "The scenery was breathtaking, wasn't it? All those French rivers, and then the mountains and olive groves. It's been amazing and Mum is a star the way she has coped with the stopovers. Even last night in the motel wasn't too bad eventually. I think I'll go in and check on her." Maggie went inside and Hugh and Susie followed, deciding bed was beckoning and said goodnight.

Later, Maggie sat outside by herself. She could hear faint noises from the beach. A smoky aroma from the barbecues, combined with the salty sea, hung in the air. She nursed her wine glass and gazed up to the stars, remembering how she would often do the same in the middle of the night back at home, but her mood was now so different, melancholia no longer stifling her. She felt hopeful and uplifted. *So God. You really have turned the tables this time. Am I following the devices and desires of my own heart? Or are you saying… this is* **your** *desire for me… for us… for Mum? Time will tell. Signing out, but keeping you close. Never have I needed you more.*

*

The following morning, Ted and Bruce sat at a table outside the bistro, drinking coffee, discussing future plans for the work rota.

"He's a damn nuisance at times, but by God, I miss having Will here, Bruce. It's too much for me to keep that bar running all the time, especially as we've got our new family staying for a while. I want to be able to spend as much time as possible with Gwen, and Maggie, of course. I'm a bit churned up inside this morning, if I'm honest. Would you come with me to meet everyone?"

"I'll have a word with Marta, Dad. Mike is due here any minute. He's turning out to be quite an asset. He's done bar work before and it should be fairly quiet this morning, I'll put him to the test, and see how he gets along. Of course I'll come with you, I'll just pop upstairs and freshen up."

Ted drank two cups of coffee and beckoned Ralph

over to him. "Come on, boy, we've got a very important meeting this morning. I think you should come too. I seem to remember Gwen being a bit soft on dogs."

They casually walked the distance towards the house. Already, the beach was scattered with brightly coloured towels and sun loungers. It was eleven o'clock and the sun was hot. Ted wiped his brow with a cotton handkerchief. "I've never been so nervous, Bruce."

"Don't worry, Dad. It will be alright. Come on, we're nearly there."

They could see a figure in a wheelchair on the front terrace, her head shaded with a floppy wide-brimmed hat. A white short-sleeved blouse revealed pale, thin arms, and a flowered skirt covered both her legs, supported by a footrest.

Ted inhaled and exhaled slowly, and proceeded to walk with Bruce towards the gate.

"That must be her, Bruce."

Bruce stepped to one side to allow his father access onto the terrace. Ralph plodded up towards Gwen, and sniffed under the folds of her skirt.

Gwen looked down at the dog.

Ted moved closer.

Gwen raised her head towards the two men approaching.

"Gwen. Gwen, it's me, Ted."

There was no response.

"Gwen, it's Ted."

Bruce grabbed one of the chairs from the nearby table and placed it next to Gwen's wheelchair, and Ted sat down, thankful to be resting, as his legs had suddenly dissolved into a jelly-like state.

"Oh, Gwen, my love."

Ted took hold of Gwen's frail hand and instinctively placed it by his cheek.

"Oh, Gwen." His tears were those of both joy and sadness, his eyes searching for some kind of recognition, but Gwen was looking at Bruce. She turned her head towards the tall, sun-bleached blond, broad man and lifted her other hand towards him. Bruce, seeing this gesture, moved closer and clasped both his hands around hers. Gwen began to murmur, "Hello, hello, hello." She repeated this over and over very quietly, barely audibly, staring at Bruce the whole time.

Maggie stepped outside from the house on to the terrace.

She saw Ted and Bruce by her mother's side, both men holding her hands.

They looked up as she came closer.

Gwen continued murmuring, "Hello" gazing up at Bruce.

Maggie stood still and watched… another moment in time for her to keep alive in her head and her heart. Gwen was transfixed by Bruce, staring up at him, trying to formulate a sentence but her words were unclear and muddled.

"She can see *you*, Ted, she can see you in Bruce. The past is her present. There is some recognition in her eyes." Maggie moved towards her mother and spoke gently. "It's Ted, Mum. Your Ted is here."

Gwen continued to hold Bruce's hand; her grip alarmingly strong for someone so frail.

Ted turned towards Maggie.

"We just came in, Maggie. I hope you don't mind, but I could see Gwen from the path. I can see it's her, even though she doesn't know who I am."

"Give her time… this is a wonderful moment… just wonderful."

Maggie could feel her tears falling freely, and she welcomed a reassuring hug from her father.

She wanted time to stand still. She wanted the past, present and future to knit together and engulf that moment, wrapping a comfort blanket around them all… safe, solid, latching onto what could have been, and what was now.

Hugh and Susie had witnessed the reunion from the patio doors. They ventured slowly out, unsure what to say or do, so gave their immediate attention to Ralph to ease their awkwardness.

Ted gathered himself together, and beamed broadly at Hugh. "You must be Hugh. Come on, lad, come here." Ted had an infectious warmth, immediately creating a relaxed atmosphere. This was his strength, and the reason he was loved by so many.

Susie was also generously hugged, and introduced to Bruce, who remained fixed to Gwen via his hand. He laughed. "Your Gran may be a little frail, but she has the firmest handshake I've ever known."

The ice was broken. The mood was buoyant and cheerful. Maggie felt a mixture of relief, and joy. "Let me get you all something to drink. This is a day for us all to remember. I think there's a bottle of something a little special in the fridge. Thank you for your generous welcome pack." She was still unsure what to call her father, ridiculous as that might sound.

Ted provided a solution to her dilemma as they toasted this momentous occasion, clinking and raising glasses. "To my new-found family, my daughter and my grandson, and please, if you're happy to do so, call me Papa. You too Maggie, I can be Papa to you all. And Gwen… I will always be your Ted, even if you have no idea who I am. Bruce… she has certainly taken a shine to you, my lad. I suppose it was inevitable, as you are the handsome chap I once was myself." With a smile and twinkle in his eye, he continued, "This is a glorious day, and I can only thank you, Maggie, from the bottom of my heart, for having the courage to fulfil a dream that *I* never had the courage to ever even hope for. You have made this happen. You are your mother's daughter. You're a marvel." Ted was beginning to get emotional again, and Maggie intervened.

"I cannot possibly accept such praise, and I can only say that in my view, God brought us all together, and so let's be thankful for our own miracle."

There was more clinking of glasses, and more wine poured, and the morning was clearly turning into quite a party, even though Gwen was oblivious to the fact she was the centre figure for such merriment. She entered into the spirit with a smile, her eyes turned towards Bruce for most of the time.

Everybody relaxed into conversation about the trip down, describing Alfred as a hero and how the staff at Bridge House had given them the royal send off.

Bruce was soon to receive a call from Marta, who was feeling the pressure back at the bistro. "You stay here, Dad, I'll head back and hold the fort. You've an awful lot of catching up to do." He bent down to hug Gwen, who was still focussed on his presence.

"I'll see you again soon, Gwen. Keep your hat on, the sun is strong today."

"Maybe I had better take her inside." Maggie gestured to her mum, suggesting it was time for a rest, and turned the wheelchair towards the patio doors, and Gwen's mind became absent once more.

"What about lunch for everyone?" Ted was eager for them all to eat at the bistro, but Maggie responded, "Won't it be too much if you're short staffed? I can prepare salad and cheese and eggs here, if that's enough for lunch. I think Mum is a bit tired, too, so I'll let her have a nap, and we can sit outside here on the terrace."

"That will be marvellous, Maggie. Now Hugh, tell me what your plans are, and Susie, have you been to Spain before?" The three sat outside whilst Maggie settled Gwen, now so much easier to do with the mechanical bed. She covered her legs with a sheet and emptied the catheter bag, a procedure she was now adept at managing. *Sleep a while, Mum. You have your man just close by. All those who love you are not far away. Close your eyes.*

A cold buffet was prepared and set out on the terrace table and lunch was soon under way.

"Gwen still has the same look about her, you know, Maggie. Her expressions are still there even though her eyes can't register. When she's had a rest, can I take her out for a walk? In the wheelchair, of course. Maybe this evening might be better. It does get so hot in the afternoons. Hugh and Susie would like to come and see the bistro and I'd like to show them around Nerja this afternoon, if that's alright with you."

Maggie replied, "Of course. I might have a rest, actually. I feel pretty exhausted, and you must too, with all this emotionally charged excitement."

Ted sat back in his chair. "I think it's all this excitement that's keeping me going."

They all finished lunch, and Hugh and Susie cleared away, giving Maggie a moment alone with Ted.

"Has it upset you to see Mum the way she is now? I've become used to it, but for a first time not having seen her for so many years, it must be a huge shock, but I must say you're hiding it well." Maggie held Ted's arm as she spoke.

"I didn't really know what to expect and I think I imagined the worst in my mind, but your mum has a look about her, that despite the illness and added years, is still there. Her eyes are different, because they used to sparkle when she spoke, and of course she's not been able to say much today… but she is still Gwen, and I recognise that wonderful person beneath all her frailty. It is upsetting, but I didn't want to let our first gathering together be full of woe and sadness. It's been a happy occasion and as time goes on, I will spend more time trying to find something that might just spark a memory for her. You never know, Maggie, we've been blessed with a miracle already and who knows what God's plan is for any of us?"

Hugh and Susie appeared. "Come on then, Papa. Show us the sights of Nerja."

The three wandered away from the house, along the pathway towards the other restaurants, and Maggie watched until she could no longer see them. It wasn't until they had gone from sight, she noticed Ralph was still lying in the shade under the table.

Looks like you're staying with me, boy. Come on, I'll get you a little treat from the kitchen.

And the sun continued to warm the air, casting a shimmering effect over the beach above the shoreline. This was to be their new life. For how long, she had no idea. All anxiety had dissolved from her mind. The here and now was a very good place to be.

Chapter Eighteen

The early days finding their way around this wonderful coastal resort was fun and exciting. There were many small coves and beaches nestled around the periphery of the town; some hidden away, and some with long expanses of small pebble sand in easy view. There were many restaurants, but very few empty tables during the peak eating times. Nerja was a buzzing and thriving holiday resort, but not over-commercialised like some of the bigger towns to the west of Málaga. They soon became familiar with the lanes and shops, knowing short cuts in between the villas, and hotels.

A beach that Hugh and Susie were particularly fond of was one further away towards the east of the town, approached by dozens of steps leading down towards the rocks, transforming into a sheltered cove, adorned with beach restaurants and fishing boats. Ted had told them that once, that particular area had been just a simple fishing beach, with only a shack to get a drink from, but over the years more and more cafés and bars had been built and it was now a thriving part of the town, always very busy, with a younger community favouring the furthest point where live music would play well into the early hours of most mornings.

Hugh and Susie met up with like-minded people keen to explore their individual musical tastes, often jamming together just for the love of playing without any financial reward. It was known as the 'hippy beach' by the locals, and it was not difficult to see why.

The days turned into weeks. It was obvious to everyone that being in such a free-spirited place, it was all too easy to lose sight of the world they had left behind, and when the conversation turned to what was actually going to happen back at home, the only decision made was the avoidance of actually making one.

Not wanting to be financially dependent on Ted, a mutual agreement solved the issue, and Maggie and Susie both started working at the bistro, sharing the care for Gwen between them. They managed to organise a shift system and took on the help of a Spanish carer who attended to Gwen a few afternoons a week to allow some free time for Maggie… time she relished.

Maggie had contacted Bridge House to say Gwen would not be returning. Meredith was no longer there, which came as no surprise, and the new manager terminated the contract, consequently cutting off any further financial support.

This had been a huge step to take, and Maggie had wrestled with her conscience, terrified in case she was making the wrong decision, but there was no other alternative on offer now. They were here, and there was no going back.

She felt concern for Hugh, too. His job at the recording studios had been given to someone else. Maggie knew he was reliant on the money Craig had given him, but that wouldn't last forever. It was obvious to everyone just how happy he and Susie were together in this creative corner of Spain. He was making music, and that was certainly an ambition of his, but there was little hope of generating an income in the immediate future. He was playing at the bistro occasionally and gradually getting a band together and that was his focus for remaining in Nerja; something he and Susie had discussed and were intent on doing, if at all possible.

For Maggie, everything seemed a little surreal but not in a bad way, just completely different to any way of life she had known before. She sometimes felt she was on permanent holiday, despite working, and for most, this would be a blissful situation to be in. It all seemed too good to be true, and she wondered when the bubble would burst.

But the bubble was buoyant and showed no signs of disintegrating. The only cloud on the horizon was how to finalise things back in England. The flat and all its contents, her car, her social security benefits… all these problems would escalate in her mind, causing her anxiety, and a solution had to be found, and quickly.

It was over dinner one evening when the tentative subject of 'home' was broached.

"One of us will have to go back, and I think it will have to be me." Maggie looked across at Gwen. "I know Mum will be fine. You can share the care with M, can't you, Susie?" Ironically, the Spanish carer was called Maria, so yet again the reoccurring M theme continued, and she was known affectionately as M.

"You won't be able to do everything yourself, Mum. What about all our stuff and furniture?"

"Well, we need to make a decision, don't we?" Maggie watched for a response.

"About actually living here, you mean… if this is to be our home? Well, all I can say is for you, Mum, it has to be, all the time Gran is still with us." Hugh lowered his voice, not sure if Gwen understood any of what he was saying. "We didn't come out with the intention of it being long term. Well, Suze and I didn't, did we?" He turned to Susie. "But it's all kind of fitting together here, and if I can get this band up and running soon, we might be able to do some gigs over in Marbella and those other rich people's paradises. I need to start earning some proper money and I don't even know if I'm allowed to do that here."

"We'll have to ask Papa. He'll know all about that. I think it's all okay for now, but he does worry about Brexit because that changes a lot of the rules for working and spending time over here. The trouble is the rules haven't been finalised yet for when we leave the EU completely. All a total fudge-up, if you ask me." Maggie was helping to feed Gwen as she spoke. "I've tried to read up about it but there's no way of finding out exactly what the consequences are going to be, except that we won't be part of Europe anymore, well not in the Union. I don't like the idea of that at all. I feel guilty because I didn't even vote in the referendum, but I couldn't get out that day. I have to be honest; I didn't think it would make much difference at the time, but I was wrong." She continued, changing the subject. "I wonder if Will is coming back. It's very strange the way he just disappeared. You two haven't even met him. I think he's a bit of a wayward son, from what I can gather. Papa doesn't talk about him much."

"Ha! Sibling jealousy, I expect, Mum. Didn't want the family boat rocked. Where has he gone, anyway?"

"Valencia, I think. That's where his mother lives. Anyway, I'll leave the flight booking to you, Hugh. I'd probably end up in Glasgow if it was left to me."

*

It dawned on Maggie as she entered Málaga airport that she had travelled more in the last month than she had in the last 10 years. Feeling way more confident than she had been on that first trip, she sailed through security, and made her way to one of the bars, deciding on a glass of wine rather than a coffee. She looked for somewhere to sit but all the tables were taken, although one had a spare seat with a man sitting alone, staring at his phone. Maggie pondered… *I'm in this time paralysis again. I quite like the feeling, sort of suspended in a timeless zone.* Her thoughts shifted to England and its problems.

What in God's name am I going to do with everything in the flat? I won't have time to sell my furniture and I can't imagine anyone would be desperate enough to need any of it anyway. And there's my car. Well, that's scrap, for sure. I wonder if I can sit at that table.

Assuming the man to be English, she said, "Excuse me, would you mind if I sat here?"

"Not at all."

"Thank you." Maggie placed her wine on the table and fiddled with her bag, checking for her passport, again, an involuntary preoccupation whilst being at an airport.

"Are you going back to England?" Her table share spoke with an accent she couldn't place.

"Yes, I'm just going for a flying visit… oh dear… dreadful pun."

"Is it Gatwick you're flying to, for your flying visit?"

"Yes." Maggie suddenly felt awkward. "I have some things to sort out. I'll be back in a few days though, if all goes to plan… not that it ever does… go to plan, that is. Are you flying to Gatwick, too?"

"No I pulled the short straw and got Luton. Couldn't get a Gatwick flight. All was sold out, but I will be heading to London to see my grandson. My first, he's only a couple of weeks old." The man put his phone away and sipped his lager.

"Oh, how lovely. What's his name?"

"Charles Henry. Very posh. My daughter has a high-flying job in the city, so I hope she's going to cope with being a mum and working. These career girls… her sister is the same. They like the finer things in life. I'm Max, by the way."

"Oh, I'm Maggie. Nice to meet you."

The waitress came over to their table.

"Can I get you a drink Maggie? I'm having another beer."

Maggie was taken aback. *Shall I? Oh go on.* "Thank you, a white wine please."

Max continued. "So, do you live in Spain?"

"I'm not sure."

Max gave her a quizzical look. "Not decided, then? It's a big step. We moved here about five years ago. It was great to start with. I'm a keen DIYer, so buying an old, dilapidated shack was right up my street."

What is that accent?

"It was a hell of a challenge, even for me… not wanting to sound big headed, but my job was fixing up properties, so I knew a thing or two… Ha! Well, I thought I did… I'm of the impression these old Spanish houses are held together with anything that was going free. I ended up almost rebuilding mine and even now there's ongoing issues. Ah well, all part of the Spanish dream, I suppose."

"Where are you from? I can't place your accent." Maggie was enjoying listening to his voice, which almost sang as he spoke.

"I'm Scottish and Irish, so a real mix, but I would say more Irish than Scottish. I was born in Scotland but lived in Ireland for a long time. Eventually we moved further south, but then when the business got too much… I'm no spring chicken anymore… we decided to try life abroad. We used to come here on holiday, like everybody did when flights became affordable, and we liked it."

The waitress brought their drinks.

"Cheers." Maggie raised her glass. "So, are you travelling alone?" *Did I actually say that? He'll think I'm chatting him up… Idiot.*

"Yes, my wife died a year ago."

Full marks, Maggie… hit on a sensitive issue straightaway.

"I'm so sorry, I didn't mean to pry… I was just…"

"It's fine. Don't worry." Max sipped his beer. "She had early onset dementia; it was terrible and a quick decline, I mean really quick. I thought she would live for years, just gradually going slowly downhill but the type she had was fast-acting and there were all kinds of other things associated. I'm no medic and I didn't understand half of what the doctors said, but one day she just drifted away."

Maggie could not quell the impact of his words. She drank her wine and tried to say something appropriate but couldn't find the words. "I'm… I'm… oh dear, I'm so sorry…"

There was a loud sobbing, and it was coming from her. It was as if the last few years had been bottled up with a specific date for opening, and this was it.

Max looked startled, and grabbed several serviettes from the container on the table, passing them to her.

Please Lord, let the floor open up right now… of all the places to have an emotional breakdown.

"I'm so sorry…" She could barely speak but tried with every ounce of control she could muster, "It's just… I'm having the same thing happen to me… no, not to me… my mother. You see, she also has dementia and I brought her to Nerja… we drove down in a campervan, well, a motorhome, and I was looking for my father… and I've found him, and he's found my mother, and she's a shadow of who she was, and it's all just so unfair, and I'm so sorry… I don't even know you, and here I am just blubbing. I don't think I've been quite so embarrassed in all my life."

Maggie looked up, half expecting Max to have made a quick exit from the table, but he was sitting looking at her, his expression one of compassion.

"I think you need another drink." He beckoned the waitress and ordered another wine and beer, and then he spoke very calmly.

"The same thing happened to me. I was in a supermarket waiting in the queue. The woman in front of me was with her mother and they were just talking together, and I heard her say, 'Julie would have loved to have been with us today.' My wife was called Julie, and it just triggered the most appalling outburst of emotion I have ever experienced. I was horrified at my own response, and the sobbing just overtook my whole body. Grief does that. You don't respond to things you would expect to get sad about, and sometimes you think you're becoming desensitised to everything, and then suddenly, like the flick of a switch, you break down, and there is nothing that will stop it. So I understand. Don't feel embarrassed. I'm not quite sure I understood what you were saying about your father, though... you lost me a bit there." Max smiled at her, and Maggie, managing to calm herself, started to laugh.

And now he will think I'm a hysteric.

"I have no idea where that all came from. I have to say, you are incredibly kind. Thank you for not running headlong in the other direction. I think I would have."

Max smiled. "I don't think you would have, actually. You've been through hell and you will always be sympathetic to anyone living the same nightmare."

Maggie sipped her wine, and continued to tell Max, with a little more clarity and composure, why she had gone to Nerja. She spoke about The Courtyard Bistro and how her life, and also Hugh and Susie's had changed beyond recognition; her thankfulness that she had taken the chance to get her mother away from the care home into a beautiful part of the world where she could hear and smell the sea, to live amongst those who loved her until her days would end. They talked for quite some time, but the conversation was brought to an immediate halt when Max checked the boarding times. "Umm, I think you had better go to your gate. They're closing the one to Gatwick now."

"Oh Lordy… Let me give you some money for the wine."

Max stood up. "Don't be ridiculous. Just run like hell to gate C. You can get me a drink next time. Hurry now."

She thanked this random stranger who had been given a summary of her life story, and hastened, partly running, partly walking with speed, following signs for departure lounge C. She raced as quickly as possible along endless corridors and ran into the correct area just as it was closing.

"Please, please can I be let through. I'm so sorry, I didn't realise."

An airport official put his arm across the barrier. "Wait here please."

This is ridiculous. How could you be such an idiot?

"They 'ave closed the gate. You cannot board now." This Spanish gentleman was in no way going to bend the rules and it became clear that Maggie wasn't going anywhere. Certainly not today.

"Please… I need to get on the plane. Surely you can open the gate for me?"

"No. It is closed." She had been officially dismissed and she felt completely foolish.

Making her way very slowly back along the same corridors, needing to catch her breath, she made a phone call.

*

"How did you manage to miss the plane, Mum?" Hugh was trying to understand Maggie's garbled conversation over the phone. "You were there in loads of time."

"I got talking to this man and his wife had died and she had dementia and time just ran away, and I had no idea how late it was getting. It's airports… they're kind of timeless."

"So you got chatted up and missed the plane." Hugh was laughing, "Honestly, Mum, you are sometimes quite unbelievable."

"Hugh, I feel a complete idiot. I can get a bus to Nerja. I can't ask Bruce to drive all the way back here again and get me. Honestly, I can't believe I've been so stupid. I'll see you when I get back. How embarrassing!"

"See you when you get here, Mum."

Chapter Nineteen

They say God moves in mysterious ways, and there was a very good reason for Maggie not to fly back to England that day.

The phone call came at four o'clock in the morning. It was Bruce.

"Maggie, I'm sorry to wake you in the early hours but it's Dad. He's not well. I had to call an ambulance and they've taken him to the hospital at Vélez-Málaga."

Maggie sat upright in the bed. Disoriented, she looked around her and saw Gwen fast asleep.

"Bruce, no, this is awful. Do you know what's wrong? I mean, how bad is he?"

"They think it's his heart. He's on blood thinners, so it could be a bleed... all depends on the results of some tests they have to do. He looked shocking, Maggie. I heard him shout out, and went to his room with Marta, and he was clutching his chest and was so pale and sweating. I knew it was his heart before the paramedics even got here. They've managed to stabilise him, but I'm going to drive to the hospital now and wondered if you could come, too. I might have to leave you there, depending on his condition, so I can sort things out this end, although Marta is telling me she can cope."

"Yes, Bruce, of course. I'll get ready and wait for you on that road nearest the promenade." The conversation ended, and Maggie struggled to think what to do next. *Get dressed. Wake up Hugh. Take some paracetamol.*

"Hugh, wake up." She was gently shaking his shoulder, but it was Susie who woke first.

"Maggie, what's wrong? Is it Gwen?"

"No, it's Papa. He's had a suspected heart attack and been taken to hospital. Can you keep an ear open for Gran? Bruce is taking me to the hospital. God, I hope he's going to be alright."

Maggie quickly dressed, cleaned her teeth and drank some water. She grabbed a bag and remembered her mobile and the charger, impressed by her recently acquired mastering of technology, and made her way out of the house towards the nearby road. Bruce was waiting for her. He looked stressed and very tired.

"Just as well you didn't make that flight, Maggie."

"Well, now you say that, I suppose it wasn't meant to be, was it? But I felt so completely stupid, to be honest. How far is it to the hospital?"

"About half an hour, maybe less as it's so early and there won't be much traffic. Dad looked dreadful, Maggie. He was struggling to breathe. It shakes you up when something like that happens. I didn't know what to do for him, but the paramedics were with us really quickly. I've never been so relieved to see an ambulance."

They drove the rest of the way in virtual silence, each deep in thought considering the possible outcomes.

At the hospital, they went straight into the emergency department. Bruce was able to navigate their way with ease. Once at the reception area, he spoke to the nurse behind the desk. Maggie listened to them both speaking Spanish, wishing she could decipher what was being said.

Bruce turned towards her. "He's in the assessment unit. All we can do is wait."

Again, silence resumed as they both sat, anxiously looking up every time a uniformed person walked past. After about an hour, a doctor came towards them. *What is his face saying?*

Again, Maggie had to wait whilst Bruce conversed with the doctor. She tried to understand by their tone the nature of what was being said. Bruce turned towards her. "He's not completely out of the woods yet but they say he's going to survive. He's definitely had a heart attack. A clot in a coronary artery so it could have been fatal, but they've managed to disperse the clot with drugs. We just have to hope he pulls through this next twenty-four hours. He's been on a tablet called warfarin, a blood thinner, for some time now but he hasn't been getting his levels checked and not taking the right dose. I never interfere with his medication, I just let him get on with it. Dad is always so independent and full of life; I never even consider his age half the time."

"Don't blame yourself, Bruce. I was wondering if him seeing Mum has upset him. All kinds of stuff goes through your head, doesn't it?" Maggie was feeling more and more anxious.

"No, he has been so happy since he's known about you and your mum. The doctor was almost certain it's the warfarin that's messed things up. He's supposed to have regular check-ups and tests, and they work out the next dose, and I think he's just become a bit blasé about it all. Anyway that's going to change from now on. He's going to need looking after. Let's just hope he pulls through these next few hours. They don't want us to see him just yet, so we can go to the hospital café and get some coffee, if you like?"

"You go, Bruce, I'll wait here. You've been up so early, and driving too. I'll go when you're back."

Bruce made his way towards the café and Maggie sat down again and tried to collect her thoughts.

I could have been in England by now. This is all so bizarre. Please God, don't let my father die.

The next few hours were spent in the waiting area with Bruce and Maggie swapping waiting, allowing for refreshment breaks for them both. Multiple phone calls home were made to give updates on Ted's condition. It was lunchtime when the doctor returned. He looked calm.

They were told they could go and see Ted. The clot was apparently 'no longer in situ' and Ted was already making good progress.

They both stood either side of the hospital bed.

"Good grief Dad, that was quite a shocker, wasn't it?"

Ted looked very tired, and his face, not surprisingly, did not have his usual healthy glow, but he was able to talk quite normally, and seemed almost perky for someone who had been so close to death just hours before. "That pain was something I wouldn't want to repeat. It was like a brick in my chest, with a sort of pressure running up my neck and down my arms. Pretty unpleasant, but they've been marvellous here, I can't praise them enough, and those paramedics, well what I remember about them… they were just wonderful. Made me feel like everything was going to be alright. I said some pretty desperate prayers in my head. Anyway, it seems I'm going to be fine now, so I just need to get home and have a nap and…"

Bruce intervened, "Yes, you do need to rest, but you're resting in here for starters, and then we need to see what plan we can come up with. You can't be going back to work, that's for sure. Maybe you need to actually retire, Dad? You've been overdoing things and not taking the correct medication. That's what the doctor said."

Ted looked sheepish. "I know. I've forgotten to go for those blood tests lately, I need to smarten up my act a bit.

Maggie spoke. "Why don't you stay at the beach house with us for a while, Papa? You can have that downstairs bedroom. We can look after you and you'll be with Mum, too and I can badger you to go for your tests, and check you're taking the right tablets… and give you some TLC, eh? Just have a think about that whilst you're in hospital."

"I think that's a brilliant idea, Dad." Bruce was

smiling for the first time since he had been in the car with Maggie. "I've tried getting hold of Will, but he's not picking up his phone."

Ted shook his head. "I don't know what has happened to that lad. I just hope he's alright."

Bruce wished he hadn't mentioned his brother. "Don't be worrying about him, Dad. He'll be fine. He's big enough to look after himself."

The doctor came towards the bed. He spoke in Spanish to both Bruce and Ted, checking the notes on his clipboard. The decision was made for Ted to remain in hospital for the next couple of days and then it was imperative he took things easy for a while, doing gentle exercise when he felt able to. The doctor was adamant Ted must no longer work. He was formally instructed to retire.

"Doctor's orders," said Bruce. "You're going to have to do as you're told for a bit, Dad."

After a short while, Maggie and Bruce left the hospital, leaving Ted to rest as instructed, feeling huge relief that the worst scenario had not happened, and Ted was going to be alright.

Once back at home, Maggie sat with Hugh and Susie and discussed with them what the doctor had said, and her idea about Ted moving in with them for a while.

"It makes sense. Bruce and Marta are so tied up with the bistro. If he comes here, then we can keep an eye on him without being overbearing. Somehow, I don't think Papa would want a lot of fuss made." She yawned, feeling the effects of her broken night.

"It's the least we can do, Mum. He's been so generous towards us, hasn't he? Pretty much changed the course of our lives. He's quite a man. Gran had good taste, that's for sure."

"I put my idea to him, and he seemed quite keen, but

right now I think I'm going to have a lie down myself, if you don't mind holding the fort here, or are you both working? I've completely lost the plot today."

"And yesterday," laughed Hugh. "Just as well you missed that plane, Mum. You would have been worried sick in England with all this going on."

"There never seems to be a dull moment these days. I keep going over and over why it was I didn't get that flight."

"Someone called Max, you said," Hugh winked at Susie as he spoke. "Mum's got a fancy man, Suze."

Maggie was quick to respond. "No such thing. We shared a table and got chatting… he was an extremely good listener. I got a bit emotional talking about your Gran. *Don't say just how emotional.* His wife had dementia and died — all very sad. Right, I'm off for a lie down, just for half an hour before you both head off to work."

Gwen was sitting in the living room, once again glued to 'The Sound of Music' on the iPad. Maggie kissed her head and gave her a warm hug as she passed by. "Where have you got up to, Mum?" Astonishingly, Gwen replied, "Trees."

Maggie looked at the screen. "You're right, Mum. It's when the kiddies are all hanging upside down in the drive when their father comes home. Well spotted."

She lay on the bed, and with the film soundtrack in the background, fell into a deep sleep.

*

It was almost a week before Ted was discharged from hospital. Getting his blood levels right had been the priority, and making sure he was as protected as possible from further episodes. He had been attended to by the physiotherapists, and was walking well and no longer as breathless. A bed had been put into the spare room downstairs in the beach house, and Marta had brought over his personal belongings and some of his books. Life at the bistro had continued as normal without Ted being present, although many of the regulars had expressed their concern at knowing how ill he had been. A collection for a heart charity had raised a substantial amount and Ted felt humble and grateful for having such a good family and friends. He was inwardly relieved not to be staying at home. It would have been too tempting to venture downstairs to the restaurant, and this way he could concentrate on getting completely well. During his time in hospital, he realised just how lucky he had been, and did not want to cause the family or himself that kind of grief and worry again. To spend more time with Gwen was what he was looking forward to most. "I'll get my girl singing again, just see if I don't."

Chapter Twenty

"Are we in Africa?" Gwen was becoming more vocal these days due to more interaction from those around her. Ted replied, "No, my love. We're in Spain. It's as hot as Africa today though. I think we'll leave our walk together until it cools down later."

He poured them both a glass of non-alcoholic sangria, having made a conscious effort to live a healthier lifestyle. "D'you remember when we worked together, Gwen, in the café at the church? Look, I've got my photo album here from years ago. Let's have a look at some of these pictures. It might just spark a memory for you." The album was faded and had a musty smell.

"Look, there's my father, Reverend Godfrey, and my mother, and look Gwen, there's St John's church, and can you see the café in this picture?" A lack of response from Gwen could not be blamed on Ted, who always enthused over any activity wholeheartedly. He was recovering well and was enjoying more free time than he had in years. "Now Gwen, if you look closely at this one, you can see you and me together. That was a rare occurrence in public, wasn't it, but it's when we went to see that theatre production of your very favourite film, 'The Sound of Music'." At the mention of this film title, Gwen pointed to the iPad on the table.

"Let's look at some more pictures before you get absorbed in that again." They sat together, Gwen pointing at the pictures but with little, if any recognition of what she was looking at, however, Ted pretended she was completely aware of everything and chattered on, regardless that his commentary was probably falling on deaf ears. Later, once the sun was less intense, they took their evening stroll along the promenade from the house, Ted pushing the wheelchair slowly with very little exertion, as far as they could go without having to tackle challenging slopes, and Ralph plodding along beside them. They would do this most days, and finish their daily exercise with an ice cream, most of Gwen's melting and dripping down her arm, but nevertheless enjoyed.

Ted knew they were often mistaken for man and wife, and he would never correct this assumption, revelling in the fact that in his own mind that is exactly what they had become.

With very little to concern himself with, now his role at work had been delegated to other family members, Ted's health made excellent progress. Each day he and Gwen would enjoy breakfast on the terrace, and then there would be the morning walk before the scorching sun became a hazard rather than a bonus, followed by a trip down memory lane for them both, with Ted playing old familiar music that sometimes raised a smile or even a glimmer of recognition when Gwen tried to sing along, her own lyrics bearing little resemblance to the performers', but together they would make their own joyful sound, not caring if they were in tune or not. If Hugh was around, he would also join in, being the one with the enviable voice. After lunch, they would both have a siesta and continue their day before supper time, finishing with another stroll along the promenade.

This regular routine encouraged Ted to gain strength and enjoy a gentler pace of life. There were usually other members of the family in the house, and also the carer, M, who would help wash and dress Gwen, making sure her nails and hair were of salon standard. It was without doubt a happy dwelling, and the positive ambience was reflected in Gwen's mood, which had lost its previous anxiety and tension that had been present before when in England. The daily dose of sea air, freshly prepared food and constant varied company offering mental stimulation was, it would seem, a tailor-made care plan proving to be successful. But the disease would not plateau for long, despite all attempts to sustain an even equilibrium. Her dementia was as potent as everyone's resilience to fight it, and tell-tale signs of its progression would sneak their way in, causing concern when simple tasks that had been possible one day would present as a challenge the next. Standing and walking seemed to cause Gwen the most difficulty and even with Ted and Maggie supporting her either side, she would forget how to lift her feet. It was distressing to see the slow decline, but overall, her quality of life was still at a level considered good by many people's standards.

Chapter Twenty-One

It was a scorching morning in early August when an unexpected visitor stepped inside the bistro.

That particular day Maggie, Bruce and Susie were all in attendance. It was too early for customers, so when the door was flung open, all eyes turned in that direction to announce they would be open in half an hour.

Will stood, hands on hips, observing the enquiring faces, and clapped his hand on to his forehead. "Must be in the wrong place... Oh, hang on, just a minute, now let me see..." At this point, Bruce came out of the kitchen.

"Will, mate, where have you been?" It was an attempt to dispel the antagonism displayed on his brother's face. Bruce became concerned as Will continued.

"Oh, it's happy flippin' families here, isn't it? Didn't take you lot long to get your feet well and truly under the lucrative table, did it?"

Bruce intervened. "Will, you can pack that in. Come upstairs and we can talk this through together. You can't just barge in here..."

"Oh, I'm barging in, am I? Not so long ago I was indispensable. Now I'm clearly completely dispensable... disposable even..." He sniggered and made his way to the bar. "Still okay for me to venture this side of this 'ere bar, is it, everyone? Or am I barred or banned or whatever?"

Will stumbled towards the bar and made his way to the stock of cooled lagers in the fridge.

"Cheers everyone! Here's to happy reunited families."

Hugh was sizing up the situation and could see things could very quickly get out of hand.

He made his way towards the bar, winking at Susie as he passed her by. "Don't be drinking on your own, erm, Will, isn't it?"

Will eyed Hugh up and down, clearly unimpressed by his matey response.

"Don't start trying to humour me, whoever you are. Another member of the Waltons, I expect." Hugh grabbed a beer and sat on a stool next to Will.

"Cheers, Will, and by the way I'm not trying to humour you, okay? Let's just get that clear."

Maggie was astonished to see Hugh behave in this very uncharacteristic way, but was curious to see what his next move would be. Hugh was always the supreme pacifist and she hoped Will would not become angry or violent.

Will concentrated on pouring his lager into a tall glass, spilling a small quantity on the bar counter. "I've lost my touch... never used to spill a drop."

Bruce was hovering by the kitchen, unsure whether to intervene or leave Hugh to pacify his brother. He wished more than anything else that Will would decide to leave before the doors were officially open to customers. He decided to join them at the bar.

"So, it's a welcome home to Will, is it? I've seen more convivial ways of introducing yourself to your family."

Will looked up at his brother. "Uh? Oh, have we got to be on best behaviour then? Since when? Since we had to accommodate refugees?"

"The two men did not rise to the bait. They were both aware this was a volatile situation. Bruce spoke. "Ooh, a bit harsh, Will, mate. Cheers anyway. So what took you so long to show up?"

"Where's Dad?" Will turned to view the far side of the bistro. "And who's that hippie?"

Susie blushed, grabbing a trolley nearby in an attempt to busy herself rearranging the cutlery. Hugh could feel himself becoming agitated. He was not prepared to put up with rudeness directed at Susie. "Susie is my girlfriend.

She's here helping out. You've been missed by everyone that I've spoken to." At that moment Mike entered the bistro, flustered, knowing he was late for his shift.

"Sorry everyone, I had a puncture. Fixed it though, so here I am."

He stood still and looked at the three men sitting at the bar. He hesitated and glanced across at Maggie. She was quick to act.

"Mike, can you come with me to the kitchen? There's some boxes need shifting into the bar."

They both hurried out, and Maggie whispered "It's Will, the brother who did the disappearing act. All a bit tense, so I would lie low if I were you. I'm not sure how we're going to get started here today. It's almost opening time."

Back at the bar, Bruce was also wondering the same thing. He needed to get back to work, but didn't feel comfortable leaving Hugh to diffuse the situation.

"Will, I've got to get back to the kitchen. What are you going to do? You can stay here, but come on mate, don't start making a scene. We've got customers, and a few who know you are likely to come in. You don't want them seeing you like this. Why not get a bit of fresh air, and have something to eat?"

Will interrupted, "Well, you seem very concerned for my welfare all of a sudden. Funny that. No one seems to have been in too much of a hurry to find me. I mean, Valencia isn't a million miles away, is it? A visit would have been…" He trailed off, his voice becoming slurred.

Hugh was weighing up the best approach. "Will, I could do with a bit of fresh air too. It's so hot in here. I had no idea August could be like this. I'm more used to English summers, you know, blink and you'll miss it. Fancy a smoke?"

Will followed Hugh outside knocking against the

tables, but remaining upright.

Bruce breathed a sigh of relief, and walked across to Susie.

"Sorry about that. He's such a prat when he's drunk. He's a pretty cool guy when he's on good form and working. You wouldn't recognise him. I think we'll have to assume Hugh is tied up right now, so just try and keep things on an even keel if you can." Susie nodded and continued to sort out the cutlery and refill the condiment containers.

Maggie was in the kitchen with Marta. Bruce apologised once more for his brother's inappropriate behaviour.

"He's screwed up, that's the trouble. All the time things are going well, he's good company, you know, but when he goes off the rails, he's a bloody car crash."

Maggie gave Bruce a hug. "I was quite taken aback at Hugh. He read the situation well."

"Yes, he used a bit of psychology, didn't he? Quite the counsellor. I hope he's okay out there."

Hugh was standing with Will outside the bistro, and managed to get him to walk away from the entrance and stroll down towards the beach. Hugh rarely smoked cigarettes, preferring an occasional spliff, but he was doing his best to formulate some kind of relationship with this offensive member of the family. He rolled a cigarette and passed it to him. "Here, have this" Will accepted, lit up, and inhaled hard. Hugh proceeded to roll one for himself.

"So, why so angry, Will? The last thing any of us wanted was for you to feel threatened in any way. Mum just wanted to find her Dad. There was no hidden agenda. Mum isn't like that. Your Dad is really generous, I'm not going to lie, but that's why we're all working together to try and help out, to give something back, especially since your Dad had his heart attack."

Will stopped and stared at Hugh.

"What? A heart attack? So nobody thought to let me know! Really! I've heard it all now."

Hugh regretted his blunder. "No-one could get hold of you. Bruce thought you were in Valencia and spoke to your mum, but she hadn't seen or heard from you for days, even weeks. He's okay, is Papa. He's doing really well."

"Papa!! Papa!! For pity's sake…"

"Okay, I'm handling this badly. You said you didn't want me to humour you, so I'm not gonna do that. I'm just trying to talk to you like I would anyone who's clearly pretty damn traumatised. We call him Papa. It's what your Dad suggested. Mum doesn't call him Dad; she calls him Papa too. He's an amazing man, Will, you're so lucky to have a father like him."

Will turned towards Hugh, staggering slightly, but steadied himself as he spoke.

"Well, that's just it, you see… erm what's your name?"

"It's Hugh."

"Okay, Hugh… well you see, our family isn't quite so straightforward as you've probably been told. It's all very well everyone being all cosy and calling each other affectionate names to bridge all those missing years, but you see, the thing is, I'm at a serious dis… dis… disadvantage here. Your 'Papa' is an amazing man… yes, you're right there… not wrong. So your mum has an amazing father, and so does my brother Bruce, also a pretty damn good guy if you ask me… yep, he's a far better human being than me."

Hugh continued to listen, straining to decipher slurred speech.

"So Hugh… where do you fit in with all this?"

"Well I'm your nephew, I guess."

"Half nephew… not all the way nephew, actually not even a liddle bit nephew."

They were walking on to the beach now and Hugh steered them both to an area away from most of the sunbathers.

"Not sure what you're getting at, Will. You've lost me, mate. Half nephew… full nephew… does it matter?"

"Different dads, Hugh. That's the thing… different dads."

Hugh stared out to sea. "Different dads? Who's got different dads?"

"My dad. Hugh… Hugh, look at me and watch my lips. My dad is not Ted. My dad is someone my mum had a fling with. Well more than that, she ended up hooking up with him for a while, but that's all finished. My dad isn't who you think he is. That's the big con… conun… conundrum, my friend. You see, your mum is the real blood daughter and Bruce is the real blood son, but me… I'm just a bloody mongrel! Ha… Yeah… a stray, a misfit."

Hugh didn't react. He was quiet and tried to figure out what Will had said, wondering if it was the alcohol talking, but realising it was more likely to be true, given his extreme behaviour since their arrival in his life.

"But you've been brought up by Pa…" he faltered, "by Ted, haven't you? I mean he's been there for you all along the way. He *is* your Dad, Will. I think my Mum would have given anything to have had a man like him for even just a year of her life growing up. You are lucky, Will. Don't let all this anger build up and distort what the real truth is. The real truth is that you've had a father to care for you and protect you, and provide for you, too. Have you any idea what a difference that would have made to my Mum's life? She had a terrific mother, and her loyalty to Gran is like no other, but she could have had the stability that your father gave you. She has never had that. She's never had any man guide her, benefiting her with their wisdom and strength of character. He may not be your biological dad, but that counts for so little, Will. What matters is the love and the loyalty. My own Dad has always been pretty detached. I'm not going to harp on about him right now, because this is about you not me, but Will, don't throw your life away by getting pissed and blaming your own inadequacies on others. You've got one hell of a brilliant life, and you've got the opportunity to make something great for yourself! Okay, I've said enough. Here, have another cig."

Will took the cigarette and sniffed. His fragile inebriated state was showing his vulnerability.

"I'm a mess, mate. It's all too late."

Hugh put an arm around his shoulder. "It's never too late. Look at Mum and my Gran and your Dad. You should see him with her, Will. They are trying to capture a lost love against all the odds, but they are clutching at what they've got, knowing it will be taken from them probably quite soon. You can't just give up. You might not have his blood inside you, but you've been given his strength by having him by your side all your life. It's not too late."

*

Hugh encouraged Will to head back to the room he had been staying in, as he was clearly exhausted and needed to sleep. Making sure he got there safely, he then made his way back to the bistro alone. He received a warm thank you from Bruce and resumed his work, out amongst the customers, alternating between the bar and the restaurant.

Maggie asked if he was alright. "Yes, Mum. I'll explain later. There's a bit of a story to tell."

*

That evening, Maggie was back at the house with Gwen and Ted. She wasn't sure whether to mention Will's appearance and thought it best to wait until Hugh returned to fill Ted in on exactly what had happened.

Bruce was with Hugh and Susie when they arrived back. Maggie had prepared some supper, and opened a bottle of wine. Gwen was on the front terrace with Ted, and they were attempting to reconstruct a child's jigsaw puzzle, albeit with slow progress.

"Gwen, you can't put that piece there," Ted laughed "Look, it's blue, and the dress is red." Ted's patience never dwindled. The scene was that of domestic harmony, and Maggie was reluctant to upset her father by discussing his absent son's return.

Hugh was keen to eat and helped himself to some bread. "Hi, Papa. Hey Gran, look at you getting all clever with that puzzle. Bruce is here. I bet your eyes light up when you see him."

Gwen continued to move the puzzle pieces around the table, unaware of new company.

The difficult subject was broached once everybody had sat down and helped themselves to tortilla, Parma ham and bread. Bruce chose his words carefully.

"We had a visitor today, Dad."

"Oh yes, and who was that?"

"I'll give you three guesses."

Ted looked up and knew immediately who they were referring to. "Was it Will?"

"Yes, he arrived this morning. A bit worse for wear, but young Hugh here sorted him out. Tell him, Hugh."

Hugh felt a little embarrassed and was economical with the truth in order to prevent adding to Ted's stress. "Yeah, he was just a bit upset about a few things, but we had a chat and I walked him back to where he's staying. I'm not sure whether he's with a friend there, but it's a room just near to the Balcon."

Ted's expression relaxed a little. "What are his plans? Did he tell you?"

"No, not really. I'm sure he'll come and see you, though. He was worried when I said you'd been ill."

"He can be a liability. I'm fully aware of just how difficult he can be. Thank you for having a chat with him though, Hugh. Maybe he'll calm down a bit and get back on track with work. I'd love to see him, but not if he's drinking heavily."

Bruce intervened. "I'll see him tomorrow, Dad. I think I know where he's staying. Anyone want a beer, talking of alcohol?"

It wasn't until much later that evening when Ted and Gwen went for their stroll, that Hugh told Maggie exactly what revelations had come to light.

"Different fathers? Maggie looked astonished. "Papa isn't his dad?"

Bruce continued the tale. "It's been the silent skeleton in the closet, to be honest, and never discussed. A bit like your situation with your mum, I suppose, never letting on why your Dad wasn't on the scene. But Dad has been the backbone of our family. He never singled me out and always treated Will just the same, to the point where I forgot about the history most of the time, but Will has clearly been harbouring resentment, and with these latest revelations, I guess he feels he's an outsider."

"But that's ridiculous. He's blaming the wrong person, it seems to me." Maggie poured more wine.

Bruce continued, "Dad is the good guy. He always is

189

and always has been, and in some way, I think that is the psychological twist. You would almost expect some kind of reaction once in a while, and Will almost tries to provoke one like he's testing him. It's unfair, and not a very pleasant side to his nature. The drinking all stems from his insecurity, but like you say, on the surface, it would seem without reason. It's those complicated collections of involuntary thoughts that play games, even when you try to dispel the demons, they just won't go away. Will struggles with a lot of baggage in his head. If only he could just let it all go and just accept. It is what it is. He's his own worst enemy most of the time."

"Do we tell Papa we know about this?"

"I'll tell him it has all come to light. He probably won't discuss it with you. His generation find this kind of thing a bit taboo. He's on his way back now — I can see them both coming along the pathway. I'd better head back to Marta. Lovely supper Maggie. Thanks, and I'll see you all tomorrow."

*

It was several days later when Will made another appearance at the bistro. This time there was no dramatic entrance. He beckoned Hugh, Maggie and Susie over to the bar.

"I've come to say I'm sorry. My behaviour the other day was unforgivable. Please accept my apologies. All I can do is prove to you that I'm not that idiot you witnessed. Hugh, you were a bit of a life saver, mate and I've though a lot about what you said. Maybe we can start again?" He looked at Maggie "Can you give me another chance, Sis?"

Maggie sensed this was a genuine apology. She gave Will a hug. "Don't think any more about it, Will. It's so good you're here. So many customers ask after you. You can tell them yourself now."

And without further hesitation or awkwardness, Will resumed his former role at the bar, as if nothing had happened. He was back.

Chapter Twenty-Two

Day to day life continued throughout the rest of the summer, with everyone sharing the workload to accommodate the increasing numbers of holidaymakers. Hugh and Susie became confident in hospitality, spending their spare time down at the hippy beach creating their own individual music, forming a band together with other talented musicians who had now become firm friends.

Maggie could see a huge difference in Hugh that summer. His confidence was growing, not only with his guitar playing but also with his outlook and appearance. The sun had bleached his now shoulder-length hair, and his suntanned body was firm from swimming and spending so much time in the open air. Susie also looked the epitome of health; so brown, and relaxed. They had become part of the beach community and it suited them both. Maggie could see there was little chance they would want to return to England and so the decision to give up the flat was something that had to be done and couldn't be put off for much longer.

Gwen and Ted were inseparable. Ted's tenderness towards Gwen was touching and even though her frailty became ever more evident, he continued to stimulate her mind with constant chatter and discussion about whatever it was they were doing. They had started to attend the services at the Anglican church on the Sundays that Gwen was well enough to make the journey. Maggie loved going along with them and often found it difficult to keep her composure when poignant and spiritually moving hymns were sung, causing her to reflect on the transformation of their lives. She gave thanks to God for giving her the opportunity to find the missing link in her life and for that person to be someone so utterly dependable and loving. It had been the right thing to do, and for that she was as grateful as she was relieved.

*

After much discussion, it was decided that Hugh and Susie would return back home to the flat and pack things into boxes for storage just for the immediate future. The landlord was happy to keep the bigger items of furniture, deciding he could earn more by managing the property as a holiday let.

Maggie's job at the bistro was secure and Ted was even more insistent about paying for the beach house now he was living there himself. She increased her hours, arranging more cover for Gwen with M, happy in the knowledge that her mother was content to have Ted by her side most of the time, and she was able to spend quality time with her mother too, without feeling as drained as she once had. Maggie would often reflect on those lonely days she had spent at home in England trying to be everything and everybody to her mother, but mostly failing, leaving her utterly exhausted and hopeless. Life was different now and it was good. It was a weekday when a vaguely familiar figure walked into the bar area and sat down at one of the tables.

I know him… where do I know him from? I don't believe it! The man from the airport.

Maggie spoke first. "Hello. It's Max, isn't it?"

He smiled and produced a large box of paper tissues from a leather rucksack. "I thought I would come prepared this time."

Maggie laughed out loud. "Oh, my goodness. You cannot imagine how many times I have thought about that incident. Don't remind me. Let me get **you** a drink — it's definitely my turn. What brings you here?"

Max replied, "I remembered you telling me about this bistro, and thought I would come and see how you're doing… you know, with your mum and your dad. Oh yes, and did you make the flight? I had to make a dash for mine shortly afterwards."

Maggie tried to hide her embarrassment. "Well, no, actually I didn't get on the plane, but as it turned out, it was for the best. My father had a heart attack that night and was rushed into hospital."

Max looked alarmed. "Is he alright?"

"Yes, he's made a complete recovery and has finally stopped working. He stays with Mum most of the time now."

Will came over to the table Max was sitting at. "Hi, what can I get for you?"

"A beer please. Thank you. Are you able to join me, Maggie or have I come at a busy time?"

Will interjected, "It's quiet, sis. Why don't you have your break now, with your friend here?"

"I'm Max. I met your sister at the airport not so long ago."

Her sibling connection to Will was cemented at that very moment. Max knew nothing of the family saga, but with a natural and simple introduction from someone new on the scene, the attachment was formed. It was an admission of acceptance by Will, who had referred to Maggie as 'sis' ever since his apologetic return. Maggie thought at first he was simply humouring her, but the name stuck.

Maggie sat with Max, choosing coffee to drink. She had been making a conscious effort to drink less wine, admitting to herself it had been a crutch that she no longer needed. There were no doldrums to wallow in anymore.

"Where is the house that you're continually having to

work on? Is it near to here? I can't remember whether you told me or not. I was a bit all over the place that day."

"It's not that far away at all, actually. Along the coast and then into the campo there's a place called Torrox. It's a pretty village and my house is just on the outskirts. Maybe when you have some time off, I'll show you. That's if you'd like to see it."

Wow this is new unfamiliar territory! It's just a friendly gesture… keep calm.

"Oh, well yes, yes of course that would be really nice. I've mostly stayed within Nerja since we got here in June. I haven't ventured far at all, what with Mum, and now working here, the weeks just seem to fly by, you know." *Try not to sound so utterly boring.*

Max smiled. "Great. Well, let me know when is good. How *are* things with your mum?"

"She's becoming more frail, but she seems happy enough and loves being pushed along the little promenade we have in the front of our house that runs along by the beach. She's always loved the coast. Papa, my father is so good with her. At first, she didn't recognise who he was, and I don't think she really knows now, but she accepts him being there and seems to thrive in his company. Who knows? You can't tell what's going on in her head most of the time. It doesn't really matter so long as she's at peace and not agitated."

"Exactly that. Julie didn't know who I was in the end, but she still sensed the familiarity. Maybe that's the same with your mum. She may well remember your dad's voice from all those years ago. It's a touching story theirs, isn't it? I doubt many people would have gone to the lengths you did to reconnect them."

"Max, it was *me* wanting to find my father. I didn't even think about the possibility of them both getting back together. It was Papa's idea to bring her here."

"Yes, but you're the one who did it. You made it happen. You should give yourself credit, but I get the feeling that's not something you're very good at."

Max cocked his head to one side and looked at Maggie, making her blush. She didn't want to behave like an awkward adolescent but could not deny that this man with his singing accent and perceptive words evoked feelings that had been buried for decades, until now.

I do believe he likes me and I'm floundering… Just be normal. He's seen you at your utmost pathetic, and he's still come to find you even after that.

"You're making me feel self-conscious. Let me get you another beer." She walked over to the bar, making another coffee for herself, and finding a cold beer from the fridge.

"Thank you." He took the glass. "I think I'll have a walk around Nerja. I must admit I haven't been here for quite a while. It's a nice little town. A lot bigger than Torrox. How's about I pick you up when you've finished here, and we can go for a bite to eat?"

Maggie hesitated. She would need to get back home to see how things were there.

Just say yes. "Thank you. I should be all done around three o'clock."

"Great. See you at three." He finished his beer and bid her and Will farewell.

Maggie felt flummoxed, and couldn't remember what she had been doing prior to Max arriving. Will was smiling. "He seems nice. Great accent. Where is he from?"

"Ireland and Scotland. Not sure which came first but his accent is a bit of both. Would you mind if I popped home just for an hour?"

"No, you crack on. It's early yet. We'll be fine here."

Maggie walked the short distance to the beach house, reliving her conversation with Max, and desperately trying to recall what she had said to him at the airport. *I can't believe he's come to find me. I must have come across as a complete nutter. What if he's not who he says he is? What if... Stop. You're having a bite to eat, not eloping together... just enjoy feeling flattered.*

Maggie stopped before opening the gate to the front terrace. She could hear music, and recognised it immediately to be 'Moon River'. From where she was standing, she could see Ted holding Gwen up, and gently rocking her from side to side to the music, as if they were dancing together. His arms were wrapped around her body supporting her, with his face touching hers. There had been many moments she had wanted to capture, and this was without exception a beautiful sight to behold, to keep etched in her mind. Such tenderness and love without expectation or promises. Not knowing about tomorrow, or even sure if there would be a tomorrow. Living for that precious treasured moment. So many could learn from those with limited time. Maggie didn't want to interrupt, but Ted spotted her and smiled.

She entered the room feeling intrusive. "Papa... you both look so beautiful together."

"She always loved this song, Maggie. We used to sing it together. I think she remembers in her own way." He gently lowered Gwen into her armchair. "You're home early. Is everything alright?"

Maggie filled the kettle. "Someone I met at the airport when I missed the plane, the night you went into hospital, came into the bistro. He's asked if I would like to go for a bite to eat this afternoon. I just wanted to check you were okay with that, as Hugh and Susie are not here."

Ted's eyes sparkled as he spoke. "Ooh, Maggie, have you got a suitor?" Maggie was laughing.

"A what? That's very Dickensian, Papa. A suitor? Well, I'm not sure. He's just asked me to join him for something to eat. If that's a suitor, then yes. Probably more like he needs some company. His wife died not so long ago. He lives up in the campo in Torrox, I think he said."

"That's a nice little town, is Torrox. There's a coastal part too. Lots of apartments there and there's a long promenade with goodness knows how many places to eat. We should go there sometime. Your mum would like that. No, it's fine, you go ahead and have some time with your friend. We'll be alright here, and I can fix up something for supper."

"That's why I popped home. I'll prepare something now for you to have later. Here, have this tea, and I'll put Mum's in her beaker."

Maggie chatted to Ted as she prepared the food, telling him about her encounter with Max at the airport, and about his wife Julie, and how sympathetic he had been about the cruelty of dementia.

"I often think about how this has all come about, Maggie. The fact that me and your mother can share such simple things has been quite a revelation to me. I've not had any experience with dementia before, but there are certain aspects of it that are good, because it makes you appreciate just how fragile life can be. I see it this way. Every day for us both is a bonus. It's something I never thought I would ever have again. She's not the woman she was, of course, but she's the woman she is now, and even though we have one-sided conversations, we can still laugh together and smile, and have companionship. I love her as I always did. I will never take for granted a single minute. If either of us died tomorrow, we have gained so much in these past few precious months. I consider myself blessed, and I have you to thank."

"Papa, my tears are dropping into this grated cheese." Maggie grabbed a tissue. "You are the most wonderful man. Please don't die tomorrow."

"It comes to us all one day, my dear. I don't mind salty, watery cheese."

Maggie finished preparing the food and made her way back to work, where tables were beginning to get occupied, and the mood was vibrant. She concentrated on the job in hand and tried not to think too much about her impending date.

*

At three o'clock, Max was waiting outside. The two of them walked down towards the beach where the popular cafés were uniformly positioned, one after another, each with their own variation of popular local dishes, paella often featuring as the main attraction.

Their choice of venue was picked for its view of the sea, rather than its culinary merits, but the food was freshly cooked, and quickly presented, the potential fast turnover of customers always being foremost in the waiters' minds.

Maggie decided she would partake in wine, despite her recent promise to herself. This was, after all, a special occasion; her first date for as long as she could remember.

She loved hearing Max speak, and noticed he was patient, never interrupting when waiting for her to respond to questions. He was impressed by her instant decision to head down to Spain, after visiting just the once, only days before, and then making a further one-way journey so soon afterwards, with barely time to unpack and then pack up again.

"Weren't you worried it might not work out? It was

quite a hasty decision. Some people plan for years to make such a huge change to their lives. But you just decided to 'up sticks' and go. Are you impulsive by nature, Maggie?"

"Well, it didn't take me long to agree to come here with you, so maybe I am. Seriously though, I wouldn't say I am very adventurous or impulsive. I don't know what was going on in my head. I was so happy to meet Papa, and I think it's fair to say he was the impulsive one. He had everything organised in a couple of days — the motorhome, the beach house, us all coming here. I didn't think it would be a long-term thing but then of course, I didn't know how Mum would be, either. She was my main worry, but there was something inside me driving me forwards, and not allowing too much time for pontificating. I think had I been given more time I might well have got cold feet. Maybe Papa knew that. Maybe that's why he persuaded me so quickly to take a leap of faith. But I'm so glad I did. Being here bears no resemblance to my previous life. Looking back, I think I was pretty depressed but didn't acknowledge it. I wanted to be the best carer, and daughter, and give Mum everything she deserved, but the daily struggle got in the way. Sometimes just getting through each twenty-four hours was all I could achieve, and that was often more like a fight for survival. But here, Mum spends most of her day outside with people around her who are living their lives, and including her in it, and in their conversations and comings and goings. She ended up in a care home in England, and they were very caring, given the limited resources, but it was Groundhog Day, with no change of faces, or activities. I could have given it longer but to be honest, it was badly organised, and having been given a chance of this for her… well, it might have been a risk, but it was one worth taking." Maggie drank her wine. "Tell me about Julie and how you were able to cope? Maybe it's different if it's a spouse rather than a parent?"

"Well, Maggie." (She loved the way he said her name.) "I can relate to the frustration you felt, and the sheer exhaustion of getting from one day to the next. I must admit, I would sometimes question if I could carry it through, but like I said to you before, her demise was pretty quick. I reckon in a year, she went from being able to have a reasonable conversation, to dying, so although a year seems a long time, each level of ability, or should I say inability, only lasted a short while. It was a kind of daily challenge to see if I could predict what was next to be affected. When walking fails, that's the real shocker. That changed things for me too, because we couldn't go anywhere much. Then you feel guilty for thinking about yourself."

Max poured them both more wine, and he looked across at Maggie as he spoke. "I don't want you thinking that I've been on the hunt for a partner since Julie died. Quite the opposite. No one can replace her, and neither should they. Something happened when you were talking to me at the airport. Well, afterwards really. I kept thinking about you, and wondering how you were getting along. I knew you were a genuine person by the way you opened your heart out like that. Don't ever feel that was a bad thing to have done, because it wasn't. There are a lot of phoney people out here, Maggie. They're shallow, you know, and seem to be only interested in themselves, running down England but never making any effort to integrate here or even attempt to learn the language after years of living here. They're intolerant of the Spanish, and just want dream homes with pools, and superficial, empty lives. Ha! I'd better shut up, you'll start to think I'm a real cynic, but what I was trying to say was you were the first 'real' person I had spoken to in quite some while, and you made an impression. That's why I'm here today, and I would really like to get to know you better, and like they say now... hang out together." Max laughed, and touched Maggie's hand.

"Do you think you'd like to do the same, maybe? You might realise I'm applying the same tactics as your Papa — no beating about the bush, straight to the point." Again, he looked straight into her eyes, and cocked his head in that endearing way.

Maggie returned his gaze. "Let's give it a go, shall we? We've nothing to lose, but I'm going to have to learn Spanish now, after what you've just said, and definitely never mention my home décor."

"Aw, take no notice of me, Maggie. But I think you know the type I'm talking about. I don't know you yet, but I can bet my bottom dollar you've never been inside a nail parlour."

Maggie immediately looked down at her hands. "Is that an observation implying self-neglect?" She was now the one to look quizzically at him.

"No, that is my way of passing a compliment. You must forgive me. It's been a while and I'm not very good at saying the right thing to a woman. Julie would laugh at my complete lack of understanding when it comes to boosting a woman's ego. She would say I was hopelessly unromantic and dangerously honest. Would that bother you?"

"Only if you ever thought you needed to be dishonest." Maggie was surprised at how easy it was to talk so openly to someone she barely knew, but was under no illusions. She would definitely take this friendship one step at a time. Being in a carefree holiday atmosphere, it was much easier to relax inhibitions normally suppressed, and she was only too aware how easy it would be to jump headlong into a relationship. She certainly hadn't been looking for anyone to share her new life with, other than her additional recently discovered family. Adapting to so much change so quickly had been more than she was capable of coping with. To include a romantic relationship into the mix could easily make the seesaw catapult its occupant headlong into a cloud of chaos. Time would tell, but right at that moment, she would simply enjoy the attention of someone she couldn't help but find to be utterly delightful company.

Chapter Twenty-Three

It was a busy time. Hugh and Susie were making regular phone calls several times a day to ask what should be stored, and what could be discarded, aware that the storage costs could escalate simply to house pointless articles, never used and unlikely to be. Maggie was working extra hours at the bistro to cover for them both, and spending time with Gwen and Ted in between shifts, and now... there was Max.

They had met a couple of times after their initial meal together, just passing time, enjoying sharing life histories. Max was quite a keen walker, and would think nothing of walking from Torrox to Nerja which was easily fifteen kilometres, getting the bus back if they had shared a bottle or two of wine together. He understood her spare time was limited, certainly until Hugh and Susie returned, but was happy to fit in with her hectic schedule.

*

Summer drifted into autumn, bringing cooler mornings, but remaining very warm in the middle of the day. Maggie was adapting to the Spanish climate, and tried to include regular sea swimming before going to work, and occasionally doing the same at the end of the day, enjoying evenings on the beach or on their terrace, watching the sun sink into the mountains. Her skin was glowing from a gradual suntan, and combined with regular exercise walking around the town or sometimes into the hills, with Max guiding them along the best routes, she began to feel energised, even though her days were often full, with little rest. She would wake early, feeling positive for the day ahead. Gwen was also benefiting from exposure to outdoor life, her cheeks pink from the sun, her hair bleached almost white around her temples. She was still able to stand and walk a few steps and occasionally joined in the conversation, trying to copy familiar sounds, and would hum to herself, especially when lying in bed in the mornings. Maggie would sometimes join in if it was a song she was trying to sing, old favourites from 'The Sound of Music' still being her preference.

Life at the bistro continued to be hectic and busy, the clientele changing from families to older couples looking forward to winter months away from adverse weather further north. Although most seemed to come from England, there were many visitors from the Scandinavian countries, Eastern Europe, and Germany, especially in Torrox, where many Germans had relocated, gaining Spanish residency. The issue about Brexit was still headline news, with uncertainty as to how this was going to affect the whole of Europe. Ted would enter into deep discussion with some of the locals on the rare occasions he left the house in the evenings. He was relieved to see Will back in the fold, with a seemingly new lease of life, and still able to participate in a few drinks with his customers without it getting out of hand. Ted was relieved Will's initial inability to accept Maggie and Gwen had now transformed into a positive for him, especially his relationship with Hugh, with whom he had bonded. He noticed he occasionally joined in with his group of friends down at the beach listening to the songs the band had created together.

Susie was also loving her new life. Her visit to England had been an emotional one when she explained to her mother she would be remaining in Spain with Hugh. Her relationship with her mother had in recent years been a rocky one, and Susie felt sad that she was unable to communicate with her in the same way she could with Maggie, but she hoped that some time apart might heal the rift that had developed, largely she suspected, because of her refusal to attend university. This was something her mother had pinned all her hopes on for Susie's future career, but it held no interest for her, as she was afraid to saddle herself with heavy debt before she had even reached her mid-twenties. The freedom that life in Spain was offering was way more appealing. However, certain elements of this freedom were to be short lived.

She had been feeling unwell, and on a few occasions, had to take time off work. Hugh was concerned and eventually persuaded her to attend the clinic for some tests. They both sat together in the waiting area, on hard grey plastic seats, feeling pensive. The doctor she was to see was female and German with impeccable English.

"Please come in." She gestured to them both to enter her consulting room.

"What exactly are your symptoms?" Her officious manner was abrupt and without the usual pleasantries one might expect when meeting someone for the first time.

Susie explained. "I feel so tired all the time. Just exhausted, and I can't eat much without feeling nauseous. I haven't got any significant pain other than a dull headache."

The doctor interrupted, "Your menstrual cycle? Are you bleeding heavily? You might be anaemic. I will take some bloods and you need to pee in this pot."

Susie took the small plastic container. "No, my periods have been really light."

The doctor turned away from the computer screen to face them both. "Can I ask you please. Are you using contraception?"

Susie replied. "Yes, we use condoms, mostly." She glanced at Hugh, both of them feeling self-conscious.

"Do the urine specimen and bring it back to me. I will arrange for the nurse to take blood."

Susie frowned at Hugh. She was inclined to be squeamish when it came to needles.

They were both directed to the waiting room and Susie disappeared to the 'servicios' and dutifully supplied the requested specimen and took it into the doctor.

Shortly afterwards, they were both summoned again.

"You are pregnant." A stark statement, lacking any kind of empathy. "I will still do the blood tests, but you will need to have a scan soon to determine your dates. I will arrange this."

Susie was speechless, and Hugh shocked. He spoke first. "Pregnant?" He looked at Susie. "Pregnant?"

Susie grabbed at Hugh's arm. "I thought because I was still having a monthly cycle, that couldn't be possible. Are you sure?"

"Yes. I have done two tests and they were both absolutely positive. Some women do have a monthly cycle right through their pregnancy. Just a light loss." She turned towards them, and softened her tone. "Do you need time to process this? I am here to help you, should you want advice if you don't wish to proceed with the pregnancy."

Susie took Hugh's hand. "I don't think we need advice of that nature. This may not be an expected baby but we both thrive on the unexpected." She turned towards Hugh. "We are going to have a baby."

Hugh nodded, trying to think of the absolute right thing to say at such a crucial time in their relationship but failed dismally. "A real baby, I mean, like, we're going to be parents? You're going to be a mum? And me a dad?"

Both the doctor and Susie exchanged raised eyebrows.

Hugh was embarrassed. "Sorry… ten out of ten for stating the obvious… I'm… a bit gobsmacked, to be honest. What do we do now then, Doctor… erm?"

"Fischer. Doctor Fischer. There's nothing you *need* to do other than try and keep up fluids, and eat little and often to help with the nausea. I will arrange a blood test now, and a scan in four to six weeks, so check we have your contact details with reception please."

And with that last comment, they were dismissed. Susie waited for the nurse to call her in for the blood test, and was swiftly summoned.

Once outside the clinic, Hugh took Susie into his arms. "We're going to have a baby, Suze. How do you feel? Are you okay, sweetheart? Look at me. You're crying."

"I'm fine, Hugh. Just a bit emotional. Also I think I'm going to be sick."

And she was.

This was going to be an unsettled few weeks.

*

They kept their news to themselves for a few more days, waiting for the right moment to make the baby announcement, which came the following Sunday after lunch at the bistro, when everyone was there, including Gwen, who made an occasional visit when on good form.

Maggie was asking Susie if she was feeling any better and whether the results from her blood test had come back. They were all sitting around a large table in the back area with an assortment of drinks and nibbles being passed around. Hugh glanced at Susie, and she nodded to him.

He stood up, glass in hand held high. "If you would all raise your glasses, please. We have something to announce and celebrate."

Maggie knew instinctively what Hugh was about to

say but said nothing.

Hugh continued, "Mum, Papa, Bruce and Marta, Will and dear Gran, we would like to tell you that we are going to have a baby. Susie isn't ill, thank God. She's pregnant."

Hugh smiled at Susie, who was positively beaming. There were cheers and congratulations from everyone, even Gwen, who always picked up on happy news and was clapping and smiling, unsure what about, but nevertheless thrilled.

Maggie hugged Susie and Hugh and then everyone was hugging each other, and Papa went across to kiss Gwen. "We're going to be great-grandparents, my dear. What do you think about that?"

Gwen's response was not wholly appropriate. "Will there be chocolate?"

"If it's chocolate you want, my love, then chocolate you shall have."

The party continued through the afternoon with copious wine and food consumed. Maggie tried hard to abstain and found the occasion both joyful, but also concerning. She was happy for both Hugh and Susie, but she was only too aware of the impact this was going to have on them both, especially as their relationship was a relatively new one.

Several glasses into the afternoon, she took Ted to one side. "I'm so happy for them, Papa, but I don't think they realise the long-term implications. Susie won't be able to work afterwards for a while, and Hugh doesn't earn much. Can they both remain at the beach house? What's happening with that? I mean, it's rented isn't it, so..."

Ted interrupted her. "It's rented for now, but I'm considering buying. It makes more sense, Maggie, I don't want to return upstairs here to live. Between you and me, I think Marta could also be thinking about babies. Did you see the way she looked at Bruce when the news was announced?" Ted tapped the side of his nose. "She will be next, Maggie, my dear, if she's not already. You wait and see. So we will have to be thinking about many things, especially with this wretched Brexit business."

Maggie looked across at Marta. *She will be a fabulous mum. She has the Spanish nurturing instinct.* "You're really worried about Brexit, aren't you?"

"Yes, I am. I'm trying to keep abreast of what's likely to come, but they won't agree a trade deal. Until we know what we're dealing with, it's like gambling, not knowing if it's a horse or a dog you're betting on. There's talk that people living here without being resident will have their time restricted in this country, and in any of the other European countries. We have to start thinking about you and Hugh and Susie, and now a baby too, becoming permanent residents. I think we'd better get some legal advice. The last thing you want to happen is to get settled here, and then not be allowed to stay. It's a bad business Maggie. I can't think of a single good thing that can come out of England breaking away from Europe like they have." Ted shook his head. "But Maggie, don't you go worrying yourself about Hugh and Susie becoming parents. We all of us floundered around with first children, never knowing whether what we were doing would help or hinder them, but their little one will have a loving family for support. We'll all be here, and the bistro is a secure business, and I'm sure it will survive, whatever Brexit throws at it. We're going to make sure of that. Both Hugh and Susie are diligent workers. You've all been good for this place. Look how busy we were today, and you all work together like a well-oiled machine. It makes me proud, Maggie. Even Gwen looks proud."

Maggie smiled. "I love the way you interpret Mum's

expressions. Maybe she does understand more than I give her credit for. She certainly seems to enjoy all the fuss she gets from everyone. And she loves being here, too. Look at her now." They both looked across at Gwen, who was patting Ralph, and saying something fairly unrecognisable to the human ear, but Ralph was lapping it all up, enjoying the attention. "Maybe I'm worrying unduly. You always seem to have such a positive attitude. It's a trait I hope I can work on."

"Maggie, you already have it. You just need to trust your instincts, my dear."

*

Ted was accurate with his prediction about Marta. She was, in fact, already expecting a baby when Hugh and Susie made their announcement, but she had been hesitant in making her news public because of a previous miscarriage, which had left her feeling nervous, preferring to wait for the twelve-week scan. Her dates were almost simultaneous with Susie's, with a due date estimated for 6th April, giving her a slight head start over Susie, who was told she should expect her baby on 14th April. But of course, babies have a habit of arriving when they feel ready to, so it was clear that sometime in early April, the family would be expanding and reinforcements at the bistro would need to be put in place.

Chapter Twenty-Four

Maggie felt her head would explode with all the plans needed to accommodate her work in Spain, and all the bureaucracy required to make their future there secure. Obtaining residential status became the family focus, dominating most conversations with, 'what was the next piece of paperwork required for the gestor?' often requiring the adept administrative skills of a qualified legal secretary, not someone who could barely understand the language, never mind the legalities. Maggie would sigh when opening yet another e-mail demanding translated copies of marriage and birth certificates and all manner of other documents.

This is impossible. Where am I supposed to get all this information from?

The one thing she had become expert at was making lists, but completing the tasks on those lists became baffling. She also had to arrange for certain items in England to be transported over with a removal company. On top of that, she was helping Susie plan for the birth, collecting little items for the spare bedroom upstairs, soon to become a nursery, and also attempting to learn to speak Spanish, which left her feeling perplexed and wholly inadequate. "There is no way I want to return to England, but the most difficult decision I had to make there was deciding on which bottle of wine to buy to get me through the day, and what to have for supper." She realised she was actually talking to Ralph, as nobody else was listening. Gwen and Ted were outside on the terrace whilst she was clearing away the breakfast dishes before heading off to work. She heard an alarming sound from outside and rushed to see what was wrong.

"Maggie, come quickly!" Ted was rubbing Gwen's back, but Gwen was struggling to breathe, coughing and wheezing at the same time. Maggie banged her fist hard in the centre of Gwen's back.

"She's choking." Maggie repeated the action again, and Gwen released some chewed contents from her mouth into her lap. "That's it, Mum, cough it up."

The panic was soon over, but Ted was upset by what had happened.

"I was just giving her some ham and bread, Maggie. She was chewing it for a long time, and then when she swallowed, she started to choke. Oh dear… I'm so glad you were here. I don't think I could have done what you did."

"Don't worry, Papa. We mustn't dwell on 'what ifs'. I'll give her some water to drink and see if that helps to clear her throat."

But it didn't help at all. Gwen choked on the water and seemed to have lost her ability to swallow. "Let's leave her a while and see how she is a bit later. Don't give her anything else, Papa. Wait 'til I get home, and we'll try again with something soft, like yoghurt."

Ted was agitated.

"I'll take her for a walk in the chair along the path here. It'll take her mind off it. And mine."

Later that day, when Maggie returned from work, she attempted to feed Gwen again with some yoghurt, but it was proving difficult to get her to swallow.

"Oh, Mum, what's happened? I'm going to have to call the doctor if you can't eat or drink anything."

They waited until the following morning just to see if Gwen was able to take anything orally, but it was clear she had a problem.

The doctor impressed upon them the need for Gwen to attend hospital. She was to be given fluids intravenously, otherwise she would become dehydrated.

During her short admission, the specialist nurse

explained that this was a natural progression of Gwen's dementia and that the swallowing reflex had become affected. Eventually, using a powder to thicken drinks, Gwen was able to take small amounts, but was at risk of choking unless given under supervision at all times. She was allowed to go home, only because there was adequate help plus a mechanical hospital bed, but it became obvious that Gwen's health was now in decline.

She lost weight quickly and very soon almost all strength was gone. It was devastating to see, and upsetting for all the family.

Chapter Twenty-Five

Even though they were now approaching December, it was still warm outside. Gwen was spending more and more time in bed, so it was moved into the living room, where it could be easily wheeled out on to the terrace. It was important to Maggie that Gwen was still to be included with family gatherings, so she could hear them talking in the background, and hear the sea, and beach chatter in the distance. Maggie was only too aware that her mother's health was spiralling downwards. She reduced her hours at the bistro to be able to spend more time with her, with help from M, who would assist with daily washing and personal care. Gwen would spend much of her time asleep. Her speech was difficult to decipher, and even raising her arm seemed to require more strength than she could muster. Everyone made a conscious effort to talk to her, and play her favourite music. Maggie had to almost prise Ted away, encouraging him to have a walk, or go to the bistro for a change of scene. He was always reluctant, but would be persuaded, knowing Gwen would simply sleep 'til he was back. The house remained upbeat and active, but there was an overwhelming sadness noticeable from everyone that the inevitable could soon happen, and Gwen's journey to be with the man she had always loved, would be brought to an abrupt end.

However, this decline in her health, like many other phases of her dementia, seemed to plateau for a while, and somehow, she was able to survive on very little nutrition, but able to take thickened drinks and small amounts of soft food like yoghurt. Her frail body became lost under her loosely fitted clothes, revealing prominent collar bones, shoulders, and pelvis. Her skin became just a thin veil without protection from body fat. Her blue-veined hands were like stems of a plant that could be crushed with the slightest pressure. The community nurses were attending regularly to check she was not developing sores, and performing bladder washouts, and teaching Maggie and M how to clean her mouth regularly. It was full-time caring, but Maggie was happy to be by her mother's side, never feeling isolated, because of the support from all her family.

It was a completely different scenario from her previous experience of caring. Here, the emphasis for companionship and regular expert advice was high on the agenda. In England, Maggie had felt isolated and unsupported. She was impressed with, and trusted the Spanish healthcare system.

*

Christmas preparations at the bistro were under way. There was definitely a market to provide a traditional Christmas menu for ex-pats and anyone visiting over the festive season. The Spanish did not celebrate Christmas in quite the same way, with their main event being held on the twelfth night, traditionally with the three kings delivering the presents.

Some items had to be imported from the UK, such as Christmas crackers and other food delicacies freely available at home. Life was pretty hectic for everyone, and Bruce and Will hired extra help to ease the load. Susie was feeling much better now her pregnancy was in its fifth month, and the nausea less extreme. Marta was also more relaxed, aware that the risk for miscarriage lessened the further her pregnancy progressed. It was a relief to Maggie that Susie had Marta to share this all with, and the previous conversations about what was now referred to as 'the bloody residencia' was overtaken by impending baby chat. This also helped with the sadness everyone was feeling for Gwen, who although frail, had an inner strength that carried her through each day, even with very little to sustain her.

It had been some time since Maggie had seen Max. He frequently flew back to England to see his daughter and her new baby, and Maggie had been so preoccupied with all that was going on around her, and inside her head, she barely had time to eat a meal these days, never mind go walking and eat out as they had done in those first few weeks of meeting up.

So, when his familiar face smiled at her as he walked on to the terrace, Maggie felt immediately uplifted, happy to see this interesting man who seemed to enjoy her company.

"Hello there, stranger." He grabbed Maggie around the waist and gave her an affectionate hug.

"Goodness, what a lovely surprise, Max! When did you get back?"

Max looked at his watch. "About two hours ago." He looked across at Gwen, lying in bed on the terrace. "Any change? How is she doing?"

Maggie walked over towards Gwen and held her hand. "She seems to be hanging on in there, but there's barely anything of her. The nurses say she's not in any pain, and I don't think she is, but her quality of life isn't much now. She just lies there, don't you, Mum?"

Gwen turned to look at Maggie on hearing her voice. "You see, she can hear, and she knows we're all here with her, so maybe that's enough for her now. She seems content enough. I don't know how she keeps alive, eating so little. All she has are spoonsful of yoghurt, and maybe some ice cream. I tried her with soup, thickened with that ghastly powder we have to put in everything, but she wasn't keen. She's always had a sweet tooth, so I give her whatever she will take." Max put his arm around Maggie's shoulders.

"And what about your Pa? How's he dealing with all this?"

"He's sad. He seems to have lost his sparkle, but he continues to talk to Mum all the time. He never gives up. They have only had a few short months together. It breaks my heart, Max."

"It makes you realise how important it is to live your life in the here and now. We all plan and ponder about what's next... what will next week or next month bring, but it's the here and now that matters. So, my lovely Maggie, are you able to free yourself for a while later on and join me for dinner? Will Ted be here to sit with your mum?"

"I'm sure I can arrange something. Where shall we go?"

"Where would you like to go?"

Maggie thought for a while. "I think I would like to go to Torrox, and maybe stay overnight."

She smiled at Max, and he responded, "Now there's an offer I can't refuse."

"I'll see if Hugh and Susie are about later, or I could ask M to come over for the evening. I'm sure she wouldn't mind."

"Right then, see what you can arrange, and I'll come over about sixish. Alright?"

"Perfect."

*

M was more than happy to stay the night, and Maggie felt reassured in the knowledge that she would probably remain by Gwen's side most of that time.

I need a bit of 'me' time. Just don't do anything like

dying tonight, Mum, will you?

She felt light-hearted for the first time in quite a while. Later that afternoon, she poured herself a glass of chilled rosé wine and packed a few items into an overnight bag. Ted had returned and was watching her.

"You seem to be in good spirits, my dear. Are you going out with that rather charming Max, might I ask?" He was smiling as he spoke.

"You've guessed it in one, Papa. I'm staying overnight. Will you be alright? M will be here, so she will sleep with Mum and keep an eye."

"You go and enjoy yourself. We'll all be fine here. I haven't seen young Hugh or Susie much today. Where have they gone?"

"They were both at work earlier, but the beach beckoned, and Hugh is trying to be with the band down there as much as possible. They've got a couple of gigs over Christmas. Things are looking up musically for him, but I still worry how he will manage when the baby comes. There are so many things they need to get. Babies don't come cheap these days."

Ted smiled. "I don't think they are too bothered about all that paraphernalia some young parents are intent on saddling themselves with. I heard Susie saying she wanted a papoose like the African mothers have. I'm sure they will be level-headed about it."

"Well, I hope so. Anyway, I'm off now, and I'll see you tomorrow." She gave Ted a kiss on his cheek, and made her way to the nearby road to be ready for Max to pick her up.

*

Torrox was inland from the coast, set up higher into the campo. The square in the middle of the village was

219

typical of most Spanish villages, with the church being the central point, and an array of cafés and restaurants. The village branched out into little nooks and crannies with small winding streets, and steep steps, lined with white bright town houses, some in poor disrepair, but most beautifully painted, complimenting the hanging baskets of red geraniums and pansies. It was all very quaint.

Max's house was set on the outskirts leading towards the next village. It was approached by a winding unmade stone path just wide enough to drive down.

"That's another thing on the list of things to do, Maggie." Max always sung his words in such a delightful way. "Anyway, here's the homestead, for what it's worth."

"You're certainly off the beaten track here. Look at those views of the hills. It's beautiful, Max."

"It's pretty isolated. I'm not really a neighbourly kind of a fella, Maggie. I like my peace and quiet, and the countryside, and walking of course. But I have to say it's different being in a place like this on your own than with a partner. It would be too easy to become a recluse.

I have to make myself get out and about into the village to see my fellow human beings. I'm not sure whether I'll keep it on or sell. Anyway, I promised you a meal, and we've driven right past all the cafés."

"What have you got in your fridge? Maybe I can conjure up something."

They both walked inside the house, which was quite dark, but the surrounding veranda which stretched around the entire house, was clearly where time was usually spent. As with many Spanish houses, particularly those in the campo, an outside kitchen was the norm as well as basic cooking facilities inside. Max's house was no exception.

There was a covered area towards the rear of the veranda adjoined to the house, home to a large double sink and cooker, with a built-in barbecue, and a huge fridge freezer too.

"It looks like you're all set up for entertaining here. This outside kitchen is better than the one we have inside at our house."

"The only person I entertain here is myself. I'm happy to eat in tonight though, if you prefer to do that. I've got some wine and a couple of beers in the fridge. Let's have a look at what else there is."

There was enough to cobble together a frittata and salad, and before long, they were both preparing a meal and enjoying several glasses of chilled wine whilst watching the sun sink down, changing the colours of the rocky hills ahead into a crimson and lavender portrait. It was beautiful. The evenings were much cooler now, so they decided to eat inside. Max lit the wood burner to take the chill off the house.

Maggie was observing the décor. She was aware Max had worked in the building industry, restoring older houses, and his expertise was noticeable, with attention to detail adding to the charm of this house. The soft furnishing also complemented the feeling of comfort, mostly in dark rich colours. Andalucian rugs over the tiled floor added warmth with many pictures and tapestries hanging on the white walls.

"I love what you've done here, Max. Did Julie have a good eye for interior design?"

"No, she wasn't really bothered about the inside of the house. She left that mostly to me. Gardening was her thing, and she made a good stab at making a fruitful veg garden here and she managed to grow tomatoes and courgettes, and spuds too. When she became ill, she lost interest in it and I'm afraid I let it all go to seed. I regret that now."

Maggie got up to check on the frittata, which was turning a golden brown in the oven.

"Come on, the food's ready. Let's eat, I'm starving."

It was a simple meal, but the homely surroundings and accompanying wine made for a relaxing pleasant evening. Maggie could feel the effects of the alcohol. Max put on some music and they both listened quietly, together, without the need for conversation.

This is frighteningly good. Don't let it stop.

When Max led Maggie into the bedroom, she wasn't sure whether to ask if he was comfortable with her sharing the same bed as his wife once had. Reading her thoughts he said, "I changed my bedroom after Julie died. This is just *my* room Maggie. No history."

She loved his perceptiveness, and walked with ease following him, knowing full well what was going to happen, and very happy to accept his love.

Chapter Twenty-Six

It was pleasantly warm with a few wispy clouds in the sky. Quite a few bathers were keen to swim, and the beach was unusually busy, but it was Christmas Day and many liked to mark the occasion with a dip in the sea. Maggie stared out from the terrace, thinking of Christmases gone by. She was keen to attend the service at the Anglican church that morning. M was joining them for the day, as the significance of Christmas meant little to her or her family, who all worked up until the twelfth night.

"Papa, are you coming to church with me this morning? A few carols will get us in the mood for the day ahead, and M will sit with Mum."

They made their way together through the streets of Nerja. There seemed to be very few people on the Balcon, considering it was Christmas Day, but it was early, and on most days, things didn't get going until lunchtime. Colin welcomed his congregation, giving Ted and Maggie a particularly warm greeting. "Christmas blessings to you both, and may the joy of this day remain with you both throughout the coming year."

Ted smiled, but his heart was heavy, knowing the coming new year would bring a sadness that would be hard to bear. Once they were seated in the pews, he lowered his head respectfully and prayed, quietly asking God to help him through what could be a difficult time ahead.

The organ was giving a buoyant introduction to 'O Come All Ye Faithful', so Ted stood up and held his hymn book, joining in with the congregation and choir in good voice. His somewhat melancholy mood soon lifted with further familiar carols achieving the desired effect to embrace this Christmas Day like no other. Maggie held his arm through 'Silent Night', finding it difficult to sing, but when finally 'Hark the Herald' crescendoed up to the last verse, they were both feeling spiritually moved, and in joyful mood.

"It's surprising what a good sing can do, isn't it Maggie?"

They left the church amidst festive greetings with other parishioners, acknowledging the day with a merry heart.

"We both know that this will be your mother's last Christmas, Maggie, so let's make it a damn good one, eh? Come on, let's pop over the road here for a quick drink before we head back. I know there's a lot to do in the kitchen, but Marta and Bruce said they would do some of the prep and bring it down to the house partly cooked."

They both sat at the café opposite the church, and Maggie remembered how only a few months ago she had sat at the very same table, waiting to find out if her father was living in Nerja. It was almost inconceivable to her that it had only been six months ago. So much had changed. Her life was here now. She felt there would be no turning back.

*

Once back at the house, Maggie listened to an English radio station churning out the usual Christmas hits whilst preparing gravy and bread sauce. She had set up a large table in the living room, albeit a tight squeeze, between the sofa and Gwen's bed. Gwen seemed to be hearing the music, her eyes more focussed than usual. She was propped up in the bed with several pillows, and wore a red and green shawl around her shoulders that Susie had crocheted herself and given to a Gwen as a present. The bistro was closing that day at four o'clock, and everyone would be coming back for a Christmas feast, with all the trimmings.

The day was everything Maggie had hoped it would be. She had a few sticky moments in the kitchen, realising the carrots had boiled dry, tasting more of salt than carrot, but other than that, the food was more than acceptable, with crispy roast potatoes, sausages wrapped in bacon (sourced from the UK by Bruce), turkey with cranberry and apple sauce, various stuffings, sprouts, parsnips roasted with honey, and bread sauce to accompany the meat. There was not an inch to spare on the table. There were crackers to pull, and a delicious crisp Chardonnay chosen by Will, who was indeed a connoisseur when it came to fine wines, and a sparkling champagne to toast the occasion. Maggie was relieved to know Max wouldn't be going back to England for Christmas. His daughters had made arrangements with friends to have Christmas lunch in a lavish hotel somewhere in London. Max was really not keen to attend anything so grand, and was more than delighted to be sharing Christmas Day with Maggie and her family. He rose to the occasion, bringing a Marks and Spencer's Christmas pudding bought on his last trip to England and some very exotic after dinner chocolates for everyone. The chatter and laughter was loud and would compete with any similar Spanish gathering. Toast after toast was announced until there was nobody left to be honoured. The music played on, and it was indeed, as Ted had expressed a wish for, a damn good Christmas.

Gwen was largely oblivious to much of what was going on, but there was a significant moment when Ted was sitting with her, and she raised her arm to touch his face. She was trying to say something, but Ted was unable to make out just what it was. He held her hand and then she spoke again.

"I see fairies." Her voice was so faint, but the word fairies could be heard. Ted smiled.

"And you haven't even had any champagne, my love. I think we'll all be seeing fairies by the end of the day."

Once the table was eventually cleared, they moved it to one side of the room and made space for dancing. Bruce and Marta, despite her blossoming bump, jived together, making everyone else look clumsy in comparison, but no one would be put off, and even Max waltzed Maggie around the room, despite her protesting.

The music became louder, and M and Maggie wheeled Gwen's bed into her bedroom, worried it would all be too noisy for her. Party poppers ripped into the air, and more crackers were pulled. The kitchen area became an unrecognisable shambles, with no surface area left uncluttered, but there would be time tomorrow to clear away the debris. After a while, things calmed, as everyone became exhausted from over-eating and over-drinking. Hugh brought out his guitar and played some melodies he had written. Susie lit candles and the pace slowed down.

Maggie and Max wandered out on to the terrace to get some air, and linking her arm, Max said, "Fancy a walk on the beach?"

They both left the party together and walked out on to the expanse of beach opposite, the moon shining across the dark eerie water, with just the sound of waves lapping over the shingle.

"It's been a fabulous day, Maggie. To be sure, you've done brilliantly with the food and all the preparations."

"It wasn't just me. I got help from Bruce and Marta, but yes, it has gone well. I'm absolutely shattered now."

Max took her in his arms.

"Thank you for making me feel so welcome today. Your first Christmas with all your family, Maggie. It's

226

one you'll never forget."

"No, I won't ever forget it, Max. And having you there too was the icing on my Christmas cake. I'm getting all emotional now. Too much wine, and sentimentality. I've no idea how long they will all be carrying on for, but I'm ready for bed. Will you stay here with me tonight?"

"If it doesn't make it awkward for you. Yes, of course."

"Come on then, let's head back."

Marta and Bruce were getting ready to leave and Susie was almost asleep on the sofa when they returned. Will was definitely in the mood for making a night of it, but decided he would head off to The Cavern in town, where a few of his friends would be. Ted was in the armchair, his mouth open, snoring contentedly.

"I'll get Papa to bed," said Hugh, who then tried to cajole Ted into leaving the comfort of his chair.

Maggie and Max waited until the coast was clear, and everyone had vacated the living room. They sat in the candlelight, and shared a brandy to finish the evening off. "I'll go and check on Mum before we go to bed."

Maggie walked, staggering slightly, into Gwen's bedroom. Her mother was sleeping. Maggie checked her catheter bag, and pulled the covers over her thin shoulders. "I'm not sleeping in here with you tonight, Mum, so I'll say goodnight. Happy Christmas. It's been quite a day. I love you and God bless you."

She quietly closed the door, and beckoned Max upstairs.

"Come on, let's go to bed."

*

The following day was a 'clear the carnage operation'. *Wow… where do I start? With two paracetamol, I think.*

Maggie was the only one up, having left Max in bed. She filled the kettle, and started to stack dirty plates and glasses. She went to check on Gwen, who was sound asleep. She emptied her catheter bag, and tried to alter her position in bed without disturbing her too much. "We had quite a day yesterday, Mum. I'm truly paying for it now though. I think we'll have a quiet one today, eh? Hopefully, M will come in."

She returned to the task of clearing the wreckage, needing to steady herself every time she bent down. *God, I feel horrendous.*

Max came downstairs, also looking decidedly fragile.

"Did you hit me on the head with a cricket bat last night?" He was holding his head as he spoke.

Maggie replied, "It was a mutual attack. I blame that last brandy."

"I think it was the two bottles of wine we had before that. Here, let me help you with this lot." Max walked up to Maggie and kissed her head. "It was quite a party."

"I'm not quite sure how I'm going to get through today, but hey ho… there's always a price to pay."

"Aw, don't think of it like that, Maggie. Today will be just fine, you see."

"I wish I could share your optimism." Maggie extracted herself from his embrace, and continued with the job in hand. "I'll be okay. I hate feeling like this. It reminds me of a time when this was the norm, and it wasn't a happy period of my life."

"Don't dwell on bad karma. It was Christmas Day after all, and you're not alone in feeling a bit rough round the edges today. How's about we clear this lot up and then head out for a walk together? Clear our heads a bit."

Maggie sighed, "I can't go anywhere until I've got Mum washed and changed. Hopefully, M will arrive soon. Shall we go for a swim later? That should kill or cure."

"I'm prepared to give it a go. Come on, I'll give you a hand."

*

The sea was freezing. Both Max and Maggie tentatively broached the icy water, not prepared to turn back unless the other one did, so it was with a deep breath and gritted teeth they submerged themselves, shouting expletives but intent on swimming, even if was for only a couple of minutes.

"Wow! That's really bracing!" Max was a strong swimmer, and proceeded with a crawl stroke in an attempt to warm his shivering body. Maggie was less ambitious, and after a very short while, headed back to the beach, quickly grabbing a large towel, wrapping it around her body, suddenly forgetting her hangover, deciding she had just discovered the ultimate cure. Max soon joined her and grabbed the other towel, rubbing his body furiously. "Hey, that's better, isn't it?" Maggie was still feeling frozen to the bone, but definitely more cheerful than earlier on.

"Yes, once I get my breath back, I think that's just about done the trick."

They weren't alone on the beach, as other enthusiasts with the same intentions to hopefully cure their previous day's overindulgences were also taking the plunge.

Max and Maggie almost ran back to the house, and decided a hot coffee with a Baileys would set them up for the day. Susie was in the kitchen scrambling some eggs. Obviously, her head wasn't in a similar bad place as theirs, pregnancy being a definite plus, giving the perfect excuse to abstain.

"Are you two hungry, as well as insane? It must be

freezing in that sea!"

"Believe me... it was, but it's made us feel a whole lot better, though not quite ready for eggs, so I'll pass, thank you, Susie. What about you, Max? Is your constitution up to some breakfast?"

Max grimaced, "No, I'll settle for the coffee and Baileys, thanks."

The mild hair of the dog did its work and Maggie was able to continue with clearing the house from the festivities, and began to plan for the day ahead. She wheeled Gwen in her bed into the living room and noticed the DVD of 'The Sound of Music' was by the television alongside the DVD player, and she decided to play the film via the big screen for them all to watch. Max pulled a face at the prospect, but went along with the Boxing Day entertainment, knowing he would be more than likely to fall asleep for most of the viewing. Ted soon joined them and also felt the best thing to do that day was to have a lazy one, watching a blast from the past with Gwen.

The day passed with very little activity. Hugh went into work to cover for the absent Will, who was probably too hungover to make an appearance, and Maggie, Max and Susie, along with M, watched the 'The Sound of Music', with Gwen lying in her bed positioned so she could see the screen, but lacking the commitment she would have once had for this old favourite. Once or twice, a vague smile was evident, maybe recognising the music or dialogue. It was hard to tell, but Maggie liked to think she was absorbing some of the film, and they were at least all together sharing the memory from her younger days, when visiting the theatre with her beloved Ted had changed the course of her life.

*

The following day, Maggie was concerned. She had called the nurse to come and see Gwen. On waking, she was aware of a change in Gwen's breathing, which was rasping with a rattle deep in her chest. The nurse who promptly arrived was English. She made some observations, checking Gwen's oxygen levels and temperature, and listening to her chest with a stethoscope. She tested the contents of the catheter bag with urinalysis sticks. She was very thorough and concluded it was probable Gwen was suffering with pneumonia.

"I will inform the doctor, and see what he thinks is the best course of action, if any."

Maggie was alarmed. "Won't he put her on antibiotics?"

The nurse gave Maggie a sympathetic look. "We have to consider all things here. As difficult a decision this is to make, we have to weigh up if prolonging life at this stage is the best way forward."

Maggie gasped and shook her head. "We can't play God! If there is a way to help her get better, then surely…"

The nurse interrupted, "We have to consider the complete picture of her overall health, Maggie. I'm not playing God, but we have to be realistic. Your mother can barely eat or drink anything. If she has antibiotics, she will have to be admitted to hospital and have them intravenously. She wouldn't be able to take an accurate dose orally. So do you want her to have the upheaval of another hospital stay? Or do you think *she* would be better remaining here with her family around her, just the way you have been looking after her all this time? You have given her a life so many people with her condition would have loved to have. I know how hard this is for you, but I have to tell you, she is now needing end of life care. We can give her regular injections of diamorphine to keep her comfortable. I can set up a syringe driver, so she has a continuous regular dose. She won't be in any pain."

Maggie sat down, inhaling deeply, covering her face with her hands. "This is it then, is it? I'm not ready. I can't say goodbye to my mother yet."

The nurse sat next to her, placing her arm across Maggie's shoulders. "You may not be ready Maggie, but Gwen is. Her time has come. We will be here to help you. You have to let nature take its course. Nothing can prepare you. No matter how much you have thought about this time coming, it is still hard to accept, and you will never be ready for it."

Ted came into the room, having walked along the beach with Ralph. He immediately analysed the situation and knew what the conversation was about.

"Oh, Papa. Mum isn't going to get any better. We have to accept that this is the end of the road for her. It's time for us to prepare for the worst."

Ted sat the other side of Maggie. "It's not the worst, my dear. She'll be released from us, but she will go to a better life. We're here with her and we can say goodbye for now, until we meet again. Keep your faith, my love. You need to be strong."

"How can you *be* so strong? How do you manage to keep so positive, even at a time like this?"

"It's the only way I can deal with life, Maggie. It's the only way I know, and I'm going to have to deal with death in just the same way."

They hugged one another. The nurse left them together and went outside to make a call from her mobile. Arrangements had to be made, and swiftly.

Later that morning, another nurse and a doctor arrived at the house. The doctor checked Gwen over in the same way the other nurse had done previously. He wrote some notes in a file and then prescribed a drug regime for the syringe driver. Then he spoke to Maggie and Ted.

"Your mother has pneumonia and probably another urine infection. I'm not going to take blood samples from her. I understand the other nurse has discussed her prognosis with you."

He was Spanish but spoke perfect English. He had a kind calm manner for which Maggie was grateful. Maggie nodded, finding this confirmation of the facts almost unbearable.

The doctor continued, "I need for you to sign a form to consent to no resuscitation, and also that you agree to the end of life care plan we are implementing."

God, this is all so bloody clinical and cut and dried.

"Yes, I can do that. I'm her next of kin so I'll sign the papers." She looked at Ted, who was visibly upset. Maggie spoke to the nurse. "Will you be staying here all day?"

She replied, "No, not all day. I'll set up the syringe driver, and write out the care plan, but I will leave you in peace. I'll give you my mobile number and you can call me any time you want to."

Maggie nodded. "Thank you. What's your name?"

"Megan."

Maggie smiled, the irony of her name almost anticipated.

"Thank you, Megan. You're very kind."

Maggie busied herself making drinks for everyone whilst the clinical operations were taking place. Gwen slept throughout everything, not even waking when the cannula was inserted into her arm. Ted stood by her, holding her hand, and gently talking her through all that was happening, but she didn't stir, or open her eyes.

Maggie wanted to know how long they thought it would be before her mother died but was too afraid to ask. *Maybe I should just let it be. What will happen will happen when it's meant to, I suppose. Dear Lord, this is so final and now so sudden.*

Ted decided to play some soft music, and made himself comfortable in an armchair next to the bed, positioned in the living room so that Gwen would never be alone.

Susie and Hugh were at work whilst all this was happening, unaware of just how ill Gwen had become.

Megan remained with them until just after lunch. "I'll go now, Maggie. Don't forget to call if you need anything at all. My colleague will be coming tonight to check the syringe driver, but it's all set up to give your mum a continuous dose of morphine. Are you happy for me to leave?"

Maggie replied, "Yes, you've been so kind. Thank you, Megan."

"Why did you smile when I told you my name?"

"Oh, it's just that everyone who has looked after Mum has a name beginning with M. It's something we've found comical, that's all. I hope you didn't think I was being rude."

"No, not at all. Well, the nurse coming tonight is called Gloria, so that's the M chain broken. She's also English. We have a team of UK nurses here because there are so many ex-pats in the town."

"It does help, being able to communicate with you properly. Maybe I'll see you tomorrow?"

Megan glanced at Gwen. "Maybe," she said.

And this was how the immediate time would be spent. It was agreed that Gwen must have someone by her side at all times. Should hours progress to days, they would divide the night sits between them. M wished to be included in this. She had become very close to Gwen over the last few months, and she cried when she saw her lying in the bed, clearly approaching the end of her life.

Hugh and Susie returned from work later and were equally upset to discover the sudden decline in their gran's physical health. Flowers were brought from Marta and Bruce, filling the room with their sweet scent. Maggie coped by constantly preparing food and drinks for whoever arrived. She finally broke down when Colin the vicar came to perform a final blessing. Everyone felt emotionally traumatised. Gwen had been the person to change the course of their lives. Even though she was unaware of the impact her former years, when she had been young and so in love, would have on her family as they grew older, she had provided the foundations for a constant love that extended to everyone she was close to. Her ability to see the good, and gain strength from adversity were characteristics so enviable. Her beauty came from within and the grace with which she conducted her life was such a rare quality. Even as she lay in her bed, she radiated calm, her expression now one of inner peace.

Gwen continued to draw breath the rest of that day. Gloria arrived at around ten o'clock that evening to refill the syringe driver and record Gwen's observations. There had been a glimmer of response from Gwen when she was turned in the bed to be made more comfortable, but she soon fell back to sleep without murmuring. Maggie was trying to remember the last words she had spoken.

"I think it was on Christmas Day, when she said she could see fairies," said Ted. "Perhaps they were angels. She looks so peaceful, Maggie, don't you think?"

"Yes, Papa she does. I think I'm going to get my head down for a couple of hours now. Why don't you, too? M will wake us if there's any change."

Both Maggie and Ted made their way to their individual bedrooms, but before getting into bed, Maggie went through to Ted's room to check he was alright. She opened the door after gently knocking. He was sitting on the side of the bed with a photograph of Gwen as a young girl in her early twenties in his hand. "Come in, Maggie. Come and sit with me for a moment."

Maggie sat down by Ted on the bed. She held his hand, and neither of them spoke for a few minutes. Ted broke the silence.

"Imagine if I hadn't been given this chance with your mother, Maggie. Imagine, if when you came to find me, you told me she had already died. This is what I keep in my head all the time. I've been given a gift from God, and I must never forget that. I could be wracked with grief and regret if I thought too much about what could have been. For whatever reason, it wasn't meant to be, and Gwen was only thinking of me and the position I was in with my family and Maureen when she left. She was selfless and soldiered on single-handedly, and I mustn't dwell on 'what could have been'. I will never ever forget what you have given me, Maggie. God bless you, my dear." Ted sobbed as he spoke the last few words, and Maggie held on to him, thinking her heart would break.

*

It was four o'clock in the morning when M gently woke Maggie from her sleep.

"You'd better come through Maggie. Her breathing… it's not good."

Maggie put on her dressing gown and went through to Gwen. She was still breathing but it was more of a gasp, with long periods in between each one.

"Go and wake Papa. I'll stay here."

Ted was soon standing at the other side of the bed. He stroked Gwen's face and kissed her hand. Her skin was mottled, the colour more purple than flesh.

Maggie lit some candles in the room and opened a window. As Gwen drew her last breath, she was held by the two people who loved her more deeply than anyone else. Her eyes closed for her final sleep.

Do not wake.
Sleep there softly with your pale skin translucent free from anxiety.
Troubled stare gone.
Sleep away your fears and free yourself.
I cannot see who you are anymore. My arms reach out but… your hand will now never again hold mine.

Chapter Twenty-Seven
Three months later.

"Maggie… Maggie!" Ted was breathless as he came into the living room, having rushed from the bistro, battling against strong winds and rain. "Are you able to cover for Marta at work today? She's been having pains all morning and Bruce has taken her into the hospital now."

Maggie wiped her hands on the tea towel thrown across her shoulder.

"Ooh, do you think this is it? She's due tomorrow, so it could be the real thing. How's she doing?"

"Don't ask me, Maggie. I'm a man. I've very little idea how labour progresses but I'm just thankful we don't have to go through it. I think the population would diminish if that were the case." Ted was smiling and had a twinkle in his eye again. The last three months had been so difficult to bear. Everyone had tried to be thankful Gwen's struggle with dementia had come to a peaceful end, but her presence was sadly missed, especially for Ted and Maggie. The void was impossible to fill, and time would be the only healer. The imminent arrival of the babies was indeed another Godsend, and there had been quite a few of those during the last twelve months.

"Susie will be jealous. She's feeling a little weary now and can hardly sleep, she's so uncomfortable."

Maggie grabbed a few essentials she needed for work, and gave Ted a hug.

"Are you staying here for a while?"

"Aye, I think I'll rest up a bit. Let me know what happens though, won't you? Great Grandpapa wants to be kept informed."

"Of course." Maggie left for work, turning back immediately to grab her raincoat and scarf. "Not very Costa del Sol, is it?"

Once at work, she busied herself in the restaurant, clearing tables, and taking orders. Susie wasn't working that day. She had gone to see her friends down at the hippy beach, and Hugh was juggling between the kitchen and the restaurant, leaving the bar work for Will.

*

It was later that afternoon when the call came from the hospital.

"It's a girl, everyone! They've had a baby girl!" The whole restaurant applauded, and a complimentary sparkling wine was offered to everyone.

Mother and baby were doing just fine, and would be home the very next day.

*

Both Marta and Bruce were proudly showing off their baby daughter. Susie was particularly interested to hear every minor detail about the birth, at which point, Ted made his way to the bar to get everyone a drink to celebrate.

"So, have you got a name yet? She is absolutely beautiful, and Marta, you really don't look as though you have just given birth. How do you young girls do it these days?"

Marta was positively glowing with pride, and didn't admit to feeling exhausted.

"I imagine I will come off this high with a bump in a few days, Maggie. I will take her upstairs soon, but all of you must have a drink to toast our new addition to the family. I can't wait to tell you her name."

"Come on, then," Will said. "Don't keep us in suspense."

"Her name is Gabrielle Gwendoline. Our dear Gwen's name will live on."

Maggie held out her arms to cradle this new young life.

"Beautiful. Just beautiful. Hello, little one. I'm your Aunty Maggie."

*

Each and every day that followed, all eyes were on Susie, who was desperate to have her baby. She hadn't wanted to know the gender before the birth, and both she and Hugh had no preference that they admitted to.

They were sitting on the beach together. It was a Sunday just one week before her due date.

Susie couldn't get comfortable and had felt unsettled all day. She was lying down with her head resting on Hugh's legs. The sun was strong, and there were quite a few people sprawled out on beach towels, content with the heat, and even braving the cool sea.

"Everything hurts, Hugh. I think I have an elbow trying to escape from my ribs."

Hugh laughed and kissed her forehead. "You've got another week of this yet, Suze."

In defiance of this prediction, and as Susie attempted to readjust her position, a gush of warm fluid escaped, soaking her legs. "Oh Hugh, Hugh, it's my waters. They've broken."

Hugh sat upright.

"Oh, shit! What can we do? Do we need to get to the hospital now? Someone will have to give us a lift. This is all a bit sudden. Me and my big mouth."

Susie was feeling her first full contraction which was strong and acutely painful. She tried to remember the breathing exercises she had been taught, but her mind was in a panic. They were in the wrong place for this to happen and without transport.

"I'll get some help Suze. Just hang on in there. I won't be a minute."

"Please hurry, Hugh, ouch, oh no, I'm having another contraction. They're so strong. This can't be right, so quickly like this."

Seeing Susie's distress, a middle-aged woman who had been sitting nearby came closer.

"Are you alright dear. Are you in labour?"

"It would seem so… I… I… Oh no, here's another one. Oh please, please, I can't bear this, they are almost continuous, and I think I'm going to do something really embarrassing if I don't get to a toilet."

The stranger spoke. "That's the baby coming, nothing else. Don't worry, there are a few people heading over this way with your partner."

Susie was now in a great deal of pain. She groaned and tried to get herself into a better position. Suddenly there were several people surrounding her, mostly her friends, but another older lady was taking charge of the situation.

"Are you a midwife, by any miracle?" She managed to raise a smile as she spoke, but then another very sharp contraction consumed her body. "Oh please, God, this is unbearable! Hugh, do something. I can't do this. Please, I need something for the pain."

In the background, a siren could be heard. "We've called an ambulance, Suze. They'll be here soon. You're going to be okay, sweetheart. We'll have a beach baby all of our own soon."

"No, Hugh, please get me to the hospital. I can't do this here."

The older lady was feeling Susie's abdomen, and asked if she could have a look to see what was occurring in the birth canal.

"Yes. Please, anything… ooh, Hugh… Hugh!"

Hugh knelt down and placed Susie's head on his knees, holding her under both arms. The ambulance was pulling up close to the beach. Very quickly, two medics were running down towards them, carrying bags and a cylinder. Seeing Susie's distress, they quickly administered some gas and air and reassured her that all would be better, now she had some pain relief.

She was groaning and rubbing her head against Hugh's legs.

"Susie." It was the female paramedic. "Listen to me, Susie. You are almost fully dilated. Don't push yet but when I tell you to, you must push hard down into your bottom."

Susie tried to nod, groaning and grabbing Hugh's arm.

"Hugh! Hugh! Help me."

"It's alright, baby. I'm here. So are quite a few others, but they've made a screen with towels. You're safe, sweetheart. Just do as the medics tell you."

"Make it stop, please make it stop, because if you don't, I swear I'm going to die…"

Hugh was sweating and looking at the medics to read their expression. Was this normal?

They didn't seem to be unduly alarmed, and were making encouraging noises to help Susie gain control.

"Now, Susie, listen to me." The female medic was positioned between Susie's legs. She had laid a thick paper sheet underneath her and was now encouraging her to push.

Susie grimaced and pushed as hard as she was able to.

"Come on, Susie, on your next contraction you push down as hard as you can. Push down into your bottom."

Susie did her best to follow instructions, holding the gas and air in her hand as if it were her lifeline. She inhaled hard on the tube, and then felt as if everything was fading into the distance.

"Susie. Susie, stay with us. Come on, you need to stay focussed."

Another massive contraction was the final wave on which she pushed with all her strength.

She could hear voices but was unable to understand what was going on. And then she was released from all pain as her baby came into the world, on a beach, surrounded by friends with the glorious sun beating down on them all.

"Oh, my baby, my baby! You're here. My darling, darling baby."

Hugh was crying and could barely speak.

"Suze. We have a son. It's a boy baby. We have a little boy."

The medics gave her baby to Susie to hold, clamping the cord, and asking Hugh to make the cut. The crowd all cheered and clapped, and then they sang a beautiful welcome chant — a spiritual mantra — as Susie held her son and cried with joy. This little beach baby boy could not have had a more loving welcome into the world.

*

Later back at the bistro….

"They've had the baby on the beach! Are you serious? You are kidding, aren't you?"

Maggie had been summoned by Bruce, who had received a phone call from Hugh.

"They're being driven to the hospital in the ambulance to be checked over, but yes, the baby was born on the beach. Well, I guess your son wouldn't have had it any other way Maggie. You have a grandson… Grandma." And the tears flowed freely, Maggie smiling and laughing at the same time. Bruce gave her a warm hug. "You have a good weep, Maggie. I think there's more emotion flowing through this family these days than any of us know how to deal with."

*

Susie was discharged from hospital that evening. She and Hugh returned to the house, driven from the hospital by Bruce, with their young son in a baby carrier. Maggie greeted them all enthusiastically, desperate to hear about the birth on the beach.

"Oh, Maggie, I was hopeless. I didn't want it to be like that at all. I thought I would be in control and calm but honestly, I was practically hysterical."

"Now, don't be so harsh on yourself, Suze. It was all so quick once your waters broke. It's no wonder you were in a panic. I think you did brilliantly, and so does young Hugo Edward here."

Maggie was given her grandson to hold. "Hugo Edward! Won't you get his name mixed up with yours, Hugh?"

"Ha! Yes, they are a bit similar, but we both love the name Hugo. It had to be done. Where's Papa?" Hugh was desperate to show off his son to his grandfather.

"He went for a walk about an hour ago. He won't be long now. Look at this little man. He's a real beauty. Susie, you are such a clever thing. Don't you dare say you were hopeless. Look at him. And you look amazing too, just like Marta was after the birth. How do you young girls do it?"

"Well, I don't think I'll be doing it again any time soon… How could anyone want to go through that more than once?"

Maggie laughed. "Come inside and have some supper.

I've made a fish pie and there's some wine chilling, but I'm guessing you'll be breast feeding, so maybe water for you, Susie."

"A glass of fizzy water will taste just as good, Maggie. I'm so thirsty, thank you. I'll just sit down for a while. Come on, little Hugo. Let's get you changed and fed."

The three sat together, gazing at this beautiful new little life, feeling blessed and relieved all was well with mum and baby.

Ted arrived shortly afterwards, sounding breathless as he walked into the house.

"Well, here he is — our little beach boy. You clever girl, Susie. Maggie couldn't believe it when she was told where you'd given birth, but it doesn't surprise me at all. You're all beach babies these days. Marta is desperate to come over, but she doesn't want to tire you."

"I don't mind, Papa. Phone her and tell her to come over with Gabby. Hugo wants to meet his cousin."

Within the hour, the house was busy with everyone comparing baby features, and devouring fish pie, celebrating the news with sparkling wine, and beer. Maggie loved having gatherings such as this, and now with the two babies added to the family, the atmosphere was one of homely cheer. She poured herself another glass of wine whilst collecting the used crockery, and silently prayed, giving thanks for this new life, and wishing with all her heart her mother could have lived long enough to see her great-grandson. *You would be so proud, Mum. Maybe you can see… maybe you're here anyway.* "More wine, anyone?"

Max arrived on the scene shortly afterwards. He was now well practised in holding newborns and could manage Hugo and Gabby in each arm. His big frame, strong and broad, was such a contrast to the two small babes he was cradling. Maggie felt touched seeing such tenderness, and was surprised at just how strong her feelings were for this man. *I love having you in my life. Stay a while. I can rest easy when you're here.*

Ted was feeling especially happy, knowing his great-grandson was named after him. Embracing his extended family, he had never felt such pride, and although there was still a deep sadness in losing Gwen so soon after finding her, these two new little lives had brought a renewed strength, hope and unlimited love. Life was good.

Chapter Twenty-Eight

And life continued to be good. Hugh took to fatherhood with huge enthusiasm, wanting to be a true 'hands-on dad', desperate to help Susie in any way he could. They would both wander down to the beach, with Hugo snug in his papoose, and Susie would relive the birth over and over again, not ever wanting to forget that beautiful moment when she held her son in her arms, and everyone present chanted together. They would sit on the beach watching the waves folding on to the shingle, as the sun sank behind the rocky hills, nursing their child, planning his future, wanting his world to be one of love and nature. Their hope was to resist the expectations forced upon so many parents from external sources, instead, giving their son their time in abundance, encouraging respect for his natural surroundings, rather than for items bought with no lasting benefits to him. It was something many parents aspired to but found the battle between their own desperate need to keep life simple and precious and the media's idea of what should enhance their children's lives too difficult to win. Hugh and Susie could only hope that the opportunity they had been given to live where the sky was blue and free from pollution, and that the freedom this climate allowed would give them the chance to fulfil their hopes for their family and future.

*

Marta and Bruce also had aspirations and hopes for their future, now they were a family. It was working well, living above the bistro, as they could both share caring for Gabby. She spent much of her time in her pram down in the restaurant with an endless stream of broody customers happy to entertain, hold and amuse her. She wasn't fazed by unfamiliar faces, enjoying the hustle and bustle that surrounded her. Ted would proudly walk her in her pram, occasionally having both babies propped up at opposite ends, causing many to turn their heads in admiration. With them both so close in age, they were frequently mistaken for twins, although they were not physically alike in any way, Hugo a blue-eyed blond, taking after his father, and Gabby, dark with brown eyes, quite clearly her mother's daughter. These two children would grow up together as constant companions, their love and loyalty a solid and strong eternal bond.

Chapter Twenty-Nine

That summer, just a year after Maggie had first embarked upon her new life, she decided to return to England just for a short visit. She felt a need to tie up loose ends, and finalise what should happen with her belongings in store. When she spoke about this to Max, he was eager to accompany her. "This time, I can make sure you actually get on the plane. I can go straight to my daughters whilst you sort out all your things from home, and then we can have a couple of days together in London if you like. Let's be tourists and do the sights. It might be a culture shock, being amongst so many people, but I'm prepared to take the risk."

So this time at the airport, they sat at the same restaurant as before, sharing a bottle of wine, but without the tears and drama of all those months ago.

*

Maggie decided to stay at a small B&B she knew of. It was close to the promenade, and she could walk to the storage unit as she had done before.

To be back in her old town, alone, after all that had happened in the last year was, if anything, a little surreal, and also induced a hefty dose of nostalgia. She sat inside the café by the beach where she had been so many times before. Previously she had been despondent, without any hope of things being different. She had to shake off dark memories, a flashback of previous mental instability overwhelming her, and decided to take a brisk walk to where her belongings had been gathering dust. Fortunately, the cost had not been excessive, as much of it was in smaller sized boxes, requiring only a small space to store. She had arranged for a van to transport what she wanted to keep to take to Nerja, and the rest she would simply discard.

Once in the warehouse, she was reacquainted with the manager, who remained disenchanted with his job, devoid of all social graces. She settled the bill and departed, feeling she had now drawn a final line, ready to move forwards. Her battered and bruised car had been kept in the car park at the warehouse, too, so she was able to drive away and aimed for the road towards her old flat. She pulled up but didn't wait outside for long. There was a board announcing holiday lets by the drive, and she didn't recognise any of the cars parked. She wondered if all the flats were now solely used for those on vacation. Accommodation for young families needing to live and work locally seemed to be sadly lacking in many coastal resorts now, which was a poor reflection of how priorities had changed.

Brexit was still dominating the headlines, with delays for the withdrawal agreement supposedly being finalised at the end of June, but this was still to be negotiated with the European Council. Theresa May was still attempting to steer the Brexit ship, but many had lost confidence in her ability to get things finalised and many were still adamant that getting it finalised was in no way going to benefit anybody. There was a lot of unrest with bitter arguments amongst politicians, social gatherings in pubs, and even within families.

Maggie was still finalising her move forwards for permanent residency in Spain. It was a big step, but now her grandson was in the process of obtaining Spanish nationality, the transition for her and Hugh and Susie was purely academic. Well, she hoped it would be, although complicated bureaucracy and the Spanish legal system were synonymous with each other. Maggie would despair when trying to decipher the various processes required to obtain residential status. All she knew was that the sooner it was completed before Brexit was finally done, the better it would be for her and her family.

The following day, she decided to take a trip to Glimstone. She hadn't got back in touch with Cathy since their last phone call when she had been informed where Ted was living.

She bought two bunches of freesia and headed off for St John's Church. She hoped that her faithful mode of transport over these last few difficult years would last out until she returned to take it to a local scrap centre. *Your final trip, Genevieve… try not to conk out on me, there's a love.*

St John's Church was cold inside, as most churches often are. Maggie made her way up the aisle and sat towards the front, bowing her head before conversing with God. *You made it all happen, and I can only give thanks, and feel humbled by your almighty power to change the way things were. I asked before for things to be different. Well you certainly didn't skimp on that request. Thank you. I will try to be the person you want me to be. I will endeavour to follow your plan. Amen.*

She sat back in the pew and gazed ahead at the altar and choir stalls. Once again, being in this church, she couldn't deny a feeling of familiarity. Despite having visited only once before, she felt as if she belonged there. It was, bizarrely, like going home. She imagined how her mother would have sat in these very same pews. She gave thanks for Gwen's life, and she knew deep inside her mother was watching over her, and that her soul was now at peace.

She remembered Cathy mentioning she lived close to the church. *Next door, I think she said.*

After a while, she left by the huge oak carved door, and walked out of the church grounds, looking at the houses close by to try and decide which one she thought it might be.

To the right of the church was a large detached house surrounded by a beautiful garden.

On the other side there was a row of stone terraced houses. She settled on the detached house, aware she was guilty of stereotyping Cathy as a wealthy middle class church goer.

Approaching the front door, she suddenly felt nervous. Was she going to tell her who Edward actually was? The door opened, but it wasn't Cathy standing in the archway. The tall female figure had her head cocked, holding a mobile phone in the crook of her neck as she opened the door. She beckoned for Maggie to enter, mouthing a hello to her. Maggie wasn't sure what to do. She spoke, trying not to interrupt the phone conversation this person was having but also feeling completely out of place being invited in.

"I'm not anyone you're expecting... sorry..." Her words fell on deaf ears, as the woman proceeded along the impressive hallway, holding another door open for Maggie to go through. *This is awkward.*

Eventually she was standing in what looked like a study. There were numerous large photographs on the wall, all in ornate frames, some dating back a long way by the look of the figures and their clothing. *I wish she'd finish her phone call.*

"I'm so terribly sorry to keep you waiting like that. I'm Ruby," and she thrust her arm out for an eager handshake. Maggie obliged, returning the gesture with slightly less force.

"These bloody caterers are completely barking mad. You try and explain exactly what you want and for how many, and they keep bleating on about allergies and food intolerances. If people can't eat the bloody food, then they should just stay at home, or bring a sandwich. We can't be delving into the science of a vol-au-vent for pity's sake, or into each guest's medical history." And her raucous laugh was accompanied by a series of snorts.

Hmm, if anyone's barking mad…

"Now, I'm so sorry to have kept you waiting but you are jolly early but that's a marvellous attribute. Come in I'll show you where to begin with the deep clean. Bloody wedding. Lord knows why she couldn't do it in a bloody registry office or in the church, for goodness' sake. I mean it's next bloody door!"

Maggie raised her voice slightly to make herself heard. "I think you've got me mistaken for somebody else. I'm so sorry. I'm in the wrong house. I'm looking for Cathy."

Ruby looked alarmed and then guffawed into more laughter. "I thought you were from the cleaning company! You don't want a job, do you?" More laughter.

Maggie tried to hide her own amusement and embarrassment and explained who she was looking for.

"Well, yes, you're in the wrong house for Cathy. She's across the other side of the church."

They both walked back towards the front door, passing the portraits once again.

"Are these photos of previous vicars from St John's by any chance?"

"Yes, they date back to bloody knows when. Hideous, aren't they? We found them in the bloody attic and we should have left them there, but someone, goodness knows who, thought it would be a good idea to hang them here. Looks like a bloody museum. This used to be the vicarage. They've built a new one now. I bet it costs less to heat than this bloody mausoleum."

Maggie was looking at the photographs and noticed immediately one was of Rev Godfrey Clarke. "This one here is my grandfather," her words so easily said, but so strange, even to her own ears.

"Well, I hope he was a better vicar than this bloody guitar-strumming born again hippie we've got now. I rarely go. Drives me bloody mad, all that chanting and clapping your bloody hands. It's more like a bloody Spanish fiesta than a church service."

Maggie couldn't help but laugh at this delightfully eccentric and wonderfully refreshing human being.

Ruby showed Maggie which one of the terraced houses to go to and waved goodbye with a singing voice and cheery smile.

Mad as a box of frogs. How weird, seeing a picture of my Grandfather hanging there like that. So random. My Grandfather… wow!

Cathy was delighted to see Maggie.

"Hello! Do you know, I was only thinking about you the other day, and wondering if you managed to find Edward. I'm so sorry, I've forgotten your name."

"It's Maggie. Maggie Chadwick."

"Of course. Come in, Maggie, would you like a cup of tea?"

"That would be absolutely lovely. Thank you. I went to the wrong house to begin with, and I met someone called Ruby." Cathy's expression required no further comment from Maggie.

"I'm surprised you managed to escape. She's off the scale eccentric that one, but quite a hoot, it has to be said. Come and sit down. I'll put the kettle on, and put these freesias in some water. They are gorgeous! Such a delicious smell. Thank you, what a treat."

Maggie observed her surroundings. The house was interesting but not what she had expected. Much of the furniture and décor was very dated. She sat in the kitchen, seemingly the main room of the house with an eating area. The small open fireplace looked as if it had been used recently. Cathy filled the kettle and was hunting in her larder for some biscuits. "I thought I had some bourbons here, but I can't seem to find them anywhere."

"Please don't worry on my behalf. I'm trying to resist biscuit temptation."

"Well, whatever it is you're doing, you look extremely fit and well, and if you don't mind me saying, completely transformed from when I saw you before in church. You're so suntanned, too. Have you been away?"

Maggie smiled. "You could say that, Cathy. I haven't actually been *here* for about a year. Since I saw you last, I have become a grandma, and an aunt. It's a long story, but the reason I wanted to see you is to thank you, because if it hadn't been for you telling me where Edward lived, my life wouldn't have taken the unexpected turn it has done. You cannot imagine how different things are now. You see, Edward is my father." She paused, and then continued to tell her the whole story, starting with her visit to St John's over a year ago.

Cathy listened intently without interrupting. She was sad to hear of Gwen's death, but was delighted for Maggie when she spoke about Ted, Gabrielle, and Hugo.

"This is quite a family saga, isn't it? You have changed the entire course of your life. I feel so happy to have played a small part in your journey, Maggie."

Maggie laughed. "Small part! You're the reason it happened at all."

Cathy became serious for a moment. "I know what Edward did was wrong from a Christian perspective, but you know, Maggie, it makes you think, doesn't it? In the eyes of God he sinned, and it would seem he's paid a hefty price one way and another, but I can't see it as a sin, can you? He was obviously deeply unhappy with Maureen, and he found love. How can that be wrong?"

"I'm inclined to agree with you. I wouldn't even be

here if he hadn't found someone he could relate to and love. It does make you question the Christian doctrine, doesn't it? But anyway, he did what he did, and here I am. I have found my father and my world has opened up more than I could ever have imagined it would."

Cathy poured more tea from the floral tea pot. "And what about Max? Now I really want to hear about him, too."

They continued to talk for quite some time, and it was late when Maggie finally left Cathy's house. They formed a friendship in that short time, with Maggie even suggesting for her to stay with them in Spain if she was ever wanting a holiday.

"Keep in touch, won't you? I can't wait to hear the next instalment."

Cathy waved her off, happy in the knowledge her new friend had found a new life.

Maggie drove back, reliving the story she had just told. She giggled, thinking about Ruby, and felt pity for the daughter soon to be getting married under her mother's cynical eye.

She was excited about meeting Max in London the following day. They would be staying in a hotel for a couple of nights before returning to Nerja. She thought about Ted and how their relationship had developed over the last year. She was missing him, and her two new babies, and would buy them all something to take back. She was happy for Hugh and for Susie. They were so in love, and had such a beautiful baby, both mutually strong in their beliefs for how they wished to bring him up. It was like a fairy tale, and she didn't ever want it to end. The road was clear, and her soul was singing, and her mother ever-present in her heart. She could think of her now and not feel pain. She recollected that first night they had slept together in the motorhome in an unknown place. She remembered the morning dew and mist, and the sun rising, and having no idea where she was, feeling carefree and wild, and yet inside, the most wonderful calm. A wild calm. She carried on driving. *Maybe a bottle of wine tonight? Or maybe not. Maybe just be content. There's nothing to fear. You've got your life… and it really is staggeringly good.*

A verse I wrote for a dear friend who lost her husband to Lewy body dementia.

I said goodbye to the you I know
Before anguish, tears and shame
I said goodbye to the you I know
Before consents, rules and blame

Give me a day, or drunken hour
Of familiar love to share
When gestures spoke a thousand words
When it was *me* for whom you cared

I said goodbye to the you I know
Before it was farewell
Give me back that knowing look
Your sleep, your skin, your smell

Give me back your strength, your pride
Your humour, wit, and mind
The very being of your soul
I searched, but could not find

I said goodbye to the you I know
And your fragile frame, too
Be still, at peace, my darling love
As I say goodbye to you.

Dedicated to Jane and Julian
Your love and endurance through the pain and anguish
are a template for life, for us all.

About the Author

I was born in Harrogate in June 1958, and have lived in the north and south of England. I now live 50/50 between Castillo de Locubín in Spain, and Winchelsea in the UK, but can never decide where home is, so I might just settle on being nomadic!

I trained as a Registered Nurse in 1976, and have worked within the healthcare services for over 40 years. Choosing to be a nurse was probably one of the best decisions of my life, alongside having my five truly loving and inspirational children. They are without doubt the apple of my eye, and always will be. With that many offspring, the chances of grandchildren are high, and yes, I have seven, and counting.

My partner of twenty-five years and I share many interests, music being one of them (he is a musician). We love travelling, and I am never happier than being behind the wheel of my campervan, the long road ahead, and no deadlines to meet. Joyful!

I have worked with, and looked after, a stadium full of interesting and incredible people, and that is from where I get my inspiration to write, as well as from life experiences. I loved writing Wild Calm, my first book, I hope of many.

www.blossomspringpublishing.com